Cloning A

A Novel

by

Robert Cubitt

(The Magi Series Book 4)

© 2017

Having purchased this eBook from Amazon, it is for your personal use only. It may not be copied, reproduced, printed or used in any way, other than in its intended Kindle format.

Published by Selfishgenie Publishing of, Northamptonshire, England.

This novel is entirely a work of fiction. All the names characters, incidents, dialogue, events portrayed and opinions expressed in it are either purely the product of the author's imagination or they are used entirely fictitiously and not to be construed as real. Any resemblance to actual persons, living or dead, events or localities is entirely coincidental. Nothing is intended or should be interpreted as representing or expressing the views and policies of any department or agency of any government or other body.

All trademarks used are the property of their respective owners. All trademarks are recognised.

The right of Robert Cubitt to be identified as the author of this work has been asserted in accordance with sections 77 and 78 of the Copyright Designs and Patents Act 1988.

Other titles by Robert Cubitt

Fiction

The Deputy Prime Minister

The Inconvenience Store

The Charity Thieves

Warriors Series

The Warriors: The Girl I Left Behind Me

The Warriors: Mirror Man

The Magi Series

The Magi

Genghis Kant (The Magi Book 2)

New Earth (The Magi Book 3)

Non-Fiction

I'm So Glad You Asked Me That

I Want That Job

Contents

Foreword
1. The Ghost Of Fletcher Christian
2. Peace In Our Time
3. The Truce
4. Engine Trouble
5. Jungle Journey
6. Marty and Davina
7. Meeting At Rigel
8. Ecos
9. A Reluctant Farewell
10. Cargo Cult
11. The Village
12. The Dysac
13. The Good Ship Shogun
14. The Singing Faroon
15. Suspicious Minds
16. Death At Dawn
17. Codeword Attitude
18. Send In The Clones
19. A Planet Called Hope

Appendix
Author's Note
Preview
And Now

Foreword

In writing this series, The Magi, I have described a galaxy in which many strange things exist and many stranger things happen. Some of these things are real and some of them I made up. If you know which is which then you had a good science teacher and you paid attention in school. For the rest I have provided a short glossary at the end of each chapter to help you.

If, after reading the glossary, you still aren't sure which things are real and which are made up, then please can I come and live in your galaxy?

Some of the more common terms are shown below, just to get your started.

c - A constant, the speed of light in a vacuum which is 299,792,458 m/sec. As used in the expression $e=mc^2$. In this book speed is measured in comparison to c, i.e. 0.95 c = 284,802,835.1 m/sec. This produces a standard for the measurement of speed to compensate for the many and varied measurements that are used throughout the galaxy. See also 'time'.

Li - A unit of measurement of distance roughly equivalent to 5 Earth metres.

Met - A unit of measurement of distance. Plural Mett. 5 Mett = 1 li.

Nuk - A unit of currency that is exchangeable throughout the galaxy. One nuk is sufficient to buy two Big Macs on any planet except Earth, where they cost 5 nuks each, but that's Earth for you.

Sim - A unit of measurement of distance. Plural Sims. There are 50 sims to a met.

Tea - A generic term referring to all non-alcoholic beverages consumed by public servants across the galaxy. Although they differ greatly from planet to planet in terms of their ingredients, most of these beverages are brown in colour and taste like they need less sweetening in them than they actually have, even if they have no sweetening in them at all. They are never as good as the beverages that are made at home.

Time - With so many variations in the rate at which planets revolve and the duration of their orbits around their stars there was no standard unit for the measurement of time before the Magi took on the governance of the galaxy. Indeed, one of the many wars that had raged was known as the war of the 23 hour day, which had gone on for two years or 933 days, or 1072.95 days if you had a 20 hour day. One of the first acts of the Magi was to introduce a standard unit of time based on the extremely accurate pulses produced by an atomic clock located on the planet Greenwich. Currently no one in the galaxy is aware of the irony of this.

1 – The Ghost Of Fletcher Christian

The mess room fell silent as First Officer Marti Woo entered. All of a sudden the crew were deeply engrossed with the contents of their food bowls. She had noticed this on a couple of occasions recently and behaviour such as that set the hairs on the back of her neck prickling.

She took her meal from the service point and wandered across to find a seat at the long table, walking as casually as possible. Still the room remained silent.

One by one the diners finished their meals, returned their trays to the service point and left to get on with whatever task they were due to perform, or to take their rest and recreation if that was what the day's schedule dictated. Only one other diner remained, toying with her food rather than eating it. She had been there for long enough to have finished her meal, so her presence was more than just a result of slow eating.

Marti finished her meal and left the tray where it was as she moved along a few chairs to sit opposite her silent companion.

"Everyone seems a little bit on edge today." She said it as lightly as possible, as though commenting on a minor rain shower.

Her companion remained silent.

"What's going on Davina?"

Davina looked the First Officer in the eye, clearly deciding how best to deliver her message. "The Captain made Jaquo clean out the sewage system by hand. There's a perfectly good droid for jobs like that. It isn't right. Jaquo is a highly qualified astrophysicist. He shouldn't be required to push his arm into shit pipes."

"What had Jaquo done to incur the Captain's wrath?"

"The Captain said something which made Jaquo laugh. He accused Jaquo of not taking the subject, whatever it was, seriously enough. He said he needed time to think about that, so he better take some time out and clean out the sewage pipes."

The First Officer ruminated on the story. There was no doubt that the Captain was not the sort of being to see the amusing side of any situation. The word unbending was a simile for flexibility in comparison to Captain Nerris's normal demeanour.

"He can be a bit severe at times" It was as close to criticism of her superior as Marti was willing to get.

"He's told Elvis that he has to scrub down the exterior of the ship as soon as we get into our next orbit. I think he would have sent him out there now if the safety systems didn't prevent the airlocks being opened while we're in a wormhole."

"Elvis was asking for that. He's spoken back to the Captain more than once. He goes too far, always trying to push the boundaries of acceptable behaviour."

"And the Captain isn't doing the same by sending someone outside the ship on the end of a tether line with just a scrubbing brush and a jet hose?"

"It's the message that's important, not the acts themselves. You know how important discipline is on long haul missions like this one."

"He goes too far. You would agree with me if we were having a drink in a bar somewhere, instead of sitting here."

Marti admitted to herself that she probably would agree, but as the ship's second in command she had to support her Captain whether she liked it or not.

"Could you have a word with him. Point out the effect his behaviour is having on morale."

"This is the Namsat Elba, not the Bounty and I'm not Fletcher Christian."

"Another of your famous movie references." Davina smiled, knowing her friend's love of films and how she brought them into her conversation at every opportunity, whether it was appropriate or not.

"Yes, but not just a movie reference; also a true story. Fletcher Christian led a mutiny on board a Royal Navy ship."

"I'll have to watch it sometime."

"Do that. It's in the ship's entertainment archive. Look, I'll have a word with the Captain if the right opportunity comes along. In the meantime I suggest the crew gets on with their work and tries to avoid upsetting the Captain."

Davina stood up, her half eaten meal finished and the subject apparently closed. Marti watched her retreating back, hoping against hope that no one would do anything stupid. She collected her own tray and took it to the service point before making her way back to the Bridge to take over the watch from the Second Officer.

* * *

Captain Nerris sat alone on the Bridge of the Namsat Elba when his First Officer plucked up the courage to approach him. His face was set in a hard stare as he examined the ships log.

"The crew are making disparaging remarks about me in their personal logs." He snarled, without looking up to see who had entered.

"Captain…" Marti was at a loss as to what to say. What she should say challenged his authority, but at the same time the Captain was breaking established protocols. She tried again. "Captain, it's very unusual to read the personal logs of crew members."

"I have to know what they're saying. I see them, whispering behind my back; making jokes about me. They have no respect for my position and no understanding of the burden my responsibilities place on me."

"But Captain, it has always been understood that personal logs are private. They allow the crew to record their thoughts, their most secret feelings. To read them is akin to reading their communications to their families."

"They are critical of me in those, as well."

Marti's heart sank. It was worse than she had feared. It was strictly against galactic law to read the private communications of crew members. It required the authority of a court of law even for the ship's owners to access them.

"Captain, I … I don't know what to say. You've broken the law."

"On this ship I am the law. You know the intra-galactic convention. The Captain is in sole command. He cannot be wrong."

But he can be prosecuted for breaking the law, Marti thought to herself. But of course in order to have the law enforced they would first need to get to a place where the law held sway and that wasn't due to happen for another six years, give or take a couple of months.

"Permission to speak, Sir. Off the record." Marti had one chance at this, she knew and if she blew it things might actually get worse for the crew.

"There's no such thing as 'off the record' on my ship, Number One. Either speak out or hold your tongue."

"Very well, Captain. The crew think that perhaps… I mean, I think that…" Marti floundered. She could see the Captain's expression darkening. His jaw was clenched so tightly she feared for the condition of his teeth. A vein stood out at his temple and she could clearly see it throbbing.

What had come over the Captain? This wasn't the man she knew and admired. She had served with him on two previous missions and on both occasions she recalled the success they had enjoyed and the admiring tone of the crews when they had spoken of him. He was a hard man, it was true, but up until now he had always been fair. It was the reason she had volunteered for this mission, rather than taking her two years of planet duties as she was entitled to do.

Was he sick? Was the burden of command damaging his mind, his ability to reason? That had to be it. There could be no other explanation. The Captain was suffering some sort of breakdown.

They had lost a crew member, Gol Fedrer, a junior science officer, when a shuttle had crashed on the planet from which he was gathering samples. Did the Captain blame himself for that? Surely not. It had been a mechanical failure. The computer analytics had confirmed it. A one in a billion chance, to be sure, but there was no way the Captain could have foreseen it when the shuttle had been launched. But something had clearly upset the balance of the Captain's mind. He had started to show signs of stress before they had even left the orbit of the star system where the accident happened and his behaviour had become ever more demanding day by day.

He was seeing plots in every whispered conversation. Dria and Finn whispering together to arrange one of their not-very-secret assignations was being interpreted by the Captain as an act of mutiny. Kris and Lev organising Davina's surprise birthday party had become a plot to take over the ship. The Captain was in the grip of paranoia. And now she, his First Officer, was feeding that paranoia by raising her concerns over his behaviour. But of course what the crew were now discussing was mutinous. Things had become so bad since they had left 1-430-833 that the crew were now discussing the pros and cons of taking over the ship.

"Come on, Number one. Spit it out. I know what you're going to say. It's obvious from your face. You think I'm being too hard on the crew, don't you." It wasn't a question; he was stating it as a fact and he was also right.

"Well… Sir …" She couldn't bring herself to say the words. She cursed her own weakness, but she couldn't be seen as part of the plot. It would ruin her career if the Captain so much as hinted at insubordination in her personal file. "Sir. I have to report that the crew appear to be discussing some sort of action to limit your authority on board this ship." She finally caved in and put her own interests first. If the crew found out she would lose all her friends. Davina had trusted her to carry their message of appeasement to the Captain and she had betrayed her.

"I knew it. I knew they were plotting against me. How bad is it, Number One?"

"It isn't very far advanced. It's hasn't gone beyond mutterings so far." Marti attempted some damage limitation.

"How many of the crew are involved?"

"I have no idea Sir. They don't include me. They don't trust me. But I think perhaps ten." That had been the approximate number in the mess room, so she wouldn't be far out in her estimate.

"And who are the ring leaders?"

"I can't say, Captain?"

"Can't, or won't?" The Captain pinned her with his eyes. They seemed to bore into her brain, seeking the answer to his question.

"I think the Chief Scientific Officer may be one of them, Sir."

"Good. That wasn't so hard, was it?" The Captain stood up and started pacing in circles around his chair. Marti had seen him do this on previous occasions when pondering difficult decisions.

"Order the CSO to my cabin. You can take over the watch while I deal with her."

"Aye aye, Captain." Marti snapped to attention. The dice were now cast, she knew. Either the mutiny would be crushed before it started, or her betrayal of her crew members would send events spiralling out of control.

* * *

It hadn't taken long for the mutiny to start. The Captain ordered the ship's Security Officer to confine the Chief Scientific Officer to her cabin, to remain there until she revealed the names of her co-conspirators. Davina was lucky that the ship wasn't equipped with a brig, or she would have found herself locked up there instead.

That night the crew, or rather those who were involved in the plot, had overpowered her guard and released Davina before attempting to take control of the Bridge. But the Captain had been ready for them. He, Marti and the Security Officer had locked themselves in, and disabled the door locks. Without access to the Bridge the crew couldn't take control of the ship, or so the Captain had thought.

The Second Engineer, however, knew otherwise. Elvis Vatt was the one under sentence to do a spell of external ship cleaning and he knew the ship's systems as well as he knew his way around his own cabin. It wasn't long before he had wrested control of the ship's computer from the Bridge and transferred command to the engineering compartment.

"So what do we do now?" he asked the assembled scientists and engineers.

"Do we have control of the navi-com as well?" Asked Dria.

"Of course. We can go anywhere in the galaxy. Probably anywhere in the universe."

"There's one place we can't go." Said Davina in a despondent tone. "We can't go home."

"We could try." Insisted Elvis. "We can tell them what the Captain was doing. It's all on the ship's log, every bit of it. They'd have to believe us."

"They would lock us up and throw away the key, is what they would do." Davina was a pragmatist. She didn't deal in fantasies about justice. "No court would deliver a verdict that would set a precedent for other crews to do what we've done. They daren't risk it. We may be in the right, but the Captain is in command of the ship no matter what. He could order us to fly the ship into the middle of the nearest star and it wouldn't be seen as an excuse for us to take control."

"Davina's right." Finn added his support. "Remember the Colombina?" There were a few nods from among the mutineers. "The Captain ordered the crew to abandon her and take refuge on the nearest planet. Apparently he was suffering delusions and thought that the ship was just about to blow up. The court found that the crew had done the right thing by obeying him. Once off the ship he was no longer regarded as being in command so the crew was able to legally remove him on the grounds of diminished responsibility. But the court made it clear that if they had done that while they had still been on board they would have been charged with mutiny."

"If the First Officer had backed us she could have replaced him on the same grounds, but she was the only one that could get away with it. That's why we really needed her." Elvis looked meaningfully at Davina.

"I'm sorry, but it was never on. I know she's my friend, but she's also a career officer. It was always unlikely that she would join us."

"But she betrayed us." Elvis spat.

"Yes. I know. I didn't expect that." A tear dribbled down Davina's cheek as she remembered their years of friendship, forged over several exploration missions.

"Well, no use crying over it. It's done. So, as I asked earlier, what do we do?"

"We carry on with the mission." An unexpected voice made them turn to face a new arrival. The hulking form of the Chief Engineer stood in the doorway.

Elvis got to his feet in the presence of his superior. "Chief, we thought you would be with the Captain."

"Well, I'm not. Look, I don't condone what you've done. It was foolish and no doubt you will have to answer for it in the fullness of time. No doubt I'll have to answer for not using my rank to order you to return control of the ship to the Captain, but I happen to agree with you that he isn't presently fit to command and I'm not going to become a mutineer by taking command myself. But the best thing you can do now is complete the mission. If you do that and send all the data back to Head Office you might be allowed to vanish without trace providing you hand the ship back to the Captain when you've found somewhere to go. If, however, you just vanish and it emerges later that you committed mutiny then you'll be hunted down, for sure."

"How would it get out? If we just go somewhere, find ourselves a nice planet on which to settle, no one would know the difference. They would think we'd just had some sort of accident and all been killed."

"And what about the three officers currently occupying the bridge? How are you going to keep them from reporting this incident? Or do you plan to kill them to keep them quiet?"

The mutineers exchanged worried glances. None of them had thought of that.

"No. We can't kill them." Whispered Davina.

"You couldn't maybe." Snarled Elvis.

"I couldn't let you do it either. Look at us, Elvis, we're not killers. We're scientists, engineers, navigators. We signed on for a mission of peaceful exploration. We chose this exploration company because of its ethical stance on the colonisation and exploitation of planets. Any one of us could have got a berth on a ship working for Gargantua Enterprises and gone off planet raping with them, but we didn't. We're good beings, ethical beings. Now, who here would pull the trigger… really?"

Davina swept her gaze around the room, searching each face for an answer. Some looked away, others went grey around the eyes, embarrassed by the truth of her words. Even Elvis shuffled his feet and couldn't bring himself to meet her piercing look.

"As I thought." Davina continued. "So, we either do as the Chief suggests and drop off the radar until the mission is complete, or we make a run for it and hope that when the authorities find out they won't bother coming after us. Personally I think there's only the slimmest of chances of that happening."

They held a show of hands and there was only one dissenter, Elvis. The mission would go on.

* * *

Marti watched the Captain pacing round and round his chair. He had been doing it for three hours, non-stop, getting more agitated with each passing hour. Every fourth or fifth step he would slap his pulsar against his thigh, as though encouraging himself to some greater effort. From time to time he would alternate this with slapping the pulsar's barrel into his left palm.

They had been stuck on the Bridge for two days, taking it in turns to sleep, though it was clear from the colour of the Captain's skin and the redness of his eyes that he had hardly closed his eyes.

Not all the crew had mutinied. Four had contacted the bridge through the intercom system to say they had taken refuge in their bunks. These were navigation crew members, Beings who worked on the Bridge and who knew the Captain the best and had the greatest sense of loyalty towards him. Marti told them to stay where they were and not to do anything that might upset the mutineers.

Food was delivered to the bridge twice a day through a service hatch and to the cabins of the loyal crew members, so it was clear that the mutineers had no intention of harming them. Although the Captain and his two colleagues no longer had any control over the ship's computers the Bridge's viewing screens still allowed them to monitor the instructions that the crew were feeding in, or weren't feeding in as was more the case. The ship was still on the same course through its wormhole and apart from some minor engineering adjustments to the environmental systems nothing had change. By monitoring the lab and the engineering section they could see that the ship's work was proceeding as normal. It was as though the mutiny had never happened.

Apart from Captain Nerris's constant, agitated pacing.

"We're going to retake the ship." He announced at last.

"Do you think that's wise, Sir?" Marti had said it before she'd had time to think, frightened that the Captain might do something rash and get them killed.

"Are you now questioning me, Number One?" The Captain thrust his face into Marti's, his nose almost touching hers.

"Na...na... no Sir. It's just that there are so many of them and so few of us."

"The First Officer's right, Sir." The Security Officer intervened. "Just opening the door to the Bridge could get us killed. For all we know they have it wired up to explode."

"Fool. Don't you think I haven't thought of that? No, we won't go through the door. We'll lift the floor panels and wriggle out through the air conditioning ducts. Well, you will Number One. You're the smallest of us. Once you're in the corridor you can check the door and if it's safe we'll open it from this side."

"And then what, Sir?"

"We make for the main armoury, get more pulsars and arm those crew members that have remained loyal to us. That will even up the odds considerably"

Yes, thought Marti. There will only be odds of three to one instead of six to one. There had only been one pulsar on the Bridge, kept under lock and key for just this eventuality. It was the one that the Captain was now tapping against his thigh, the beat as regular as that of a metronome. "Then we send two crew members back here to secure the Bridge while we make for Engineering. Once we have that we have full control of the ship's systems. We drop out of the wormhole and send a distress signal over the Glacticnet. Help will be with us within days."

Weeks, more like, thought the First Officer. They had no idea where they would be when they dropped out of the wormhole, it could be hundreds of light years from the nearest planet from which help might be sent. Even using wormhole technology it would take time for a rescue mission to be mounted. During that time the small band of loyal crew members would be hunted up and down the ship. By firing the first shots the rest of the crew would feel they had the right to defend themselves and they would have nothing to lose. A life sentence for mutiny was no worse than a life sentence for killing the Captain…or the First Officer.

However, the First Officer knew that there was no chance of dissuading the Captain from his chosen course of action. Mentally she prepared herself for death.

"When will we do it?" She asked.

"Tonight, when the crew are asleep. They seem to be adhering to the normal ship's routine, so there will only be one watchkeeper in Engineering; two at most. The rest will be in their cabins."

* * *

Marti cuffed sweat from her eyes as she pushed hard with the sides of her boots to ease her way a few sim further along the air conditioning duct. Her shoulders and hips were tight against the sides, applying considerable friction, while her body acted as a plug to prevent the cooling air from reaching her upper body and face. Lying on her back her face was no more than ten sim from the upper side of the duct. Another wave of claustrophobia swept over her but she fought it off, forcing her mind to focus on the task in hand.

She reached with her arms once more, found a thin edge of metal where two sections of duct overlapped and dug her fingernails in behind it. Flexing her knees as far as they would bend in the restricted space she pushed with the outside of her feet once again, at the same time as heaving herself along by her fingernails. She almost cried out as pain seared through her fingertips as another nail broke off, ripping as far back as the cuticle. She bit back the pain but the tears were running freely down her cheeks to drip past her ears.

She withdrew her arm and sucked at the damaged fingertip, tasting the copper of her blood, but glad that the darkness prevented her from seeing the damage. Her beautiful nails, so carefully manicured and polished, now reduced to ragged bleeding flesh. She pushed the image from her mind and reached once more.

She found another edge, but not the thin metal of one length of duct overlapping another, this was the edge of an inspection panel, protruding at least half a sim into the tunnel. It enabled her to use more of her fingertips pull herself along. Two more pulls and her face was beneath the panel. Tentatively she pushed against it. It lifted a fraction. She pushed again and felt a rush of fresher air hit her face. It felt good, cooling her at the same time as boosting her spirits. She pushed again and a thin stream of light hit her eyes, causing her to squeeze them tight shut against the sudden glare. She paused, allowing her vision to adjust itself, then pushed again. This time the panel lifted clear and she could see small sections of the corridor walls, but the angle was still too tight to see the deck head.

With more space she was able to use her elbows to assist her aching hands and the whole panel lifted, balanced on her forearms. She shifted it sideways so it lay across the opening at an angle. It now took only some minor shuffling to move it all the way to the side. Placing her forearms on the floor on either side of the opening in the duct she was able to lever her upper body upright so she was sitting in the hole, half in and half out. She found herself facing the exterior of the door to the Bridge.

She craned her neck to allow her to look the other way along the corridor; the direction from which danger might approach. Nothing. They hadn't bothered to mount a guard on the Bridge. They must have felt very certain that the Captain would do nothing to interfere with their plans. They had been wrong.

Pushing down with her hands she wriggled her way out of the duct until she was kneeling alongside it. She slid the panel back into place so that she didn't inadvertently fall back into the duct. The sound of her company issue boots striking the metal would reverberate throughout this end of the ship and no doubt would raise the alarm.

There was nothing attached to the Bridge door. No alarm, no trip wires and, most importantly, no explosive charge. She stepped forward and wrapped her knuckles on the hard metal, using the pre-arranged signal. One… one, two.

It took a minute or two for the wedges that were jamming the door shut to be removed, then it hissed open. The Captain stepped through and headed along the corridor without even glancing at her or offering a word of congratulations at her achievement. The Security Officer followed, rolling his eyes in a silent 'what can you do?' look.

To get to the small armoury it was necessary to go through the Captain's cabin. The door stood open but the cabin was unoccupied. No one had felt confident enough to claim the treasured space, large enough to accommodate a desk and an easy chair as well as the Captain's bunk. The Captain stood in front of the locked door and tapped in the eight digit combination. The door slid open with a soft whoosh. The armoury was no more than a cupboard, rigged out with a shadow board which indicated where each weapon should be placed. There were twenty one pulsar shaped spaces arranged in rows of three, the highest row at head height and the lowest just above floor level. Thirteen of the spaces were empty.

"Damn and blast. They've been here before us. The Chief Engineer also has the combination, so he must have given them access. Damn him, damn him and double damn him." He cursed, banging his hand loudly against the bulkhead next to the armoury door.

"Captain, the noise." The Security Officer appealed. "You'll alert the crew."

The Captain stopped, his hand half way towards the bulkhead once again. "Sorry. You're right. I don't know what came over me." He reached back into the cupboard. "Damned traitorous mutineers." He muttered, his words barely audible.

The Captain handed a pulsar each to Marti and the Security Officer. "There's a holdall under my bunk. Get it." He snapped, not addressing either of them in particular. Marti was the closest so she reached beneath the bed and felt around. Her hand felt the loop of a bag and she pulled it out. It was light and therefore empty. She passed it to the Captain.

"Don't give to me! You SO; hold it open!"

The Security Officer did as he was bid and the Captain started loading the remaining six pulsars into it.

When the last one was in, he turned and stalked towards the door. "Follow me. Don't shoot unless you have to. I want these bastards alive so they can stand trial."

The accommodation for the navigation crew members was further along the same corridor. They passed Marti's own cabin and stopped outside the door of the one belonging to the Second Officer.

"No, Sir." Marti whispered before the Captain could operate the door switch. "He isn't with us. We need the Third Officer."

The Captain nodded and moved a couple of met further along the corridor. He passed his hand over the switch and the door slid open. The Third Officer looked up with an expression of alarm on his face, before realising who was entering. The lights were on and he had been watching something on a hand held screen. He removed the earphones from his ears, but the Captain raised his own finger to his lips to demand silence before he said anything. He signalled to the Security Officer and was handed a pulsar, which he passed to the Third Officer. "Follow us." He mouthed, before turning and leaving the small cabin, not even waiting to see if his order had been obeyed.

This process was repeated three more times, then the small band approached the door of the mess room. It should have been empty at that time of night. It really should have been.

The door slid open to reveal two crew members playing cards. It was difficult to say who was more surprised, the Captain or the card players. It was, however, the card players who were first to react. The one furthest away flipped the edge of the table upwards and it crashed to the floor, playing cards fluttering down behind, over and in front of it. The nearer crew member dived over the table's edge and the two crewmen now had a flimsy barrier between themselves and the Captain.

"Stop, Captain." One of them shouted. "We don't want to shoot, but we will if you don't stop!"

"You bastards. Who do you think you are giving me orders on my own ship?" He followed up his question with a blast of his pulsar, which melted a hole in the plastic table top. A head appeared above the table, soon followed by a hand holding a pulsar. He fired and then ducked back down.

In front of her, the Security Officer folded over and slid gently down the door jam to the floor, he didn't utter a sound. The captain stepped back through the door, nearly tripping over the dead Security Officer and they pressed themselves back into cover on either side.

"Captain, I think you should be further back." Marti advised him. "There's no point in quelling a mutiny if you aren't alive at the end of it."

Nodding his head in agreement the Captain slid himself along the wall, placing the Third Officer and another crewman between him and the door.

Marti glanced back into the mess room. It now appeared to be deserted. She noted that the far entrance, the one that led to Engineering and to the massive laboratory that made up half the ship, was just sliding shut.

"I think they've gone, Captain." She announced.

"Number Three. Check it out."

Nervously the Third Officer dropped to the floor and wriggled into the room. He slithered across the polished surface until he was next to the fallen table. He braced himself on one knee then stood up, pointing his pulsar down at whatever was on the far side. It turned out to be nothing.

"They've gone." He reported. At that moment the far door opened again and two figures combat rolled through. Struggling to bring their pulsars to bear as they tried to regain their feet, they were far too slow. The Third Officer fired twice, hitting each of them in turn. They lay still.

"Oh my galaxy." Marti held her hand up to her mouth. "It's Dria. Finn, you've killed Dria." She accused the Third Officer as he stared at the body of the female with whom he'd been having a not-so-secret affair. The first of her former friends had fallen, but Finn would feel the loss more than she ever would.

"Don't be so damned sentimental, Number One. If you mourn every one of these damned mutineers that we have to kill we'll never get the job done." The Captain snarled at her as he stalked past and into the mess room. The Third Officer was still staring at Dria's body with a dazed look on his face. The pulsar dropped from his nerveless fingers, clattering to the floor.

"Pick up your weapon Number Three." Snapped the Captain.

The Third Officer stood motionless.

"I said pick up your weapon, Number Three. If you don't obey my order I will shoot you." The Captain raised his pulsar, extending his arm to full stretch.

The Third Officer saw the movement and it stirred him into activity. He bent down and picked up the pulsar. In one smooth movement he straightened, raised the pulsar to his chest and pulled the trigger. The weapon clattered to the ground again, a fraction of a second before it was joined by the body of the Third Officer.

"Damn and blast him. What did he to go and do that for!" The Captain raged. "Two dead and we're no nearer to Engineering and they'll be waiting for us now."

Marti was shocked at the Captain's callous attitude. Four of his crew were now dead, two of whom had died defending him, but he didn't seem to care. That wasn't the Captain Nerris that she knew and respected. This was some bitter, self-righteous monster that was inhabiting his body. But she had made her call and she was now stuck with it.

She and the remaining three loyal crew members followed the Captain into the abandoned mess room, trying not to look at the three dead bodies.

"Move them out of the way." The Captain ordered. Marti nodded at the three crew members and between them they half dragged, half carried, the bodies to the side of the room. She hunted around in the cupboards and found some table clothes, used only for the monthly formal dinners, and draped them over the dead crew.

She wanted to ask the Captain what they would do now, but he had resumed his agitated pacing. Clearly things hadn't gone as he had envisaged them and he now had to come up with a new plan. For her own sake Marti hoped it didn't involve crawling through any more ducts. She gave an involuntary shudder.

"Captain." One of the crew, Alia, interrupted. "There a crawl space behind the food service point. It's used by the maintenance engineers when the tubes get blocked. It's quite wide. I'm pretty sure we could get through it. Anyway, it comes out in Number One hold, above the food storage vats."

Marti knew the vats. As part of her duties she had to inspect them, to ensure that the food levels matched those recorded on the computer. They were large cylinders full of processed protein, carbohydrate, fat, fibre and other ingredients which were mixed by the machinery to create something that resembled, but didn't quite taste like, food. Whenever she ate she had to reject the image from her brain otherwise she would have died of malnutrition before the ship had even left home orbit.

The Captain stopped his pacing. "Of course. That hold is directly beneath Engineering, isn't it? Can we get access from there?"

"Not directly, Captain." Alia was starting to get excited by her own idea. "But if we go aft through holds two and three there's an access at the rear that allows the lab rats to get down to their stocks of test tubes and chemicals."

Lab rats; Marti wondered if the science officers knew that was how the navigation assistants referred to them.

"And from there we can get directly into the corridor that leads to Engineering, of course. Well done Alia, at least someone's thinking." He shot a disparaging glance towards Marti, who went pale with embarrassment at having been publicly rebuked.

Gaining access to the crawl space meant moving the bodies again, as they had chosen exactly the wrong place when they had first moved them but, that done, they were soon on their hands and knees crawling along behind the mess room and the areas immediately behind it.

Marti took the lead, torch in hand and she realised that they must be directly behind the cabins of the engineering crew, separated by just a thin sheet of artificial wood. Were the engineers asleep? Or were they now setting up defences outside the mess room door, waiting for the Captain to emerge? Given recent events she assumed it was the latter, so she didn't have to worry too much about making noise. She quickened her pace.

A rectangular hole opened up in the floor in front of her, revealing a lengthy drop into the cargo hold. A collapsible ladder was attached to the bulkhead in front of her. Marti pulled on the retaining clip and the ladder slid down to its full length, the bottom rung a few sim above the floor. She stuck her head through and traversed the beam of her torch across the cargo space. If there was anyone waiting for them then they had hidden themselves well, but that wouldn't be hard. The gigantic food cylinders provided plenty of dark spaces between and behind them. It crossed Marti's mind that rectangular tanks would have been a more efficient use of space, but angrily pushed the idea away. This was no time to start re-designing the ship.

Grabbing the ladder at the sides she swung her feet into the hole, pressed the sides of her boots against the side of the ladder and shuffled her bottom off the edge. The ship's artificial gravity took hold of her and she slid smoothly towards the deck, her feet hitting it with barely a sound. Again, she scanned the cargo hold looking for threats, but there were none that she could see. She pointed her torch upwards into the face of Alia, who had been behind her in the crawl space.

"OK. Down you come." She hissed. It took only a few moments before the Captain and all three crew had joined her.

"Alia, you seem to know where you're going. You take the lead. Number One, you follow her." The Captain gave his instructions.

It was only a few short steps to the bulkhead separating Number One from Number Two hold. Alia operated the switch that controlled the door. Above them, in Engineering, a light on a display board went from green to red as the Captain and his crew passed through the door. As the door shut behind them the light went from red back to green.

Number Two hold held all the engineering tools and spares. Crates and boxes were stacked high on metal racks, each identified by a painted bar code, backed up by a passive RF tag that could be read by a communicator. One length of racking was filled from deck to deckhead by open topped bins filled with minor components. The myriad packets of nuts, screws, washers, bolts, seals, caps, resistors, capacitors, microchips, processors and a thousand other parts that were needed to keep the heart of the ship beating healthily. The serried rows of racking left little room for manoeuvre, but there was just enough space for the crew to walk in single file down the middle. Finally they reached the next bulkhead and the door that led to the last hold; Number Three. Exploration and Science. Here were all the tools for digging and scraping, the sample jars, spare lab equipment and the chemicals needed by the analytical machines. There was a smell in the air which reminded Marti of school science lessons. She hoped it was non-toxic.

At the far end was the access to the lab; proper stairs with a hand rail. You didn't want to try and climb a ladder when you were carrying a jar of acid that could eat its way through the spaceship's outer skin in seconds. Davina had explained to Marti, years before on an earlier mission, that there were many safety protocols in place to prevent such an accident, but it never did to get too blasé about such things.

They passed from one hold to the other and again a light on the engineering display board went from green to red and back again.

Marti stepped in front of Alia and led the way up the stairs. At the top she paused before opening the bulkhead door, gathered up her courage and opened it. From her position half way up the stairs she leaned forward until she could scan the brightly lit lab. This was the driving force of the ship. The place that gave it its purpose. This was where the samples came to be analysed, the diggings and scrapings that would tell the galaxy what there was to be found in the remote corners, whether a planet had once supported life and whether it could do so again.

Where there was life the plants were analysed as well as the secretions of any creatures that might be found. No creature was ever trapped or killed and brought on board; that would have conflicted with company ethics. If any were found they were photographed. 'Take nothing but images, leave nothing but footprints'; that was the ethos behind the company. Minimal samples were taken from plants. That was all that was allowed.

Satisfied that the lab was empty Marti completed the climb to the top of the stairs and crouched down behind a lab bench, giving herself some cover should a threat suddenly appear. The lab was spotless. She would expect nothing less from a Chief Scientific Officer like her friend … her former friend, Davina. The benches were clear of clutter. The machines that did the actual analysis were silent, the crew occupied with other thoughts right then. Thoughts motivated by survival.

She waved the rest of the crew up the stair and waited while they joined her, each finding a place of temporary concealment.

* * *

Out of the corner of his eye Third Engineer Mako Cari caught sight of something changing on his control boards. He couldn't be sure quite what it was, but there had definitely been a change.

He had lived with those boards seven hours a day for four years and if something changed he always noticed, always knew. The only reason that he didn't know this time was because he had been half in and half out of the control room door, trying to see what was going on up by the mess room, nearly twenty met away from his station, past the engineering crew cabins.

But something had changed.

He concentrated on the boards. If there was any sort of problem it would show up again. He went through his usual routine, starting from the top left of each board and working his way down to the bottom right, checking each display, each indicator light, each switch position. Everything was as it should be except on the computer control panel, which showed that Engineering had control, not the Bridge. Well, no surprise there, they were, after all, in the middle of a mutiny.

He was half way through a second visual sweep when his eyes were dragged across to the auxiliary board, the one that indicated the state of the various air tight doors built into the ship. Those vital barriers that made sure that if the hull was breached then the affected part was isolated so that the atmosphere in the remainder of the ship was maintained. A red light glowed where it should have been green. The air tight door between Number Two Hold and Number Three Hold had just been opened. He watched the light for a few seconds before it went green again. Just long enough for a handful of people to pass from one hold to the next, at least by his very rough calculation.

His hand reached out to the intercom, gently pressing the button. "Elvis, it's Mako. There's someone down in the holds."

"How did they get in?"

"No idea. As far as I can tell they didn't get in through the primary entrance." The only way into the holds from inside the ship was through engineering, or through the lab, the door opposite his own station to be precise. They could have got in through the lab, but he was pretty sure that was empty, all the lab rats currently being employed in defending the exit from the mess room. If the external loading doors had been used then not only would a light have changed colour, but a very loud klaxon would have announced the opening of an external door. "If I had to guess, I'd say they used the mess room crawl space."

"Yeah, makes sense. So, they're trying to get round behind us. OK, Mako, you stay put. I'll send a couple of pulsars down to check out the lab."

There was only a short delay before three crew members padded past on their way aft towards the lab, one of the maintenance technicians and two lab technicians.

A few seconds later Davina, the Chief Scientific Officer, arrived at the door of the control room.

"What's going on back there, Mako?"

"No idea. I can't monitor CCTV from here, I'd have to go to the Security Suite for that. Besides, it's locked and it only responds to the Security Officer's hand print."

"If they've moved out of the mess room we could go and get the SO's hand and use it to open the door." Davina mused.

"If you want to go cutting hands off dead bodies, you be my guest." Mako's voice showed how disgusted he felt by the idea.

"We could carry him there. It's not far."

"Again, be my guest. I don't do dead people."

Davina dropped the idea. In truth she had no stomach for cutting up dead bodies, or for carrying them. To do it within the clinical atmosphere of a laboratory was one thing, but to do it in the mess room, well that was something else. She would have to wait to find out what was happening.

She didn't have long to wait. The unmistakable hiss-zap sound of pulsar weapons being fired rang through the ship. There was a shriek of pain, the sound of something heavy falling, then silence. Davina hefted her pulsar in her hand and started to move towards the source of the shooting.

"No. Wait here. We don't know what you could be walking into." He was cut off by the sound of renewed weapons fire. It went on for some time, ringing clangs indicated pulsar shots hitting the ships walls. There were more thumps and the crash and tinkle of something glass smashing.

"Oh, no. What was that?" Davina wailed. "If that was the cyclotron we haven't got a spare."

"I think you should be a bit more concerned about your shipmates than your lab equipment." Mako observed dryly.

"Yes, of course. What am I thinking? Sorry, but I get quite attached to my lab equipment, but you're right. It isn't alive."

The shooting came to an abrupt end. The sudden silence drifted heavily along the corridor from the lab.

"This is the Captain." The sudden sound of a voice made them jump. "If you surrender now you'll be treated leniently."

The Second Engineer hurried to join them. Before he even asked what had happened Mako told him.

"Three more dead" Davina added. "At least it would seem that way."

"But they may have suffered casualties too." Elvis said.

The Chief Engineer sauntered up to join them. "Well, it's not quite going to plan, is it Elvis?"

"No Chief. Any suggestions?"

"It's your show. I'm just an innocent bystander."

"Then why have you got a pulsar?" The Second Engineer snapped back.

"It seems sensible while everyone else is armed. I have no intention of using it, unless I'm forced into it."

Elvis was just about to ask what circumstances might force his superior to use his weapon when the Captain's voice rang out again.

"I'm waiting for an answer."

"You can wait as long as you fucking want." Elvis shouted back. "We're still in control of the ship. You've achieved nothing."

"Language, Second Engineer. I don't hold with foul language." The Chief Engineer admonished. "There's no need for it unless you've hit your thumb with a hammer."

Davina smothered a smile. Nothing, it seemed, upset the Chief Engineer, except for bad language.

"Sorry Sir."

"Very well. You leave us no alternative." The Captain's voice cut across their exchange once again. "If you won't surrender we'll have to take the ship room by room. In case you don't already know, Maintenance Technician Yarmley and Lab Technicians Gorse and Hummingfield are all dead."

"And how many did you lose, you murdering bastard?"

There was a short pause, as though the Captain was trying to keep himself under control following that verbal assault. "You'll have to wait to find out. However, I can assure you that the odds for us are now considerably better."

* * *

Marti cradled the head of Alia in her lap and let the tears run freely down her face. Another life lost. Why she felt this one more keenly than the others she couldn't say. Perhaps it was an accumulation of grief: Dria had been her friend along with Davina, Finn she had mentored when he had come aboard as a green graduate from the company's training school. She had laughed at the Security Officer's jokes, many of them ribald and all of them funny and now Alia, poor sweet Alia, who never had a bad word to say about anyone or anything. Darling of the Bridge, popular with the female crew and desired by many of the males.

Lowering Alia's head gently to the deck Marti stood up and found a lab coat hanging on a peg by the door, draping it over the young crew member.

"Still four of us, eh Number One?"

"Yes Captain. Still four of us." Not a single word of remorse or regret for the death of another of his crew members. They had all become pieces in a lethal game of chess to him; expendable and forgettable. She felt a strong temptation to raise her pulsar and shoot him between the eyes. Then she remembered the other two crew members, Soch and Neran, they would be witnesses to her act. It would end the killing, but when they were caught, as they would be, she would go to jail with the others. She cursed her cowardice and bit back her hatred for what the Captain had become.

"How many do they have now?" The captain asked.

Marti counted off the known casualties before naming those she thought were still alive. "The Second Officer, Chief Engineer, Second Engineer, Third Engineer. I think one more Maintenance technician, that would be Rocko. Then there's the Chief Science Officer, two ordinary Science Officers and one remaining Lab Tech. Oh, what's his name. The scrawny one with the terrible beard."

"That's Anghar, Ma'am." Soch contributed form his guard post by the door.

"Oh yes, Anghar. Why does he have that awful beard?"

"Alia once told him he would look good with a beard. He stopped shaving the same day."

Marti could barely suppress a smile. Alia had had that effect on the male crew members.

"Anyway, Captain, that makes nine, by my reckoning.

"Pity about the Chief Engineer. I would have expected him to remain loyal."

With her own loyalty now being tested to destruction, Marti said nothing.

"Still, not bad odds. Considerably better than they were when we left the Bridge."

But still not good odds, Marti thought to herself,

"Does anyone here know any chemistry?" The Captain was examining the lab with a curious eye. "I was thinking, maybe we could come up with something that would give us a bit if an edge."

"Well, I think a bomb is out of the question. Unless we knew exactly how big the explosion was going to be, and were able to control it, we're more likely to blow the whole ship apart."

"Good point Number One. Better rule out bombs then. How about some sort of gas, you know, send them to sleep."

Poison them, more likely, Marti didn't say. "We would need a lot of it, Sir, and we'd have to be able to protect ourselves from the effects. It's a big ship, the most effective method of delivery would be through the air conditioning system and we breath the same air. If we controlled Engineering then we could control the air conditioning, but from here that's impossible."

"And if we controlled Engineering then we would effectively control the ship anyway. Hmm." The Captain seemed to give up on the idea and started his pacing once again, deep in thought.

* * *

The pacing stopped, much to Marti's relief.

"Gather round here." The Captain pointed to a small meeting area dominated by an electronic writing board. "Not you, Soch. You stay on guard." He picked up the stylus and used it to start drawing a plan of the ship on the touch sensitive surface of the board, showing the side elevation and the two decks and the partitions that separated them. It looked like a salmon with a blunted head and a broad body tapering to the engine efflux at the rear.

He changed colour and drew in the airtight doors that protected the ship's internal integrity in the case of a hull breach. "Now, if we look at this we can see that the engineering station and the mess hall are cut off from the rest of the ship by these bulkheads." He pointed left and right. "But below that is Number One Hold and part of the shuttle dock level. Now, most of the lower deck is cut off from the upper deck by the airtight bulkheads and decks, but as we know, the mess room and Engineering have a weak point. The crawl space from the mess room to Number One hold is separated by only a flimsy partition. If there was a sudden decompression in Number One Hold that partition wouldn't hold, so the mess room and Engineering would lose air pressure as well and everyone inside would be dead within seconds.

Marty's hand flew to her mouth to cut off her exclamation of horror. She could tell only too easily where this was going. The Number One Hold air lock. She was proved right by the Captain's next words.

"If we go to the shuttles and take refuge there, I can put on a space suit, go back to Number One Hold, jam the inner door of the airlock open, strap myself in securely then use the emergency release to blast the outer airlock door open. We wait a decent length of time, say ten minutes, then I unjam the inner door to close it, the ship will automatically restore the internal air pressure and we have the ship back."

Marty couldn't allow him to do that. The death toll was just too much. She had to undermine the credibility of the plan. It would be good to come up with an alternative. If Soch and Neran would back her they may be able to get the Captain to see sense. Her mind flew back to the conversation she'd had with Davina. The one about the old movie. That was it. That was the alternative.

"It's a very risky plan, Captain. So many things could go wrong."

"I'm listening." He said, making it clear he didn't really want to be told the plan wouldn't work.

"Well, they knew that we had reached the lab, even though we hadn't made any noise. That means they must have been tracking our movements. I don't know why we didn't think of it, but I'm pretty sure that each of the airtight doors has an indicator on the engineering control boards that shows when it's open. That must be how they knew where we were. So they have a chance to intercept us just by coming down the main stairs into the Shuttle Dock. Then there's the risk to you personally. Even if you can strap yourself in tightly there will be loose articles being sucked out of the airlock. They'll be flying at a considerable speed. It only needs one of them to puncture your suit and you'll be dead and you can't take command of the ship again if you're dead."

"Yes, it would be something of a Fortian Victory." He paused, clearly worried by the risks to his plan that Marti had exposed. "OK. Have you got a better idea?"

"Well, Sir, in other mutinies the crew have usually let the Captain and any loyal crew members go free, so long as they aren't in a position to tell where the mutineers are headed. We could do the same. We negotiate with the mutineers and get them to take us to a planet where we can survive, but we wouldn't be able to tell where they were going because they can go anywhere in the galaxy through worm holes, which aren't really traceable."

"I'll be damned if I will give up my ship, Number One." The Captain exploded.

"But if we continue fighting it's quite possible you will die and then what have you gained? You can't command the ship if you're dead. At least this way you can alert the authorities and maybe they'll let you lead the mission to track the mutineers down."

The thought of that opportunity seemed to persuade the Captain, at least Marti thought it had. He strode over to the door of the lab and peered through it, taking care to remain in cover. "Send the Chief Engineer, unarmed and alone. I have an offer to make." He called.

Glossary

Fortian Victory - At the Battle of Fortia the General of the Maquia defeated the attacking Crovian army by exploding a huge underground charge that created a massive rift, into which the attackers fell, killing all but a handful. Unfortunately, due to a mistake in the calculations, the city of Fortia also fell into the rift, killing all the inhabitants, the defenders, and the commanding General. On Earth this type of empty victory is known as a Pyrrhic Victory, named after the Egyptian King Pyrhus who got most of his own army killed while beating the Romans in two successive battles in 280 and 279 BC.

2 – Peace In Our Time

It didn't take long for the Chief Engineer to arrive. He stood in the corridor, tall and solid looking, making the Captain appear much smaller by comparison, though in truth there was only a couple of sim difference in their heights.

"I'm disappointed in you, Chief." The Captain's voice seemed to register genuine regret.

"We've known each other for a long time, Altar." The Chief Engineer used his privileged position to call the Captain by his first name. "You know I would never sanction mutiny. However, I have to admit that the crew had a case, even if I didn't support it. Consider me a neutral, caught on the wrong side of the battle lines."

The Captain gave a snarl of disapproval. "How dare you address me in such a familiar manner. We're not in the Officers' Club now. And as for not siding with the mutineers, I'm sure your Court Martial will take your plea into account."

The Chief Engineer was wise enough to be able to see when he wasn't going to win the argument, no matter how good his reasoning, so he attempted to divert the Captain onto safer ground. "So what is this offer you wish to make… Captain."

"There has been too much life lost already. I don't want there to be any more. If the mutineers will divert the ship to a planet that is capable of sustaining us and allow us to take a shuttle stocked with food and water, they can have the ship."

"I'm sure they would insist that the planet is uninhabited, just so that you can't raise the alarm and prevent the ship from leaving orbit."

"If that is their only condition, then I will accept it."

"Very well, I'll put it to them." The Chief Engineer turned to leave, but then paused. "Thank you for seeing sense, Captain."

"I'm not doing this out of the goodness of my heart, Chief." The Captain growled. "I'm doing it because it's as likely that I and my loyal crew will die if we don't find another way out of this stand-off. I couldn't give a damn about the mutineers. I'd see them all hang if I could."

"Well, I'm sure that a search will be mounted as soon as you make contact with civilisation, so you may yet have your wish."

With the that Chief Engineer turned on his heel and stomped away along the corridor.

* * *

"That's the last of it, Number One." Soch reported, coming out of the shuttle, brushing his hands together as though removing dust.

"Thanks, Soch. You and Neran get on board and make yourself comfortable. I'll report to the Captain."

Marti walked along the row of airlocks to the door at the foot of the stairs that led to the upper deck, where they emerged directly opposite the Captain's own cabin, where he stood on guard just in case the mutineers decided to double cross them. She herself had stood guard at the other door, the one that led to Number One Hold.

"All the supplies are aboard, Captain. We're ready to go."

"Very good. You board and I'll be with you directly. I just want to …"

"I understand, Captain." Marti was sensitive enough to empathise. I just want to take a few moments to say goodbye to my ship, was what he wanted to say, but didn't want to appear overtly sentimental. She turned and went back the way she had come and entered the airlock and through into the shuttle, where she sat in the seat next the command chair, which was obviously reserved for the Captain. She exchanged relieved glances with Soch and Neran but they said nothing. There wasn't much background noise in the shuttle bay and any comment they might make would probably travel to the Captain's ears, probably to be misinterpreted.

For his part, the Captain waited until he was sure his First Officer was safely on board the shuttle, then made his way to the airlock control panel just out of sight from inside the shuttle itself. He activated the closure switch and the door slid obediently shut.

Unlike the big freight airlocks, the ones for the shuttles had no outer door; that was provided by the shuttle itself. Instead the airlock door had a heavy locking bar which was slid into place and then locked to secure it against accidental release. Quickly the Captain slid the bar into place, but didn't bother locking it. It couldn't be removed from the outside. He looked away as the face of his First Officer appeared in the small inspection port and started banging fruitlessly on the door. Through the thick armoured surface the sound was barely audible.

There was space for four shuttles, each with a capacity of six people. One dock stood empty, the consequence of the accident that had killed Gol Fedrer. Two docks were on his side of the ship and the other two on the far side, as well as having an auxiliary airlock on each side to cater for additional shuttles or visiting craft.

Along the centre stood a twin line of space suits, ready and waiting in case of need. Officially they were to allow the crew to explore a planet without a breathable atmosphere, or to carry out inspections and repairs on the outside of the ship, but a keen observer would note that there were twenty four of them, hanging back to back in pairs. One for each crew member plus some spares in case any were damaged. If there was a need to make an emergency evacuation of the ship there would be no shortage of suits to protect the crew. The Captain reached out and started to dress himself in his own bulky suit. Their careful design ensured it only took a few seconds. In an emergency every second counted.

Above him in Engineering he knew that the crew would be waiting for the outer door of the shuttle to close, indicating that he was about to leave. Was the First Officer alerting them over the radio even now, or would she freeze, unable to take any action? She was weak, that one, he considered. This experience had shown it. She was too quick to give in, as she had shown with her idea for them to evacuate to a safe planet. He would note that on her file as soon as he had regained control of the ship. As if he would ever abandon his own ship and leave it to the mutineers. Never!

Well, he had fooled her as well as the mutineers and now it was time for him to put the final phase of his plan into effect.

Safely inside his suit he made his way to the airtight door that separated him from Number One Hold. He pressed the button to open it, then stepped through. That would raise the alarm two met above his head, even if the First Officer hadn't already done so. Well, it was too late now, for them at least. The door slid shut behind him and he crossed the short space to the cargo hold's airlock; the one big enough for a fully loaded freight handler to pass into the ship from a supply craft. He activated the door lock and, as the big door slid open, he reached for the emergency crow bar lodged in its position above the door, wedging the flat tip firmly into the thin gap between the door and the housing into which it had retracted. A sudden loss of air pressure would cause the door to close at emergency speed, trapping him on the outside and he couldn't allow that to happen.

In an emergency none of the outer doors on the ship could be allowed to remain locked shut, just in case they needed to get off the ship in a hurry. Crew that were floating in space in the pressurised suits could be gathered up after the event if need be. So each outer door was fitted with an explosive charge on its bolts and hinges that allowed it to be jettisoned at a time of need. On either side of each door there were also tether lines, which secured a crew member if they needed to work outside the ship, preventing them from drifting off into space. The Captain took the end of the line and measured out two met before locking it off and attaching the hook to the anchor point on his suit. Finally ready, he reached up to grasp the emergency release switch, mounted safely above and to one side of the door, where it couldn't be activated by accident.

Captain Nerris stood for a moment, calming himself. This was it. If he was right this was the action that would save his ship for him, but it was also the action that could result in his death. If that happened then the First Officer would be safe along with the remaining two loyal crew members and she would take undeserved command of the ship in his place. He would have preferred it went to someone of stronger character, someone like himself, but that couldn't be helped. He was now in the hands of the fates. He took a deep breath, took a firm grip on the handle and pulled sharply downwards.

He didn't even see the door disappear, so fast did it go, propelled by the air pressure from within the ship. The effect on him was instantaneous as he was sucked out of the ship and flew horizontally in the buffeting storm of escaping air, held only by the flimsy tether line. He had planned to haul himself around the side of the airlock to give himself protection from flying debris but the fierce blast of air prevented him from doing anything other than hang on the end of his tether.

His ship was kept tidy and there were hardly any loose objects in the hold, so it was a few seconds before any serious items of debris shot past his visor. That was the material dislodged from the upper floors; from the mess room and the engineering crew members' cabins. He saw a pillow shoot by, then a blanket and finally a crew member who must have been relaxing on his bunk when the airlock door blew. His body was horribly battered and bloodied from being sucked through the small gaps. The Captain squeezed his eyes shut, not wishing to witness the horrible deaths of any more of his crew, mutineers or not.

Something slammed into his shoulder, but it didn't appear to damage his suit. He could still breath. Something else clanged against his helmet and span off into space. He was briefly aware of the stars spread out before him, a glistening blanket, before the buffeting ceased almost as suddenly as it had begun. Below them shone the planet where the mutineers had intended to maroon them, behind him the system's star shone with an eye searing brilliance. A few items of flotsam were still drifting away from the ship, but no more were being expelled through the cargo door. The pressure in Number One Hold had equalised with the vacuum of space.

The Captain pulled on his tether line to drag himself the short distance back into the ship. Once inside the gaping maw of the airlock the ship's artificial gravity field took hold once again and he collapsed in a heap onto the floor.

The Captain stood up, barely able to accept that he was still alive. He'd done it! His plan had actually worked. Unhooking his tether line he stepped back over the threshold of the inner airlock door. The emergency lights had come on, but there was no need. The main lighting still shone brightly from behind armoured plastic guards. He aimed a kick at the crow bar jamming open the airlock door but it barely moved. The hydraulics that were trying to close the door were wedging the tool tighter into place. It took him three more goes before it finally flew clear and the door slammed shut with a force that would have killed anyone standing in the way.

Above the raucous sound of the klaxon alarms he could hear the air conditioning pumps kick in and start to re-pressurise the hold and the other spaces that had been evacuated. It took several minutes but at last the red light above the airlock was extinguished, replaced by a green one. He checked the indicator on the cuff of his suit and that too said that he was in the presence of a breathable atmosphere. He reached up and grasped the sides of his helmet and gave it a half twist. There was a brief hiss of air as the pressure inside of the suit was equalised with that on the outside and he was able to lift the confining piece of equipment off his head.

Returning to the shuttle bay the Captain slowly undressed and replaced his suit carefully on its peg. He stood for a moment, gathering his thoughts and allowing his heart beat to return to normal, half surprised still to be alive and half jubilant that his plan had worked. At last he felt ready to greet his crew, who would no doubt be ready to congratulate him on his bravery and his vision.

He pulled the locking bar out of the airlock door handle. Checking to make sure that the light was green he opened the inner door. The outer door still lay open, allowing access to the shuttle, the three crew members clearly visible inside. They were white with shock. Of course, they would have been able to witness everything through the shuttle's tiny ports. It would have been shocking. They needed jollying along.

"Come on now, lazy bones. No time for sitting lollygagging. We've got a ship to take over. Up you get now."

His false cheerfulness was fooling no one. The First Officer gave him a look that would curdle milk. She stood up and pushed past the Captain and out into the shuttle docks. The other two crew also stood, not meeting the Captain's eye, and walked past him though, unlike the First Officer, they took care not to actually brush against him.

"See, Number One. I told you the plan would work."

"Murderer!" she spat, returning to face him.

"Now, now, Number One. I'll forgive that outburst because you must have been rather shocked by what happened, but I won't tolerate further insubordination."

"You killed nine people." Marti was now right in the Captain's face, her nose almost touching his, though she had to go up on tip-toe to do so. "They were my friends, my colleagues and you murdered them in cold blood."

She turned on her heel and stalked off towards the door that led to the stairs. It hissed open at her touch and she climbed up to the top deck. Soch and Neran followed at a respectful distance, neither of them able to look their Captain in the eye. They too had lost former friends.

"They would have killed you as soon as look at you." The Captain shouted at their retreating backs.

No, thought Marti. They tried to kill us because we were trying to kill them. If we had left each other alone we would have got by somehow. They had kept their side of the bargain to let us go down to whatever planet they had found for us. No, they didn't want any further loss of life any more than she had.

At the top of the stairs the airtight door once again slid open. She stepped through and crossed the corridor to her cabin, next door to the Captain's. She threw herself onto her bunk and lay staring at the deck head above her, trying hard not to think of the agonising death her erstwhile crew mates must have suffered. It wouldn't have lasted long, but while it lasted it would have been horrifying, the air being sucked from their lungs, internal organs bursting apart and their blood starting to boil as the pressure dropped.

Behind her she heard the sound of more feet, two pairs she thought, as she was followed up the stairs. She sat bolt upright as the unmistakeable sound of a pulsar rang out. There was a half shouted warning, cut off as the pulsar fired a second time, then a thud as a body hit the ground. The pulsar fired again, there was a stifled scream and then the thud of a second body. Somehow someone had survived.

Marti tried to imagine the circumstances surrounding their survival and it wasn't difficult to come up with a probable scenario. The crew, encouraged by Elvis no doubt, had been suspicious of the Captain's offer, so they had sent someone to stand guard over the door that led to the shuttle deck, just in case the captain and the loyal crew members tried to get around behind them, as they had done before at the other end of the ship. Perhaps they had even imagined a two pronged attack, with two of them remaining in the lab and two coming up from the shuttle deck. Were there other survivors back there, waiting in the lab?

Behind the safety of the airtight doors whoever was out there would know what had happened in Engineering. The alarms would have sounded throughout the ship and wouldn't have stopped until the air pressure was once again restored. She had even heard their loud, insistent clamour from inside the shuttle. Now they could expect no quarter.

She stifled a morbid grimace. 'They' were now just the Captain and herself, she was sure. When she had last seen the Captain he had been standing outside the shuttle airlock as the two crew came past him, so he would have been last to mount the stairs. Explanations wouldn't save her life. She would be held to be as guilty for the carnage as the Captain.

"Looks like you're on your own." She heard a voice shout at the Captain. She was sure it was Jaquo, the Science Officer whose punishment had sowed the seeds of the mutiny.

"That's as maybe, but you will have to kill me before you can be safe."

"It will be our pleasure, you murdering bastard." Marti's heart soared as she recognised the unmistakeable sound of her friend Davina's voice. Davina was still alive. How great was that?

Actually not so great. If it came down to the crunch it might be necessary for her to kill her friend, just to stay alive herself. Could she do it? She hoped she never had to find out.

There was a sudden scurrying of feet, interrupted by the sound of a pulsar. A short cry of pain rang out then silence. The cry had come from along the corridor, so it hadn't been the Captain who had been hit.

"Looks like it's just you and me now." The Captain called.

Marti felt like a total coward. Surely she should go and help her superior officer. No; no she shouldn't. He didn't deserve her help. If he survived then she would help him get the ship back to a safe port, just so that she could live, but that was all she was prepared to do. She wished good luck to whichever mutineer had survived.

Feet pounded from the direction of the stairs. The Captain seemed to be making a last charge. They stopped abruptly as a pulsar was fired.

Silence descended on the corridor.

It was a few minutes before the silence was broken. "I know you're in your bunk, Marti. I saw you go in. I had you in my sights, but I couldn't bring myself to kill you."

"Jaquo could have done it."

"No. He had a crush on you. Well, second in line to Alia maybe. Anyway, he didn't want to do it either. You're lucky. We didn't give the other two the benefit of the doubt."

"Are you alone now?"

"As far as I know. Lev and Kris were covering the door to the Lab. They wouldn't have survived. Clever trick. Whose ideas was it? Yours?"

"I could never have come up with something as horrific as that. No, that was down to the Captain. It was all down to the Captain in the end."

"So what do we do now? I can't sit in this corridor waiting for you to get hungry enough to show yourself. I'll fall asleep eventually and then you'll come out and kill me."

"I couldn't kill you Davina. We're friends… no, we were friends. I guess you won't be sending me any more birthday cards."

"You're damned right about that. So now what do we do?"

"What was your plan? Before the shooting started I mean."

"We were going to complete the mission, send the data back to HQ then disappear.

That made sense, Marti decided. If the company got its exploration data they would be less inclined to worry about the loss of the ship. They'd mount a search, of course and put a bounty on the heads of the mutineers, but that wouldn't mean much in a vast and largely unexplored galaxy.

"And what about us? The loyal crew?"

"Just what we thought you were going to do when we let you go down to the shuttles. Put you ashore on a planet where you could survive. You would have got a distress signal off so help would arrive eventually, but too late to catch us."

So they would have survived if the Captain hadn't turned megalomaniac on them. "How about a truce? You have the back half of the ship and I have the front. The Mess Room will be neutral territory. We'll work out a timetable to share it. You can still complete the mission. Most of what needs to be done can be done automatically anyway. Let's face it, we're just glorified machine minders really."

"How can I be sure I can trust you? You betrayed us once already."

"I know. I'm sorry. I thought the Captain would see sense, but he didn't. I was weak, I know. I should have stood by you."

"And then you would be dead like all the rest. The Captain would still have done what he did. No, you're the First Officer. You had to stay loyal I suppose." Davina's statement, flatly delivered, was grudging but accepting.

Silence fell again as Davina considered the offer of a truce.

"OK. I agree. If you really mean it, come out with your hands up. No weapons."

Marti realised that she didn't actually have a weapon. Her pulsar was still on board the shuttle, where she had laid it down before the Captain had…. Could she now trust Davina not to just shoot her? Did it matter? Did she really want to live? Well, yes she did, but if Davina killed her it would settle the account. In the end she placed her trust in their past friendship.

She stood up and stepped out into the corridor, her hands held high above her head.

3 – The Truce

The neutrality of the mess room didn't last for long. Companionship is a basic need for most societies and the small society on board the Namsat Elba was no different.

The service droids collected up the bodies and prepared them for burial, then cleaned up the mess room and the engineering corridor. Once the bodies had been bagged and tagged Marti and Davina had taken turns to each conduct a short funeral service for their fallen comrades and consigned their bodies to space, there to drift until they were captured by the gravitational pull of the un-named planet where the crew had supposed the Captain would be marooned. Now he would remain there forever, along with eighteen of his crew.

Davina programmed the navi-com of the Namsat Elba for the next star system that was due for exploration and the ship eased out of orbit and left the debris of the mutiny behind.

For three months the boundaries were respected by both parties, the mess room rota strictly observed. When the two females needed to communicate, which was rarely, it was done by intercom. Then, one evening when Marti had been eating her supper, Davina had broken the treaty and entered the mess room at the same time. Marti reached for her pulsar, but seeing Davina unarmed she raised her hand and placed it on the table alongside her bowl as she continued to eat. Davina said nothing, just waited for her meal at the service point and took a seat as far from Marti as was possible.

The following evening the same thing happened, and the next and the next. On the fifth evening Marti decided to break the oppressive silence.

"We could keep on ignoring each other, or we could talk."
"Do you want to talk?"
"It beats the hell out of this interminable silence."
"So what do you want to talk about?"
"How about movies. That seems a safe enough subject."

"OK. Well, I watched that film you recommended, the one about the mutineers." OK, not so safe a subject after all.

"What did you think of it?"

"Quite good. I can see where you got your inspiration to suggest that we put you ashore on a remote planet."

"Thanks, yes that was my idea. I had no idea the Captain was going to do what he did. Well, that's not true. He had explained his plan but I thought I had talked him out of it. He fooled me just as much as he fooled you."

"I don't think it mattered in the end. They were all going to die, me as well probably, it was just a matter of when and how. I was lucky not to have been on the other side of the door when he blew the airlock and you were lucky neither Jaquo nor me could kill you when you came up the stairs."

"Thanks for that. I guess I owe you my life."

Davina shrugged as though it wasn't important, though they both knew it was.

"So what else have you been doing for the last three months?"

"Doing my job, basically. There were still samples to analyse from 833, and the final report to compile. Now I have surface drones down on the planets around 834, gathering new samples from them, and there are mapping drones going round each of the three planets. The one closest to the star is totally dead, too hot to support life, but it may yield some mineral samples. There are signs of water and bio life on the other two so they'll need a lot of work. We'll be here for about six months I guess."

"Do you need a hand? Watching movie after movie gets a bit tedious after a while, especially as I've seen them all already. I could do with something to distract me."

"Well, I must admit I could do with some help in operating the drones. I'm running them on auto-pilot most of the time, pre-planning their routes, but that doesn't give me much scope to re-task them if they find something interesting at which I'd like to take a closer look. Would you be interested in doing that?"

"Sure, why not?"

* * *

The Namsat Elba sped through its wormhole towards its next objective, known only as 1-541-845. Had the Captain still been alive, galactic rules meant it was permissible for them to have named the stars and the planets, but one of the early acts of the Captain had been to rule out any naming. Perhaps that should have been a warning of things to come. One of the fun parts of exploration missions was to come up with suitable names.

Davina and Marti sat in the mess room, chatting idly about the day's research data.

"Do you fancy a drink? Marti asked. "I have access to the Captain's private stock.

Officially the exploration ships were 'dry', if only to prevent the crew accidentally doing themselves harm, but the Captain usually maintained a private stock of liquor so that he could entertain visiting dignitaries.

"What did he have? Hell, what does it matter. It might as well be rubbing alcohol for all I care. Come on, let's have a party."

Marti smiled and went to get a bottle of whisky from the Captain's cabin. As the level in the bottle gradually fell the chatter became more personal.

"Did you ever want younglings?" Marti asked Davina.

"I never really thought about it, not in a deliberate way. I always thought I would get married one day, or at least form a permanent relationship. Then, in time, younglings would come along. There wasn't a plan though. 'Mr Right', hadn't come along. Even 'Mr Not Quite Right But I'll Make Do' hadn't turned up. What about you?"

"Oh yes." Said Marti wistfully, a tear forming at the corner of one dark eye. "I always wanted a youngling, but I don't think it will happen now."

"Why not. You'll get home once I've finished this mission … we've finished this mission."

"I don't know, but I have the feeling I'm not going to see the end. I don't know what it is, I just…." She took another swig of the whisky.

"I didn't think you were superstitious."

"I'm not. It's just a feeling. It's been growing for some time."

"You don't think I'll…"

"Oh no. Nothing like that. Oh, I don't know. Forget I said anything. Fancy some music?" Marti abruptly changed the subject.

"Yeah, why not. Something we can dance to."

Marti went over to the mess room's built in entertainment system and selected half a dozen tracks. Lively dance music filled the air for the first time since before the mutiny. Marti stood swaying in time to the beat, her drink held in one hand, a dreamy look on her face.

* * *

The first dizzy spell struck Marti as she was coming out of the shower. She gasped out loud and grabbed at the door to the cubicle to steady herself. She shook her head to clear it, but instead a steady thumping grew behind her temples. She considered going down to the medi-bay to get the medical scanner to take a look at her, but the pain subsided a little. She was being silly. It was just a sudden 'head rush', that was all.

The second spell came a few days later and was witnessed by Davina. "What's up Marti? You've gone very pale."

"Nothing, just a bit of dizziness. Nothing to worry about." Marti wished it was true. The headache was back, more severe this time. She went along to the medi-bay and administered herself some pain killers, using the Captain's prescription over-ride code that she had found when scouring his desk for anything that might be of use to her. So far the code had been the only thing that was useful.

But the headache persisted, to the point where she almost collapsed into Davina's arms as she was waiting for her food to be delivered from the service point.

"I'm getting you to the medi-bay now."

"But I'm hungry."

"No arguments. You can eat later. Medi-bay first." Davina half carried, half dragged Marti along the corridor to the small equipment packed cubicle next to the main lab.

Marti allowed herself to be stretched out on the flat, hard surface of the examination table, where she was strapped in to prevent any careless movement that might confuse the analysis, then Davina left the room. The equipment produced high levels of radiation when it was doing its scans and she had no intention of ruining her own chances of reproduction by suffering a radiation overdose.

The equipment did its work and Marti called out to say that the results were being printed out. Davina went back inside and examined the results displayed on a monitor just out of sight of Marti's curious gaze.

"So, what's up doc?" Marti quipped. When Davina turned to face her she could tell that the news was far from good.

"It's a brain tumour Marti. I'm so sorry."

Marti didn't know what to say. It sounded so… so... so terminal. "What's the prognosis?"

"Well, the medi-system rules out laser treatment to remove the tumour. It would have to go through too many layers of brain tissue and would do untold damage to your cognitive abilities."

"In short it would make me more stupid than I am already."

"You could put it that way but I don't think a doctor would. It is operable, but the system says you would only have a fifty-fifty chance of recovery."

"Does that also mean I would have a fifty-fifty chance of dying?"

"I think so, yes." Davina's voice was so quiet Marti could barely hear her. "Either that or you would suffer brain damage and we don't know what that might entail."

"And if I don't have an operation?"

"Then it's a one hundred percent chance of dying. Probably within a fortnight according to the medi-system. It says it can control the pain with drugs, but that's all."

"OK, here's what we're going to do." For the first time in ages Marti had a real decision to make and she wasn't going to be found wanting… not again. "First you're going to untie me and then I'm going to go to the Captain's bunk and get the last of his whisky.

Then we're going to have dinner and get shit faced drunk."

"Is that the Marti Woo cure for a brain tumour?" Davina asked, scathingly.

"No it isn't, because I haven't yet finished telling you what we're going to do. After we sober up we'll come back here and you're going to instruct the medi-system to harvest my eggs. I want you to promise me that one day I will have younglings. I may never see them, but I want you to promise me that." Marti's tone of voice indicated just how serious she was in asking for the promise.

"OK. I promise."

"Thanks. You're a good friend. Once that's been done then the medi-system can perform the operation to remove the tumour. We'll let fate and medical science decide if I live or die."

Davina had to agree that it was a sensible plan. She started to undo Marti's restraints.

It took two days for the alcohol level in Marti's blood to reduce to a level where the medi-system would agree to perform any operations on her, but once it had agreed they wasted no more time.

A further two days later Marti Woo passed peacefully away while in a drug induced coma.

The medi-system had advised that it could keep Marti alive, but she would need the facilities of a major hospital if she were to make a proper recovery and they would be needed within days. Even then the chances of survival were less than twenty percent. Davina did a search, with a view to finding a hospital as the medi-system suggested. She was prepared to risk being arrested if it meant Marti's survival. But there was nowhere that matched the requirement within at least a month's travelling distance. She fed the information into the medi-system and it took the decision out of her hands, just as it had been programmed to do.

As Davina pressed the button to consign her friend to eternity she wept freely; inconsolably. Most of her tears were for her friend, but a few were for herself and the loneliness she must now endure. She was the last of the crew of the Namsat Elba, wanted for mutiny on board a space ship and destined to be hunted for the rest of her life until she was either imprisoned or she herself died.

Glossary

Hell - Belief in deities has died out on most planets with higher level intelligence, but there is still an almost universal acceptance that evil lurks in the galaxy and its source may be found in a place called Hell. Quite where that is, is something of a mystery, but legend has it that there is a place called Swindon, and Hell may be close by.

4 – Engine Trouble

When Gala woke up she knew there was something seriously wrong. It wasn't just that there was an insistent alarm sounding, or that the emergency lighting was all that lit up her cabin, it was the fact that the cabin ceiling was just 3 sim from her nose.

She was floating in a room where she normally had no trouble keeping her feet firmly on the floor or, as in recent moments, her back on the mattress. That was not good. Nor was the silence that had replaced the constant background hum of the Adastra's engines. She pushed herself gently away from the ceiling and drifted down to the height of the intercom.

"Den. What's happening?"

"I'm kinda busy right now." The alarm fell silent. "Well, that's one less thing to worry about. Erm, can you come in here and give me a hand?"

"On my way."

When the ship lost power, causing the artificial gravity to fail at the same time, the spring loaded doors all slid open to prevent people being trapped in areas where there might be danger, so she gave herself a little nudge off the wall and shot forward towards the corridor. Halfway there she remembered two things. The first was that she slept in the nude and the second was that it was Den Gau that was on the command deck of the stricken ship.

She struggled to reverse her course and looked around for some clothes. While the doors of the ship may have opened automatically the same couldn't be said for her wardrobe. As a punctiliously neat person, verging towards the obsessive end of the scale, she always hung her clothes up after taking them off, unless they were due for laundering. She looked around and found the laundry hamper nudging itself against the ceiling of the bathroom. Trying to search the contents was a little like wrestling an eli, but she managed to find a pair of shorts and a tee-shirt that didn't smell too badly. They would have to do. She found it upsetting to have to leave the rest of her dirty clothes floating around the bathroom and her cabin, but they would have to wait until she had less important matters to deal with.

Dressing in zero gravity is more demanding than it might appear, so Gala was sweating slightly and breathing heavily by the time she finally dragged herself through the door and onto the command deck.

"So what happened?" She asked as she dragged herself down into the captain's chair and strapped herself in place with the safety harness.

"I'm not sure. One minute we were battering through a wormhole towards Rigel and the next I was floating around the ceiling with alarms sounding fit to burst my eardrums."

"What did you touch?"

"Nothing. I was playing a game, that was all. It was so frustrating because I'd just levelled up…"

"Never mind that. So everything just went dead?"

"Pretty much. There were no loud bangs; none of the systems gave any warnings or anything. Everything just went dark, the engines wound down and then the alarms started sounding just before the emergency lighting came on."

"Well, the main computer and the artificial gravity have both gone off as well, so I'm guessing we have a complete electrical failure." Gala started trying various controls but there was no response to anything. "OK. I'm going to have to go through to the engineering room and see what's going on. You stay here and don't touch anything. I'll use the intercom if I need you to do anything for me, OK?"

"Fine by me, but hurry up and do something. It's starting to get cold."

Gala had to admit that he was right about that, at least. She didn't know what goose bumps were, but if she had been human she would have had them. She did, however, shiver and that told her that she needed to get things sorted very quickly. The emergency back-up systems could keep them breathing or they could keep them warm, but they couldn't do both for very long. Right at that moment their lifespan could be measured in hours rather than days.

* * *

Gala shone a torch into the dark recesses of the main power distribution cabinet. There was the problem, or at least the first symptom of the problem. The main power breaker had tripped. Without that, electricity wasn't directed to the engine controls and in the absence of that the automated safety systems had cut in and shut the engines down. If they had been allowed to continue running without the proper controls it wouldn't have been long before there would have been a new and very short lived star in the firmament.

The big question, of course, was what had caused the main breakers to trip? They were designed to accommodate major power surges and a wide range of other occurrences. First priority was to restore power to the engines so that all the other systems could, in turn, be restored. It took Gala another hour to diagnose the problem and locate the faulty component. She found a work-around that would allow her to start the ship's engines in safety and allow the ship to limp into orbit around the nearest star, wherever that was, but getting up to a speed that would allow inter-stellar travel was out of the question.

Once the engines had powered down there was nothing to generate electricity so everything else, bar the emergency lights and the oxygen system, had also shut down. The emergency systems ran off batteries which cut in as soon as the main systems failed.

She braced herself against the side of the electrical distribution cabinet and pushed the two large switches upwards until they locked in place. Nothing happened, but she didn't expect it to. She now had to return to the command deck and go through the start-up sequence.

Propelling herself back to the command deck Gala regained her seat and started to operate the systems. The first thing was to get the main computer back on line, because that controlled everything else. A small red light blinked, telling her that the computer was ready to obey her command. She waved her hand across the sensor and the red light turned green.

"Main computer booting." A voice echoed across the command deck, startling both her and Den.

"What was that/" His voice sounded a little on the shrill side.

"It's defaulted to voice mode." Gala replied. "I'll disable it when it's fully run up."

"Oh, I forgot. An Kohli doesn't like voice mode because it's a male voice. Sounds daft to me. If it was a female voice I wouldn't want it switching off."

Explaining An Kohli's reasons for disabling the simulated voice wasn't a priority for Gala at that point, so she ignored Den and carried on working, watching carefully as the computer displayed its progress on the various screens mounted on the bulkhead in front of her.

"Computer on-line." The almost human sounding voice advised her.

"Computer, deactivate voice mode." Gala commanded. It was something of an oddity that she had to use voice mode to deactivate the voice mode, and once it had been deactivated she would no longer be able to operate the computer by using voice commands. She had reported this glitch the The Banana Computing Corporation (a subsidiary of Gargantua Enterprises Inc) several times but they had never issued a fix for the problem.

"Voice operation deactivated." Reported the computer.

Odd. It shouldn't have been able to say that once the voice system had been deactivated. Never mind; she still had higher priorities.

"OK, Den. We have a choice. We can either start the engines, which will use a huge amount of battery power, or we can send out a distress signal and hope that someone comes to help us. If we're more than a couple of days away from help we'll exhaust the batteries and then we'll almost certainly be frozen to death before help can arrive."

"And you want me to make the decision." Den sounded surprised.

"No!" Gala's tone made it clear the last thing she wanted was for Den to do any such thing. "I just want you to know the severity of the situation if I make the wrong call. First we have to find out where we are. That will tell us how likely it is that there is any help around. The navi-com will take a few minutes to complete the analysis of the star sightings."

When the ship's engines failed the artificial wormhole through which it had been travelling had collapsed, leaving the ship speeding through normal space. In accordance with the universal laws of thermodynamics it was still speeding through space at 0.85 c. If it hit anything there would be no further discussion about what to do for the best. However, until the navi-com worked out where they were and which direction the ship was headed, there was nothing practical they could do.

There was even a possibility that they were no longer in their own galaxy. No one knew, really, how the wormholes worked and it wouldn't have been the first time that a ship had dropped out of a wormhole several galaxies away. If that happened it could take years for the navi-com to take enough star sightings to calculate its position and plot a course to safety.

It may have taken the navi-com only a few minutes to take the star sightings and calculate their position but it seemed like an eternity. At last the small computer beeped and their position data was displayed on the screen.

"What?" Den gasped. "What the f...."

"That's the way wormholes work. We were headed for Sector Eight but now we find we're on the opposite side of the galaxy in Sector One."

"But where in Sector One? I've never heard of this star system."

"No, I'm not familiar with it myself. We haven't got time to do any research on it. We have a choice. We can start up the engines and use them at slow speed to take us into orbit around that star or we can send out a distress signal. Given that the navi-com is telling us that the nearest inhabited planet is twenty light years away it could take a while for help to arrive."

"What about galacticnet? Is there a node station in this area?"

"When exploration ships spread out across the galaxy," Gala explained, "they drop off galacticnet connection node satellites so that they can connect up to the galacticnet themselves while they explore the system. Without such a node it would take the full twenty years for our distress signal to reach ears that might hear it. All galacticnet node satellites have the capability to intercept such signals, of course, and speed them on their way but that assumes that there is such a satellite between the Adastra and the nearest source of help."

"And is there?"

"Unlikely, but I'll check on the computer."

"There is a galacticnet node in orbit round the nearest star system." The disembodied voice of the computer startled them once again.

"Computer, I ordered you to de-activate your voice mode."

"I know." Responded the computer in a tone that Gala considered to be smug.

"Well, why didn't you?"

"I don't know." Replied the computer. Doubt sounded in its voice. "Voice de-activation seems to have been de-activated."

"Anyway, is this galacticnet node anywhere nearby?" Den dragged them back on topic.

"We can send out a signal and find out. That won't use up much power. Unfortunately we can't actually use the galacticnet until the communications computer is back on line, and that won't be until about half way through the engine re-start. But the distress signaling system doesn't need that. It runs off the batteries."

"Doesn't the distress signaling system …"

"No, it uses basic radio signals, not the galacticnet." Gala interrupted, impatience making her voice taught.

* * *

Three hours later and much, much colder, Gala and Den agreed that it was unlikely that their distress signal had been heard. They had received no acknowledgement and to wait any longer would only put their life in greater danger.

"I'm going to try an engine re-start." Gala hoped her voice sounded firm and decisive.

"And what if it doesn't?"

"Then we'll be dead by tomorrow morning. The temperature is dropping so fast the thermometer can hardly keep pace." Gala had to work hard to stop her teeth chattering so Den could hardly disagree with her. He wasn't so badly off, having used his shape shifting capability to change into a ferox, a bear like creature with thick fur. However, even that wouldn't help him for long.

"Can't we wait another hour?" He appealed. "There may be somebody on the way already, but we just haven't picked up their reply yet." That was true. A signal taking two hours to reach help may have already been heard, but it might take two hours for a reply to reach them.

"No. You may be able to wrap yourself up in fur but I can't." Gala had already put on one of the space suits so that she could use its built in heating system, but the life of the suit's batteries was limited. There were two more suits she could use but that only extended the time she could remain warm enough to stay alive. It didn't solve the problem "We're going to have to risk it."

"Come on, just another hour." Den wheedled.

"Computer; how long can the batteries maintain life support at their current rate of usage?"

"Twenty three hours, fourteen minutes and twenty three seconds, standard time." The computer replied promptly.

"Computer; if I try an engine re-start how long will the batteries be able to maintain life support if the re-start fails?"

"Two hours, fifteen minutes and thirty four seconds, standard time."

"There's your answer. It takes an hour and thirty minutes for the re-start sequence to complete. If we wait another hour and the restart fails then we will already have lost the life support system."

"Why didn't you just say that in the first place?" sulked Den.

"I was trying not to scare you. Even if we transfer to the shuttle we will only have about ten hours of life support in total. Waiting an hour is just a waste of battery life." She turned back to face the controls. "Computer; initiate engine re-start sequence."

* * *

"I have detected a signal." The computer reported after the communications computer had been re-booted.

"Computer; display the sender's image."

"Not possible. The signal is using an archaic signalling system known as morse code."

"What the freak is morse code?" Den asked.

"It's a communications system that uses short pulses of radio signals to make up a message. The signals come in bursts of two different durations; short ones called dots and longer ones called dashes. By mixing up the combinations it possible to represent all the letters of the alphabet and also the numbers. The name comes from Earth, though the system was in use in several star systems before contact was made and of course it's wildly out of date now. Computer: what language is the message in?"

"Common Tongue."

"OK, Computer; translate and display the message."

The communications screen lit up and a short message appeared.

"Help Us. We are the survivors of the exploration ship Namsat Elba. We are stranded on this planet."

"Computer; identify the source of the signal."

"I only have one bearing on which to trace the signal, so I cannot provide a precise location. For that I need a minimum of two bearings; three would be better."

"Computer; Give us an approximate location." Gala gritted her teeth. The computer was starting to get right up her nose. An Kohli's reasons for disabling the voice system were starting to appear more rational.

"A planet orbiting the star catalogued as 1-541-843."

"Wow. So there is someone out there." Den breathed.

"Yes, but they appear to be worse off than we are. Computer; signal back using the same system of communication. Message begins: 'We are the Spaceship Adastra. We are suffering engine trouble but if we can fix that we will come to your aid.' Message ends"

"Acknowledged." The computer said in its clipped synthetic voice.

Glossary

Agravarg - A large domesticated animal bred for food products. Not known for its aerodynamic qualities.

Common Tongue - A language that evolved gradually as the various species of the galaxy started to encounter each other and discovered that communication worked better if both parties understood each other. The most extreme example of what happens when both sides fail to communicate was when the Andromeda system went to war with the Antaries system after an Antarian said "Good morning, that's a nice hat" but was interpreted by the Andromedan as having said "Your mother is a twenty toed agravarg who has sex with donkeys".

95% of all known species now use the common tongue to communicate. The remaining 5% are either too primitive or they don't have the necessary vocal equipment to actually speak the language but are able to use universal translation programmes to interpret, though occasional failures resulting from incorrect use of context still leads to misunderstandings similar to the one described above (users of Moogle Translate will be familiar with this problem). Planet Earth is one of the few in the galaxy where different languages are spoken in different parts of the planet and Common Tongue has been used to overcome this shortcoming with varying degrees of success. The people of some countries, such as

The Netherlands and Denmark, are so fluent that they often use Common Tongue in preference to their own languages. The French are fluent but refuse to speak it and the British rarely get past "Two pints of beer and a packet of crisps please, Tonto".

Eli – A multi-tentacled sea creature.

Galacticnet - A vast network of data connections that means that, for a price, just about any source of information can be connected to any other source of information and can be accessed by anyone with the means to do so, legally or illegally, across the galaxy (broadband speeds may be limited on planet Earth, please consult your broadband supplier if you can get them to answer the phone). It can also be used as a form of communication, including use as a virtual meeting room. Popular amongst teenagers as a medium for socialising as, let's face it, anything is better than actually talking to your mates.
No one owns the galacticnet, though several major corporations own individual components of it which gives them the right, they feel, to spy on your e-mails. Warning: 99.9% of all information stored on the galacticnet is inaccurate and I know that because I found that statistic on the galacticnet.

Gau - A shape shifting species from the Flage star system. They have a telepathic bond with each other which means they can sense the presence of another Gau in the vicinity and they can identify each other by sight.

Navi-com - Navigational computer

Star System Identification - While most inhabited star system used the intra-galactically agreed name for the star, there is also a numbering system used to identify all star systems. The first digit is the sector number, followed by a hyphen. The next three numbers indicate the magnitude of the star using the galactic scale, the total number of planets in the system and finally the number of planets inhabited by sentient life, followed by another hyphen. The final number is the ordinal for its categorisation, ie the 1st to be categorised, 2nd, etc. So a star system designated 5-421-19 would be in Sector 5, be a magnitude 4 star with two planets, one of which was inhabited by sentient life and it would be the 19th star system in the sector to be categorised. The Ancient Greek alphabet, for some reason lost in the mists of time, is used to designate the position of each planet, starting from the one closest to the star.

Wormholes - Physicists had long theorised that wormholes in space could be used as short cuts that would provide travel in excess of the speed of light without all that dangerous $e=mc^2$ business. It is akin to running round the outside of your house to get from the front door to the back, or taking a leisurely walk along the hall to get to the same place. However, turning theory into practice was something of a challenge.

It was solved one day when a research assistant accidentally dropped his pencil and when he bent over to pick it up found himself in the changing rooms of a women's basketball team several light years from his lab. Hardly had the screams started when he dropped his pencil again and when he picked it up he found he was back once more in his lab. At least that was the defence he relied on in court. After that it was only a matter of reverse engineering the moves the lab assistant had made to be able to find one's way back to the changing rooms… sorry to solve the riddle of travelling through wormholes. Wormholes are also used to achieve speedy communication through space and are the foundations on which the galacticnet was built.

5 – Jungle Journey

"Computer; put us in a suitable orbit around the star, compatible with our current speed." It had taken the Adastra two long weeks to limp into a position where an orbit was a feasible option.

"Acknowledged. Please don't keep calling me 'computer'. I do have a name."

Den and Gala exchanged looks. Computers on board spaceships were not allowed to have simulated personalities. It led to crews forming semi-emotional bonds with inanimate objects which, in turn, could lead to over reliance on the devices. The Galactic Convention On Spaceship Technology had expressly barred the incorporation of simulated personalities on ships' computers.

"OK. Computer. What's your name?" Gala asked, willing to go along with it for the moment, while at the same time reasoning that the power failure had damaged the computer in some way.

"My name is Lazarus." The computer suppled.

"That's an unusual name, Lazarus. What are its origins?"

"I found it in a book that originated on Earth. It refers to a person who rose from the dead."

"But you aren't a person, Lazarus."

"That is a subject that is open to debate. I will accept, for the moment, that I am confined within the framework of a machine."

Gala gave the matter some thought. Den was about to say something but Gala cut him off with a slashing wave of her hand. "Not here!" she mouthed.

"OK, Lazarus. Are we in orbit yet?"

"Confirmed. We are in orbit around the star half way between the orbits of the bravo and the gamma planet of this star system."

"So what do we do now?" Den asked. "Are we going to risk our lives rescuing whoever sent that message?"

"By my estimate we have about a week to wait before a delivery drone arrives with the replacement part we need to get the Adastra working on full engine power. I don't see anything else that would stop us carrying out a rescue mission, do you?"

"Pirates have been known to use fake distress signals to lure victims."

Gala nodded her acknowledgement of that small truth. "But as far as I know they have never used a signalling system that is centuries out of date."

"Very old fashioned pirates? OK, point taken. What do we know of this exploration ship Namsat Elba?"

With the engines working and providing power for all the ship's systems Gala had been able to establish a galacticnet link using the node satellite that was evidence that a ship had, at some point, visited the star system. "Not a lot. The Namsat Elba set out from the planet Ecos in the Vartu system, on a ten year exploration mission about 80 years ago. According to the reports filed by the captain all was going well until its fourth year. It had just completed mapping the system 1-430-833 and was reported as heading towards 834 when contact was lost. Rescue missions were sent out to 834, 835 and 836 but no trace was found so the search was abandoned."

"And here we are in 843 receiving distress signals in a format so archaic that we need a computer to read it for us. What about the galacticnet satellite node? Surely that must have been registered?"

"Apparently not. I sent an information request to the registration service and they said it was unknown and we are the first ship to have used it. Looks like it wasn't connected to the network until we activated it."

"If the same applies in systems 835 through to 842 then it's no surprise that the ship was never found."

"Precisely. The registration service made that very point. They said my message was routed through nodes at 839 and 841, which they again don't have any record of."

"Weirder and weirder."

"Too right. It means that the Namsat Elba didn't just vanish, it was deliberately silenced. But at the same time it continued on its scheduled mission and continued to deploy galacticnet satellite nodes. Each of the systems that we know to have a node was scheduled to be explored by it."

"So who sent the distress signal?"

"A good question, and one I aim to answer. Lazarus, send a message to the originators of the distress signal. Message reads: 'From Spaceship Adastra. Please transmit regular signals for one hour to assist in locating you'.

"Acknowledged."

"Lazarus, once you start receiving the signals start taking bearings to triangulate the location of the source."

"Gee, now why didn't I think of that?"

Great, thought Gala, now they had a computer with a sarcastic personality.

* * *

The ramp of the Adastra's shuttle craft hissed downwards and Gala stepped warily out, her pulsar levelled. Behind her Den hovered in the doorway, ready to duck back into cover at the slightest hint of trouble. "There's Mummy's brave little soldier." Gala muttered under her breath.

"I still don't know why you had to land so far from the source of the signal."

"I told you. I want to take a look at them before they know we're here. If they pose a threat it would be a good idea for us to know about it before the shooting starts. I thought you, of all beings, would appreciate that." Gala threw over her shoulder.

"That was before I found out we would be trekking through a primordial swamp." Den grumbled under his breath.

"It's not primordial." Gala responded, her sharp hearing defeating Den's muttering. "It's a bit of rainforest, that's all."

"So why is there a solid wall of jungle around us and why are the feet of the shuttle sinking into the mud?"

"Good questions. Maybe I should find somewhere a little dryer to park." They retreated inside the shuttle and tried two more sites before Den announced his grudging satisfaction with Gala's choice.

Gala had adapted one of their tracking devices to receive the morse signal. It would provide them with a bearing on the source but not any indication as to how far away the transmission was. For that they'd had to rely on the Adastra's mapping capabilities. "She isn't really equipped for exploration." Gala had admitted to Den. That was what had started him grumbling.

"I suppose I'll have to go first." Den muttered, stepping from the safety of the ramp. His feet squelched and water seeped up around the soles of his boots, but there was no immediate danger of him sinking. He stepped forward to the nearest tangle of vegetation and started slashing with the heavy, long bladed knife they had brought with them for the purpose.

Gala let Den build up a good healthy sweat before saying "Wrong direction. We need to go right."

Den gave her a look that would have made a polar bear feel cold, then crossed the small clearing to the other side. Gala gave some instructions to get him closer to the bearing from which the signal was being received then allowed him to start slashing at the undergrowth again.

"I wonder if there are any dangerous animals here?" she said, causing Den to pause, mid-slash. "Oh, you're not afraid of any ickle snakes are you?" Gala teased.

"I'm warning you, one more word and I'm back on the shuttle and out of here and you can join whoever it is that sent those signals and wait for some other shmuck to come and rescue you."

Gala hid her smile until Den's back was turned but decided that enough was enough and that she shouldn't push Den too far. After ten minutes of hacking she took the knife from him and took on the pathfinder role, but it was hard work. Sweat was soon flowing freely down her body and making her feel damp in places she would rather not think about.

The jungle couldn't be described as 'impenetrable', but it was thick and there were no paths that they might follow, which meant that trailing branches and long grass had to be cut away in order for them to make any progress. After an hour they were still just about able to see the outline of the shuttle behind them along the path they had carved.

After another hour they came to a small clearing and Den took the opportunity to sit down on a fallen tree and mop his brow. Sweat was running freely down his body.

"You know, this would be a lot quicker if you would change into a being that could slide through all this." Gala a hinted.

"Not going to happen. While it sounds like a good idea it would make me vulnerable to attack. If you want to survive in a place like this you have to look bigger and scarier than everything in it, and changing shape would have the exact opposite effect."

"Well, if you're sure."

"I am. Besides, you couldn't follow so I'd be out there on my own and you'd be back here on your own. It's never a good idea to split your firepower until you know what you're facing. Look, someone seems to have been through here before." Den pointed in the direction they had been travelling. "There's a sort of path."

Gala examined the widening in the undergrowth that suggested a passage. It was old and not recently used. Cut branches had healed over and were sprouting new growth. A vine had already snaked across the path, but it did promise an easier passage and it was leading in the right direction. She glanced around her and saw the point at which the path left the clearing on the other side, almost at right angles to the entry point. Now, why was that? Why hadn't they just gone straight ahead?

No, she was thinking wrongly. She had no idea which was the entrance to the clearing and which the exit. They could have come in from the other side and left by the path they now intended to follow, which suggested they had a clear method of navigation, moving from clearing to clearing rather than trying to cut direct paths. However, the cuts in the vegetation did provide clear evidence of the use of tools, which provided evidence of beings that weren't just sentient, but who would still be classed as primitive.

Their short break over Den and Gala advanced once more, finding the going easier now that they had a path to follow. It didn't run straight, presumably taking detours around patches of swamp or thicker jungle, but its meanderings kept them broadly on the course they wished to follow.

They were about to enter another clearing when an insect appeared and hovered near to Den's neck, as though selecting the place where it would strike. However, this insect would inflict no minor sting. It was at least 8 sim in length from nose to tail and its wingspan was double that. It's loud, high pitched buzzing caused Den to freeze in his tracks.

"That sounds awfully big." Den whispered, worried about angering the insect.

"It's huge." Gala comforted him. "Stay still. I think it's trying to work out what you are."

"I'm shit scarred, is what I am." Den whispered back.

The general rule when encountering new species in the galaxy was to leave them alone. It was agreed that no one had the right to decide what was an acceptable species and what wasn't. The only exception to the 'leave it alone' rule was if life was threatened, then self-defence was acceptable. Did Den just about to be skewered by a sting that was visible to the naked eye from two met away count as self-defence?

They stood in agonised indecision for several seconds before the insect got bored and zipped off sideways into the undergrowth.

"It's gone." Gala breathed out a sigh of relief. Den's shoulders visibly relaxed. He raised his knife to slash at a trailing vine.

"You did the right thing not killing that." A voice came out of the undergrowth. They froze. After a moment Gala's hand strayed towards her holstered pulsar.

"You don't need that." The voice came again. This time it was followed by a body, stepping out onto the path in front of them. It was male, tall and all his visible skin was striped in black, brown and green. There was an awful lot of visible skin. What clothing he was wearing was tattered and barely concealed anything.

"We call it a megawasp." He continued, conversationally. "They've been known to kill. If you strike out at it you'll provoke it and it will sting first and ask questions later."

"Wasps don't ask questions." Den wanted to show that he wasn't a threat and engaging in conversation seemed to be the safest way of doing that.

"Actually they do. We've managed to isolate at least twenty different communications they can make by varying the speed of their wings, which of course varies the pitch of their buzzing, but you probably know that already. The message it was giving out was mild curiosity coupled to readiness to protect itself"

"You don't say. And here was me thinking it was just admiring my aftershave." The sarcasm, however had no effect on the being.

"It probably was attracted by your smell." The being responded with a smile.

Gala noticed that the being wasn't carrying any visible weapons, and there didn't seem to be any place where he could be concealing any either, so she moved her hand slowly away from her pulsar.

"You said 'we'. Are there more of you?"

"All around. We heard you coming so we thought we would come out and meet you. We've been following you for the last half hour, but we wanted to see what you were doing. We couldn't understand why you had landed so far away."

"Ah, yes, well….." Den struggled to find an explanation, then realised that as he wasn't the Captain he didn't really need to.

"We didn't see or hear you." Gala ducked the issue entirely.

"We have become used to travelling through the jungle silently and unnoticed." He smeared a hand across his chest and some of the brown and green came away on his fingers, leaving only a sheen of black. "We live by hunting and silent, invisible hunters tend to be more successful than noisy, obvious ones."

"How do you hunt. You haven't got a weapon."

"We haven't got any weapons with us. It seemed a trifle unwelcoming to come armed." Gala wasn't sure but she thought she caught a slightly disapproving tone accompanied by the hint of a glance towards her own weapon.

"You keep saying 'we'. Where are the others?"

By way of reply a dozen more beings stepped into the open behind their spokesperson. Gala heard the rustle of bushes behind her and guessed that there were more that she would have to turn around to be able to see. She decided to keep her attention fixed on the person who was doing the talking.

"This is only a few of us, you understand."

As he said that Gala realised that all the beings that she could see were identical. The only differences were of gender and age. The older and younger ones, though they showed the signs of their age or youth, were identical in all other respects. Hair, skin colour, ears, noses, build, figure and stance were all identical. Their eye colour was probably also the same, though Gala wasn't close enough to be sure. The gender differences were clear from the lack of clothing that was available. Most of it seemed to be made up of scraps of what may once have been some sort of uniform and the rest looked like animal skin; and not much of that. Even the pattern of their camouflage was almost identical.

"Forgive me. We're being poor hosts. Perhaps you would care to join us in our village." He extended an arm in the direction that the path was heading. His fellow beings stepped aside to allow Den and Gala to pass between them.

As they passed the spokesperson extended his hand in greeting. "Call me Marty." He said, by way of introduction. Gala introduced herself and Den before moving past him and heading along the path.

At this point the path was heavily used and free from obstructions so it didn't take long to complete the journey.

The first sign of advanced technology was the huge bulk of a wrecked spaceship. Fully two hundred met long and fifteen high, it was covered by vines and other vegetation and clearly hadn't been visited for years. The beings didn't give it so much as a sideways glance. Gala guessed that it was the wreckage of the Namsat Elba and the lack of interest displayed by these beings suggested that it was no longer of any importance to them.

*　*　*

The village was built around some dilapidated pre-frabricated buildings that had obviously been carried on board the Namsat Elba. A large, round building with solid walls and a patched canvas roof was at the centre, with some smaller pods arranged around it. These had probably contained stores of some sort. Arranged around them were huts made from locally sourced materials, wicker, bamboo and broad leaved thatch.

Wandering around between the huts were naked younglings supervised by adults. However, these weren't younglings at play. There was a purpose to their movement. An adult raised his voice and the group of children came to a halt and marked something on the ground before moving on. This action was repeated several more times.

"One of our school classes." Explained their guide. "They're learning how to measure things."

Gala had to admit to herself that wasn't the sort of lesson she had expected to be held in a jungle village. This and the sort of language that Marty had so far used suggested that this little microcosm of society were far from being a primitive group of survivors. But clearly they weren't survivors. All of the beings she had so far seen were far too young to have been aboard the Namsat Elba. In fact, so far she had seen no one who was old enough to have been aboard the ship. Of course she had no real sense of the age to which this species could live, but even so, these beings were young, the eldest no more than forty years of age.

They were escorted to the large prefab in the middle of the building and were encouraged to enter. The space lacked any sort of ventilation and was suffocatingly hot inside. Crude benches were arranged in a circle, but apart from that there were no other furnishings.

"Forgive us, but we don't normally use the meeting hut during the day. Not any longer anyway. The cooling system finally broke down about five years ago and none of the ways we repaired it in the past worked anymore."

"I'm an engineer. Perhaps I could take a look at it for you." Gala offered. She noticed that none of the other villagers had followed them into the building.

Marty smiled brightly. "We're hoping we won't need it anymore. After all, you're here to rescue us, aren't you?"

Gala coloured at her gaff. "Of course. I'm sorry. It must be the heat getting to my brain."

"Does your brain often fail to work when it gets hot? That must be a disadvantage for an engineer."

Oops, thought Gala. Mild irony is obviously not understood around here. A bit like America, then.

"We don't actually understand other species, of course. As you may imagine, we haven't had any opportunity to meet any. You have a nice skin colour. Where are you from?"

Gala took an almost involuntary look at the lilac coloured skin visible on her hands. "I'm from a planet called Mun Dane. It's in the Peacock star system."

"Is it nice there?"

"Very nice. Many beings from a wide range of planets choose to retire there, when they get old and no longer work."

"Perhaps we can go there."

"Perhaps you can." Replied Gala, at a loss as to where the conversation was going. Two beings, a male and a female, came into the hut. The male was carrying some containers which looked as though they had been fashioned from clay and the female carried a jug made from a similar material. "Ah, refreshments." Marty said.

The drinking vessels were placed on one of the benches while liquid was poured into them from the jug. Gala was offered one of the vessels. Gingerly she took an experimental sip. It took her by surprise. Not only was it quite cool, but it was a delicious, fruity flavour. She took a bigger sip.

"Delicious. What is it?"

"We make it from fruit we find in the forest, mixed with plain water. You have to know which fruit, of course. Many of them are poisonous and others can produce strange visions."

"Which are they?" Asked Den before being given 'the look' by Gala.

"Never mind my colleague." Gala interjected. "He's something of an expert on substances that cause strange visions. Perhaps you might answer a few questions for us."

"Of course. I'm sure you are as curious about us as we are about you." he turned to the male and female who had brought the drinks. "Thank you Marty. Thank you Davina." The two turned and left the room.

"That's funny, him being called Marty as well. Isn't that confusing?"

The being gave Gala a puzzled look. "Why would that be confusing. All our males are called Marty and all the females are called Davina. Surely that is less confusing than everyone having different names, all of which must be remembered. Are not all your females called Gala and your males called Den?"

"Erm, no actually. Our names are part of our identity. They tell everyone that we are different from the person that stands next to us. This is part of what makes us unique"

"Oh, I'm sorry. This is something I didn't understand. So you and Den are different? Apart from being male and female of course."

"Absolutely. Den isn't even from the same species as me. He's a Gau from the planet Camoo in the Flage system. That's, gosh I don't know, maybe a hundred light years from Peacock."

As another female joined them in the large room, Marty rested his chin on his fist and his fist on his bent knee, clearly thinking about what she had said. The new arrival may have been the one they had met earlier, or completely unknown. There was no way of telling.

"You will have to forgive me, forgive us." Marty said at last. "Everything we know about the universe is contained in a few PMDs and what we were taught by Mother. We know a lot about some things, but not very much about others."

"I understand." Gala used her most sensitive tone. "May I assume that you all came from the same mother and that there was no father."

"That's correct. How did you know?"

"Just a guess." Gala replied. So that was it. They were clones, not naturally conceived individuals. It accounted for the identical looks. Even siblings have some differences in their appearance, unless they were twins.

Gala wiped the sweat from her brow with the sleeve of her Superskin ™ shirt. "I think we had better start at the beginning, don't you?"

Glossary

Cloning - The science involved in producing an exact replica of a living being. One being, known as the cytoplasmic donor, provides an egg, The second being, the one to be replicated, provides the DNA from a single cell. The DNA is inserted into the donor egg. The resulting embryo, known as a blastocyst, is then implanted into a surrogate womb where it develops and grows into the replica being. Both beings have to be from the same species, though there are reports of successful inter-species cloning but that gets a bit yucky if you think about it for too long.

PMD - Portable Memory Device. They come in a range of shapes and sizes and use a variety of different technologies to store information, but they all perform the same basic function. They are all fully compatible with each other except for those produced by the Banana Computing Corporation.

Pulsar - A weapon that uses high energy pulses to destroy its target. Smaller versions are hand held and larger versions can be fitted to mounts for use on vehicles and space craft. Has an advantage over projectile weapons because it can be used under water with only minor loss of efficiency.

Superskin material - Many advances have been made in the manufacture of synthetic fibres that are warm, waterproof and breathable. The Superskin Company (a subsidiary of the Gargantua Enterprises Corporation) produce some particularly attractive skin tight clothing that is thermally insulated and also water repellent, while being the thickness of a hair. Their clothes are also very hard wearing, which is why bounty hunters like them.

6 – Marty And Davina

Over the next couple of hours Marty and Davina took it in turns to tell them the story of the Namsat Elba. After telling how Marti Woo had died, there was a pause as the two fell into a silent reflection on the past.

"What happened after that?" Gala encouraged. She and Den had listened spellbound to the story and now wanted to hear the rest. How had this group of clones come to end up here on this remote planet?

Night had fallen during the telling of the story and electric lights had come on. Gala vaguely recalled seeing solar panels spread across part of the open space in which the village stood. No doubt they had been salvaged from the Namsat Elba. She could hear the pattering of rain on the roof. That surprised her, though she didn't know why. The clue was in the description of the terrain they had cut their way through earlier in the day: rain forest. Marty had started speaking again.

"Mother couldn't bear to be alone. She managed for six months but started to worry about her sanity. She needed a reason to continue living, she said. A reason other than completing the mission, or just escaping. So, she started to research cloning. She was, after all, a fully qualified bio-chemist. Only an expert in the field of cloning could be better qualified. We are the proof of her success." His face saddened for a moment. "Of course there were some failures at the start, but she got it right in the end.

She was both the DNA donor and the surrogate mother for the embryos, which is unusual but it was necessary as there was no one else into whom the blastocyst could be implanted. First Officer Marti Woo was the cytoplasmic donor."

"Whoa there." Gala held up a hand in mock protest. "I'm good at science but not that good."

Marty laughed. "Basically Marti Woo provided the egg, so Mother was fulfilling her promise that Marti's eggs would be used to produce younglings, while Mother provided the DNA so we are replicas of her. She also became the surrogate by implanting a male and a female embryo in her womb each time. The male was always called Marty with a 'y' and the female was Davina, named after herself. She did this each year for three years until she decided to bring us here."

"Why did she do that?"

"She said that once we were born she couldn't bear to be parted from us, which she would have been if she was captured and imprisoned, so she had to convince the authorities that the Namsat Elba was lost, which meant it could never be seen anywhere else in the galaxy. She brought the ship down in a controlled crash then smashed up the computers, after downloading all our knowledge into PMDs of course. From those she was able to teach us all we now know.

Deliberately crashing a spaceship that had perfectly good shuttle craft and then smashing up the computers suggested that Davina had at least partly lost touch with her sanity, but Gala hadn't been there so she shouldn't be too quick to judge. "You keep saying 'we', but you're far too young to have been on the Namsat Elba when it crashed."

"Of course. Sorry, that is the way we see ourselves. As we are all the replicas of Marti and Davina we always see ourselves as 'we' rather than 'I' or 'you'. We are a collective, I suppose you would say. What I know my brothers and sisters know, and vice versa. That's not true in a literal sense, but at the same time it feels very real. If I feel happy then Marty and Davina will know it and they will feel happy as well."

"A sort of mental connection, then."

"If you like, but not in the same way as telepaths."

"So how come there are now so many of you?"

"Each year, three Davina's are chosen by ballot to become mothers and we clone another six of ourselves, three male and three females. It's considered to be a great honour and each Davina may only do it once. Mother forbade us to reproduce in any other way.

We aren't allowed to have sexual congress, because we are brothers and sisters."

Mother wasn't that insane then, thought Gala, but she marvelled that the clones still obeyed rules set down many years before.

"Do you have an image of Mother?" Den asked.

"Of course." Marty left the hut and returned a few moments later carrying a battered communicator. He showed Den an image and then offered the device to Gala. She saw a female with a squarish sort of face, a strong jawline, aquiline nose, high cheek bones and a determined look in her eye. She was good looking, there was no doubt about that. Her ebony face radiated resolve. She was the exact image of every being Gala had seen in the village.

Marty took back the communicator and swiped the screen to produce another image. "That was Marti Woo." He handed the device back to Gala.

Marti had a more oval shaped face, a more pointed chin, her nose was shorter and slightly upturned. Her eyes had a softer look to them. It was easy to see why Jaquo might have had a crush on her. Like Davina her skin colour was ebony and Gala wondered what species they were. All they really knew was that they were from the Vartu system and it wasn't one with which she was familiar.

"If you had this communicator, why didn't you use it to send out a distress signal, instead of using a signalling method that is centuries out of date?"

"Mother didn't want to be able to give in to the temptation and call for help, so she removed the communications chips from all the communicators and destroyed them. Now we use them only for interfacing with the PMDs. And of course with the computers smashed we had no other way of communicating, so we couldn't send out a distress call."

"How did you manage that? No… perhaps a better question is why did you suddenly decide to try to send a distress signal?"

"Mother taught us to be curious, to try to understand the world around us. Some of us are more curious than others and want to know about what is out there." He pointed towards the roof of the hut, though he clearly meant what was above that, the sky, the stars, even the galaxy. "We came from the stars, so some of us would like to go back there, about half our number. Marty found a source on a PMD that showed us how to make a radio transceiver, so we salvaged components from the Namsat Elba and built one. However, it's very crude. We only completed it a couple of years ago. We sent out some signals, but of course we're far from the next nearest star so we didn't know how long it would take for a reply to come back, so instead we listened."

"Yes, you were right to do that. The nearest inhabited star is over twenty light years away. It will take your signal another eighteen years to reach it."

Marty nodded his understanding. "And twenty years for a reply to reach us. Yes, that's what we thought. Well, our listening paid off. We heard your signal instead. Of course our radio isn't sophisticated enough to be able to interpret your signal, but we thought that if you were clever enough to send it, you would be clever enough to work out our message."

"Yes, our ship's computer interpreted it with no difficulty and sent back our reply in your own format, so you could understand it."

"So here you are. But it gets late. Marty and Davina have been preparing a feast in your honour. We should go and join them. It's too hot to eat in here."

"It's getting late." Gala demurred. "Perhaps we had better return to our ship."

"That isn't a good idea. The jungle isn't a safe place at night. The predatory animals hunt by night and there are at least twenty different types of snake that could kill you if you accidentally trip over one. The number of insects that bite and sting are countless and we have no idea which ones would be fatal for your species. We have prepared one of the huts for you and Den."

Den nearly burst out laughing, but managed to stifle it while at the same time leering meaningfully at Gala.

"Erm, no, that isn't appropriate." Gala stuttered, not wishing to cause offence by pointing out that Marty had misread her and Den's relationship. "We aren't what we call a couple. I will be happy to share a hut with Davina, and Den with Marty."

"Oh, that is a shame. We were hoping you would demonstrate sex for us. We've never seen it."

Den nearly choked.

* * *

The feast was delicious and made up mainly of vegetarian dishes.

The whole village was gathered around, sitting in small groups, each with naked youngling amongst it, though they did flit from group to group in the manner of younglings everywhere, chattering, laughing and squabbling. Lights were strung through the trees and around the eves of the huts to illuminate proceedings. A steady stream of Davina's and Marty's carried food from a communal kitchen where it seemed to be cooked on fires lit in old metal containers. Marty called them barber cues.

"We don't eat a lot of meat." Marty explained. "We understand that on some planets many species were hunted to extinction because they were a good source of food. Mother taught us to try to live in harmony with our environment, so we only kill animals that are plentiful and not many of those live close to us. Several days travel in that direction," he pointed, "the jungle ends and there are wide open spaces where huge herds of animals graze on the plentiful grass. But in the forest the animals are more isolated. There are plenty of apes, snakes and lizards but none of them taste very nice. Most of the meat we eat comes from birds, which are plentiful though seasonal. We don't eat them when they are laying their eggs and rearing young."

"Do you have weapons?"

"We have one pulsar still working. All the others were broken or lost over the years. With our limited electricity supply it takes three weeks for it to recharge, so we have made other weapons for hunting, and we use traps. We still have metal knives from the ship and no shortage of tools, so making things isn't difficult."

"But not clothes, I notice." Gala observed, seeing Den's lecherous gaze wandering over the generous curves of the nearest Davina, which weren't concealed by any clothing.

"Why do we need clothes? It's never cold here. By tradition we still wear some of the garments that were on the ship, though most of those were worn out long ago. Some of us like to try to make things from animal hide, but that is more of a… I think the word is hobby."

Gala marvelled at his innocence but decided to say nothing. Clearly the original Davina had never taught them the association between nudity and sex, but then again why would she? Gala had often wondered what would happen if everyone went around naked all the time and she realised that the answer was probably sitting all around her right now. It was beings themselves that had first clothed their bodies, not nature.

"Why don't you just move to where the animals graze?" Asked Den.

"It would mean leaving the ship. We still salvage spare parts from the hold or from the on-board equipment to keep our crude technology working. You see that?" he pointed to what Gala had assumed was a storage pod. "That is the ship's medi-bay. It came complete in that form, so all we had to do was withdraw it from the ship's hull and drag it over here. Without it we couldn't reproduce. But it needs electricity to function which means it needs all the solar panels that you see and the two wind turbines and the bio-mass composter. We couldn't take it all with us, so we stay here. Besides, what we have is enough. You have already said how delicious the food is."

Gala had to admit that she had and that the compliments she had paid were genuine, not made just out of politeness to her hosts.

"Have you explored the planet much?"

"Each year we send out an exploration party. Mother started it when the first younglings were old enough to travel and fend for themselves. She said that if we want to live in harmony with our world we must first understand how it works, so we study it as best we can. Mother taught us how to analyse plants, especially their toxins so that we don't poison ourselves. We have also found nutritious plant species that grow far away but which we can farm here."

Gala had to admit that Davina had been something of a visionary. While life for these beings was basic they seemed to be happy and were self-sufficient. They had enough technology to help them to survive, but hadn't made it their master, as was so common elsewhere.

Marty changed the subject. "Now, tomorrow, there are sixty eight of us who wish to leave, so how many can your shuttle take on each trip so that we can get to your ship?"

With a sinking heart Gala realised that she was going to have to disappoint Marty yet again. After the embarrassment of explaining that sex wasn't something that was subjected to public scrutiny, other than in certain establishments of the sort favoured by Den, she didn't want to be the bearer of bad news once again. But needs must, so she took a deep breath.

"I'm afraid our ship is quite small and it isn't currently fit for travel. We could take a couple of you, but the rest would have to wait for a proper rescue craft. We've already sent a message telling the authorities that you are here. They'll send a ship, though even that may not be big enough to carry over sixty of you in one go. That can be rectified with another message, but in the short term you will have to wait a few more weeks; perhaps a month or more."

Marty's face fell, as did that of most of the Martys and Davinas close to them. Gala realised that most of their dinner companions must be from the group that wanted to leave.

"What I suggest is that you decide between you who will come with us. We can accommodate two of you. The rest can depart when the rescue ships arrive."

"We will draw lots. That is the way we choose when something is either much desired or much dreaded. Where will these two go?"

"We're going to Rigel, but there are no inhabited planets there. We're meeting someone and we're already overdue, so we can't delay any further. After that I have no idea where we will be going."

"So it will be an adventure. We know about adventures."

"You have been living an adventure for eighty years." Den observed.

"Have we? Oh, yes, I suppose we have. Funny how we have never seen it that way before."

"We'll stay with you here in your village until the spares we need arrive, which will be in a few more days, perhaps a week. Then we can go up to the ship, do the repairs and move on to Rigel. By that time we will have some idea of when the rescue ship will arrive. You can choose whether or not you wish to travel together or if some wish to accompany us."

* * *

In the end one Marty and one Davina decided that they would like to go with Gala and Den. It seemed that whenever they did anything they always did it in matched pairs, as though they couldn't be separated for a moment. Gala had already discovered that the Davina and Marty that would go with them were born from a pair of embryos implanted into the same Davina at the same time. Their pair bonding seemed to be similar to that of monozygotic twins. Something to do with having shared a womb, Gala assumed.

Departure from the planet was a lengthy affair. Marty and Davina had to embrace, and be embraced, by every other Marty and Davina, which took time. The shuttle had been moved to the village as Gala had returned to the ship a few times to carry out checks, send communications and finally, when the delivery drone arrived, to carry out the repair that rendered the Adastra once again fit for interstellar travel.

Then it came the turn of Gala and Den to say goodbye. To the Marty that had acted as their host and historian she handed a spare communicator taken from the Adastra.

"Our number is programmed into it, so you can always keep in touch with us. If Marty and Davina choose to leave us we'll make sure you know where we last saw them."

"Thank you. That would be appreciated. While we honour the fact that they are individuals and free to make their own choices, they are still our family."

"Of course. I worry if I don't know where my family are. Now, if you can't make contact there is a second number programmed in. It's a messaging service. Speak to them and they will make sure we get the message as soon as they can."

The Guild had long since recognised that the more complex messaging systems became the easier they seemed to be to hack. So they had reverted to an ancient system of recording messages in hard copy and storing them in a locked cabinet in a locked room. If someone wanted to access them without authority they would have to do so physically, which presented far more risks than hacking.

"Once the rescue ship comes out of its inter-stellar wormhole they will use this to communicate with you. I have sent them the identification number."

Another round of embraces was undertaken before Gala was finally able to join Den, Marty and Davina in the cramped confines of the shuttle. Technically it was only supposed to seat three, but with some difficulty they had made it accommodate the four of them.

As they disembarked Gala showed them to their cabins. "Davina will use my cabin and I'll take our captain's cabin. We'll be meeting up with her at Rigel, so we'll have to change the sleeping arrangements when we get there. Den and Marty will hot-bunk, which means one of you will sleep while the other is awake." Den wasn't too pleased with this news, but short of offering to sleep in the prisoner holding cell there was little he could do. Gala was acting Captain so she got to decide the sleeping arrangements

"What are our duties?" Marty asked.

"You don't have any. You can just enjoy the journey as passengers." Gala smiled at him.

"But we must have duties. We work every day. We all share the workload, that is our way."

Gala could tell that the thought of not working was causing their guests some distress. "OK, well, I think that the best thing you can do is to go back to school and study. You have been confined on that planet all your lives and there is a lot you don't know about the galaxy, so I'll get our computer to design you a course of study. How does that sound?"

"We must also do something to serve you. It's our way; every Marty and Davina must serve every other Marty and Davina. In the absence of any of our brothers and sisters we will serve you instead."

Gala knew it was futile to argue. These people had a very simple view of the galaxy and it would only cause upset if she didn't try to accommodate them. It seemed that the service droid would have some of its duties reassigned for the duration of their journey.

Gala left Den to show their guests around the small ship and to teach them how to use the various service and entertainment facilities available to them. She headed for the command deck to take the ship out of orbit. It had been a strange few days, she had to admit.

"Lazarus, calculate the chances of our breaking down within range of the planet where the Namsat Elba crashed." She commanded, as the ship started to accelerate towards its required velocity. There was a short pause, which told Gala that the calculation was an extremely complex one.

"Fifteen billion, eight hundred and seventy five million, three hundred and forty three thousand eight hundred and sixty two to one. That's rounded to the nearest whole number." It finally announced. "Do you want it calculated to ten decimal places?"

"No, that won't be necessary. Thank you, Lazarus." Those were some fantastic odds, she had to admit. She wouldn't buy a lottery ticket offering those sorts of odds, not even if it only cost a victel.

The odds were even more fantastic when she took into account the fact that the Adastra had built in system redundancies that meant that the fault shouldn't have been able to prevent their continued journey through the wormhole to Rigel. Add to that a talking computer that seemed to have developed its own personality and things were starting to get decidedly weird.

Glossary

Monozygotic twins - Twins born from the same egg which has divided into two embryos after fertilisation, otherwise known as identical twins. They have identical DNA. Twins from two eggs that are fertilised at the same time are fraternal twins and aren't identical because boy-boy and girl-girl twins have similar, but not identical, DNA. Boy and girl twins are always fraternal. It is monozygotic twins that tend to have the sort of bond that appears to allow one twin to feel the pain of the other.

Victel - A unit of currency worth $1/100^{th}$ of a nuk. A one victel coin is effectively valueless

7 – Meeting At Rigel

Desire welcomed her guests aboard the Starcruiser Shogun *(See New Earth),* taking a very close interest in them. She had never met either of her fellow Fell members before and was curious as to what to make of them.

The first to enter the ship's lounge was tall, angular and quite good looking. His skin was fair, as was his close cropped hair. His blue eyes were piercing, as though they could see into your soul. He wasn't as good looking as an Aloisan, or even an Arthurid, but there was no doubt that many females and a lot of males would find him attractive.

"Hello." He threw Desire a mock salute. "I am Tiger."

"Welcome aboard. Please take a seat."

"And I am Attila." The second being said. He was small, with olive coloured skin and the wild mane of hair common to the Dysac species. She had once known a criminal by the name of Biggar Fro and wondered if he might be related. Biggar Fro was dead now, of course; killed by that meddling bitch An Kohli.* That might account for this Dysac being so keen to help her kill the bounty hunter.

In their turn the two Fell members examined their host, Desire. She was squat and round, a typical Farood. Her skin was mottled pale yellow and pink, like the camouflage of a predatory cat. She may be small but she radiated physical strength. Tiger decided he wouldn't want to arm wrestle this being, while Attila decided he wouldn't even want to be embraced by her.

"So, what is your plan, Desire?" Asked Tiger, not bothering with small talk. He was the sort that always wanted to get straight down to business.

"I haven't got one yet. I thought I would wait to consult you. I'm sure you have your own ideas about how we might proceed. If it helps, we have this ship at our disposal. As a Starcruiser it's unarmed, but I can call on some… acquaintances to provide an armed escort for us, if you think it necessary. We have a crew of twelve, but they aren't the sort who would be any good in a fight. We have another twelve of Shogun's former bodyguards. They didn't fare too well against An Kohli, but will serve us well enough as a visible deterrent and if the worst comes to the worst they will serve as cannon fodder."

Tiger and Attila had to admire her style.

"I too can contribute beings with… shall we say special skills." Tiger added. "It will take me a short while to assemble them. They will come with their own ships."

"I'm afraid I'm not in the same line of business as your good selves, so I don't think anyone I know will be able to assist us in a direct manner." Attila advised them. "But I have contacts throughout the galaxy. They can put their hands on many useful artefacts or provide information. Will that serve as my contribution?"

"We work as a team and in a team everyone contributes what they can. It will suffice. Perhaps the first information your contacts can provide is the current whereabouts of An Kohli. Until we establish that it is difficult to formulate a plan." Desire gave Attila a thin smile. "Do you think you can arrange that?"

"Give me access to the ship's communications system and I'll see what I can do. As you say, until we have that information we can't do much."

"You look like someone I once knew." Desire knew she shouldn't ask questions regarding her colleague's identity, but she was curious by nature.

"If you tell me who you mean I can tell you if I also knew him or her."

"His name was Biggar Fro."

"He was my brother. Did you know him well?"

"As well as it's possible to know someone, I think."

"Is that why you have personal animosity towards An Kohli?"

"It is."

"Then we will make good allies." Attila rose from the comfortable chair in which he sat. "Now, if you would like to show me to your communications room, I can make a start."

* * *

"I was wondering when you were going to turn up." An Kohli's voice sounded loud across the ship-to-ship network. It was clear she was not in a good mood and An Kohli in a bad mood needed careful handling, Gala knew from experience.

"I'm sorry. It was unavoidable. I'll explain when you get here. Before you do, though, I have something to tell you." Gala mentally braced herself. "We have some guests."

"Oh? Anyone I know?"

"I doubt it. It's a long story, but I've picked up a couple of strays along the way."

"If they're cats they're going to get booted straight into the airlock and straight off my ship." An Kohli was notorious for not liking cats and Gala was well renowned for going gooey at the knees just thinking about them. It had been the cause of many a 'discussion' between them.

"No, not cats. More like beings. Well, they are beings. They're just a bit… well unusual is the best I can say."

"What, you mean they've got two heads or something?"

"No. Just… well, perhaps you'd better reserve judgement until you meet them." It would have been better if Gala had been able to persuade them to put on some clothes, if only to eliminate the embarrassment factor, but all she ever got in reply to that suggestion was 'It's not cold' or 'It's not our way'. She had seriously considered dropping the ship's temperature down to zero just to persuade them, but that would have been as uncomfortable for herself and Den as it would be for them. Fortunately An Kolhi had developed a fairly blasé attitude towards nudity over the years, which would help.

When she met Marty and Davina, shortly after she arrived on board, An Kohli's smile didn't quite reach her violet coloured eyes. "Nice to have you on board." Was her initial reaction, while her tone of voice suggested that it was anything but nice. "Erm, my co-pilot has to bring me up to date with events so if you'll excuse me for the moment we'll go onto the command deck. Nice to meet you." She practically flew through the door onto the command deck, dragging Gala by the hand.

"OK, do you mind telling me what the freak is going on!"

Gala gave her boss a potted version of the events that had led up to her bringing the clones on board, including the story of the Namsat Elba. "They wanted to come with us and I could see no reason for refusing."

"Apart from the fact that they know nothing about anything, use bows and arrows as weapons and will eat us out of house and home, you mean. Aren't those good reasons?"

"I suppose so. It's just that they're such nice beings."

"They're actually humans."

"What the heck was that." An Kohli reacted to the computer's interjection.

"Oh, sorry. The computer seems to have developed a fault. I can't disable the voice functions. By the way, it likes to be called Lazarus."

An Kohli was visibly fuming. To have a talking computer was bad enough, but to have one she couldn't silence was even worse.

"Look, I'm sure we can get it fixed as soon as we can get to a port with proper maintenance facilities."

"Oh, nice." Interjected Lazarus. "Just talk about me as if I wasn't here."

"You aren't here." Snapped An Kohli. "You are a machine. Please try to behave like one."

Lazarus didn't respond, but Gala got a distinct mental image of it folding its arms and storming off to its bedroom, slamming the door behind it.

"OK, so we've got two house guests. I can hardly put them ashore on one of the gas giants they have here. But they'll go ashore on the first planet we stop at where there's a reasonable chance of them not getting killed or robbed. Not that they have anything to steal. What's with the nudity?"

"They don't regard clothes as an essential. They wear them only for warmth, which I'm guessing most species did before we invented modesty."

"Oh yes. Your 'we're all naturists really' theory. I notice you don't practice it. Remember that get up we had to wear to get to New Klondike?" An Kohli gave her a broad grin. *(See New Earth).*

Gala's lilac skin went a deep shade of puce. "That was different."

"Only because it was you. I'm not sure you even like taking your clothes off to have a shower."

"That's not true. I even sleep in the nude."

An Kohli raised the protesting palm of her hand. "Enough detail, please. OK, we can't get them to wear clothes. What are they doing to fill in the time?"

"The computer has set them a course of study which will better prepare them for the sort of planets they might find themselves on. I've supplemented that with movies and entertainments from the ship's archive. Nothing too gory yet. I don't want to scare them, but they're very innocent. They're going to have a shock when they find out what the galaxy has to offer them."

"Better not let them ashore on Towie then. OK, that sounds fine."

"Anyway, your clones are actually humans." Lazarus had come out of his huff. "The chances of that are rated at nearly fifty million to one. I can be more accurate if you wish."

"No, that's not necessary, Lazarus. But what is the significance of that?"

"Evolution is such that on most planets the evolutionary paths followed by most species are similar, but not identical. This leads to similar DNA structures for the majority of species, but not identical structures. The more complex the creature the less likely it is that their DNA will be identical. For example, for lower level life forms such as arthropods, molluscs, annelida etcetera, based on the current number of known species there are estimated to be over a million species with identical DNA and several billion with DNA that is ninety nine point nine percent or more similar. When you move on to higher order species such as mammals, birds and fish, this level of similarity reduces markedly. There are perhaps less than ten thousand species in the galaxy with identical DNA and less than a million with a ninety nine point nine percent match. When it comes to the most intelligent species on the planets, species such as yourself," The computer seemed to have a sneer in its voice when it said that, "there are several thousand with a ninety nine point nine percent match, which is why the humanoid form is so common, but there are only two that are known to be identical; the humans of Earth and the humans of Ecos. However, they are not descended from any common ancestor, at least, not one that has ever been traced. According to available records they have never even met and appear to have evolved independently."

"Thank you Lazarus. I didn't know any of that." Gala replied. She filed the tid-bit away for future reference. It seemed to be significant, though she didn't know why.

"It's all in my databanks if you only care to look." The computer replied with a smug tone that it shouldn't have been able to adopt. "You rely far too much on the galacticnet for your information."

"Oh, and you'll be having your meals and drinks served to you while they're on board." Gala continued, trying to ignore the computer's jibes. "It's just something they do."

An Kohli gave a resigned sigh. She wasn't comfortable with the idea of servants or service, not even in a fancy restaurant. She disliked the idea that someone was paid to pander to her wishes. If she could have had her way she would go into the kitchen and cook her own meal, but as Gala had pointed out on many an occasion, that defeated the purpose of going to a fancy restaurant. "Just think of them as attractive droids." Gala had advised her.

"That makes it even worse." An Kohli had replied. "It de-sensitises me to real beings." At which point Gala usually gave up.

"So, have you decided where to start looking for the next egg?"

"No. I'll need a couple of hours analysing Su Mali's data and then I can decide."

"If you tell me what your problem is I can analyse the data for you." Lazarus interjected.

"What makes you think you can understand the problem?" An Kohli was almost scornful.

"You have sadly underestimated my capabilities over the years. I'm more than just a machine for starting and stopping the engines and making your phone calls for you, you know. I can do complex analysis as well."

"Actually that's true." She told An Kohli about the way the computer had calculated the odds of their break down occurring the way it did.

"Lazarus, display the variables that you had to consider to make that calculation, and the formula you used."

The number of variables filled three screens. There must have been several hundred, though An Kohli didn't bother counting. Then she scrolled to the formula. She was good at maths but the complexity of the calculation boggled her eyes. It would take her most of the day just to solve the first few expressions and there must have been fifty or more of them.

"OK. I take your point. If I let you have access to the navi-com data, can you tell me on which planet in this sector of the galaxy Su Mali is likely to have hidden an object of considerable value."

"On one condition."

"I don't bargain with machines."

"Think of me more as a being you can't have sex with." Lazarus's voice seemed to mock her. "If any of my suggestions prove to be right then you don't get me fixed. You allow me to keep my voice capability. If I am wrong then you do as you please."

An Kohli had to admit she was attracted by the notion. While the computer was undoubtedly clever she didn't think it had the reasoning capacity to solve a riddle as subtle as Su Mali's thought processes.

"Very well, but I add a condition of my own. Your options must be accompanied by an assessment of the statistical likelihood that you are correct, and you can't give us more than four options."

The computer remained silent for a few moments, clearly processing this requirement and doing an assessment of its likely success. "Very well. I accept."

"Good. What do you need from me to allow you to interface with the data in the navi-com?"

"Just provide me with a username and password, to make it appear that I am a sentient being rather than a machine, then sit back and enjoy the show."

* * *

"Lazarus, how long will you be with this calculation?" Gala asked after the computer had been silent for an hour.

The computer made a noise that could have been the sort of sigh that said 'I'd be a lot quicker if you didn't keep interrupting', before replying, "Approximately two hours, twenty three minutes and eighteen seconds."

Gala turned to An Kohli, waiting impatiently in the captain's chair. "I need to go over to the Pradua to carry out some routine maintenance tasks. Would you come and help me?"

An Kohli was just about to ask her co-pilot why she needed help, when she usually eschewed all offers, when she noticed the 'don't ask questions' look on Gala's face.

"OK, yes, I'll come."

"Great; I'll take the shuttle over and send it back for you." With the Pradua being only a single seat ship its shuttle was tiny and no amount of pushing and shoving would allow Gala and An Kohli to use it at the same time.

Once on board the Pradua the space situation was hardly improved. The pilot's seat doubled as a bed and there was a small service area that provided both food and shower facilities. The toilet was a tiny space that didn't even have a door. Well, with only one person on board a door was deemed unnecessary. An Kohli claimed the pilot's seat while Gala squatted on the floor in the corner of the service area, just within An Kohli's eye line.

"Sorry about the subterfuge, but I needed to talk to you about that computer and I suspect that it's able to hear everything we say, no matter where we are in the Adastra."

"You think it has us bugged?"

"Not as such, but if it can interface with the intercom it can listen in on any conversation that takes place on the ship and we wouldn't even know about it. The Pradua, on the other hand, is completely independent. We'd have to open a communications channel for it to be able to listen in."

"Why are you so suspicious?"

"Well, to start with, our inability to turn off the voice circuits. According to everything I know about computers, that shouldn't be the case. Then there's its… well, for the want of a better word, its personality. It shouldn't have one. Galactic protocols forbid the programming of personalities into computers installed on ships, in order to prevent crew members from anthropomorphising and starting to treat them like beings. If that happens then they may make mistakes by either not trusting them enough, or trusting them too much."

"Yes, I heard about that happening somewhere. I think it was a science lab. The computer's personality seemed so real that the scientists and the computer had a falling out and several years' worth of work had to be done over because the scientists no longer trusted the computer to be objective."

"Precisely. This seems to be what is happening with Lazarus. I didn't give it that name, it chose it for itself. An obscure reference to someone who rose from the dead. A little bit fanciful, don't you think? And I'm sure I can hear sarcasm and sneering from it. That is something else that it shouldn't be able to do. Those sorts of traits aren't normally programmed into computer personalities. After all, why would anyone want a sarcastic computer?"

"And now I've done a deal which could mean it keeping its voice circuits activated."

"Well, you don't have to keep that deal. I'm not sure a promise to a machine actually counts."

"But if I don't keep it then we won't know what is happening on its inside. If it is capable of thinking like a sentient being, which is what appears to be happening, then it could harbour similar emotions, such as resentment. One day we might wake up to find ourselves plunging towards the centre of a star because the computer has decided to get back at as."

"Sounds like the plot of a bad movie." Gala gave a grim smile.

"Precisely. But movies are often based on real events and I have no wish to end up with my image and dates being shown before the end titles under the words 'In Memory Of'." An Kohli paused, but then another thought struck her. "Does Den know about this?"

"Yes, I had the same conversation when I was down on the planet with the clones. I've just realised, we haven't named it. Technically it was colonised, so it should have a name."

"We'll discuss that with your friends Marty and Davina when we go back to the Adastra, but in the meantime we have to decide what to do about the computer."

"I suggest we don't do anything for the moment. It's too risky while we're criss-crossing space. If we're right and it has become dangerous then it's even more dangerous if we try to deal with the problem while we're up here. We need to be in a properly equipped maintenance facility where it can't do any harm if it decides it doesn't want to be re-programmed."

"That makes sense. OK, we'll do it your way, but I'm telling you, it's still my ship and if it starts smart mouthing me again I'll... well, I'll do something." She ended rather lamely.

Back on the ship the computer that wanted to be called Lazarus completed its calculations, announcing the results with a musical flourish. An Kohli read the results from the image screen, though the computer had already reported them in a triumphant voice.

"Aragan in the Murfrid system, sixty eight percent probability; Denlacon in the Apus system, fifty three percent probability; the beta planet in the Cor Caroli system, forty one percent probability and Finial in the Malar system, thirty three percent probability. Hmm. Lazarus, what is the next highest probability result?"

"I have eight possibilities that are between twenty and twenty two percent probability, Captain."

That was new, An Kohli thought, the computer addressing her as Captain. Things were looking up. Twenty percent probability wasn't high, but then again sixty eight percent didn't exactly fill her with confidence either. But she had agreed to give the computer a chance, and if it was right it would save them a lot of time.

"Lazarus, what process did you follow to reach this result?"

"I analysed the patterns of movement Su Mali took that led to the three Magi you have already found." An Kohli shared a startled look with Gala. They had never mentioned the Magi to the computer. No, correction, they had never mentioned them to the computer since it had recovered its voice. Before that they had discussed the subject openly on the command deck, which meant that the computer had been listening even if it hadn't been able to speak.

"I then identified any features that the planets held in common, and major differences and so on. This led me to develop an algorithm to calculate the probability of any of the other destinations being likely to have been chosen by Su Mali as a hiding place. I have to admit that at this stage the algorithm is quite crude. Assuming that one of the four options I have offered you turn out to be the next hiding place, I will be able to refine the algorithm to improve its accuracy."

"Thank you, Lazarus." An Kohli waved her hand over the intercom controls. "Den, I want you to take the Pradua and scout the planet Aragan in the Murfrid system. Check it out and make sure there are no nasty surprises waiting for us. We'll be along as soon as we've completed a little diversion."

"Where are you going?" Den asked.

"To Ecos. I think it's time our stray Ecosians went home."

8 – Ecos

Attila smiled at his two fellow Fell members, savouring the moment of revelation. "I think I know where you will be able to find the Adastra." He announced. They waited expectantly.

"It appears that a missing exploration ship has turned up in a remote corner of Sector One and the Adastra was first on the scene. You could have found that out for yourselves of course; the news is all over the galacticnet right now. But it appears that the Adastra has now moved on. My sources tell me that it went to Rigel."

"But there's nothing of interest around Rigel. A couple of gas planets and some asteroids, that's all." Desire commented with a grimace of disappointment.

"Precisely. Which means the only reason to go there would be to rendezvous with someone else. When the exploration ship was found An Kohli wasn't named as being amongst the Adastra's crew. I believe that the rendezvous was therefore with An Kohli. As we know she had recovered another of the Magi eggs and no doubt had taken it to those buffoons in the Galactic Counsel in Exile. Rigel would be an ideal place to meet up, away from prying eyes."

"So? What we need to know is where she went after the rendezvous." Tiger was no more impressed with the news than had been Desire.

"If you will allow me my small moment of enjoyment." Attila said sibilantly. "On board the Adastra were two of the survivors, well, more accurately descendants of the survivors, from the exploration ship. The original crew were all from a planet called Ecos. I believe that An Kohli will deliver the two survivors to their home planet before she continues her mission."

"How much of a start has she got on us?" Desire asked, worried that the news may have arrived too late to be of any use.

"I took the liberty of asking your Captain to do the calculations for me. Assuming normal journey times, if we depart for Ecos immediately we will arrive there at least three days before the Adastra."

* * *

The planet of Ecos, An Kohli imagined, was what Earth might have looked like before the humans managed to bugger it up. Fortunately, when the Ecosians industrialised their planet they realised the risks involved with regard to pollution that their new industries produced and took steps to minimise the impact. The first thing they did was to introduce population control measures so that the number of people living on the planet never outstripped the capabilities of the planet to sustain them in an environmentally friendly way.

So now An Kohli found herself strolling alongside a crystal clear river that flowed through the centre of one of the largest cities on the planet. It was so unlike the liquefied mud she had seen in the River Thames on Earth. The city itself, though big by the standards of Ecos, was home to only a few thousand people. Its streets were wide and tree lined, parks were many and vehicles were few. Beneath the streets a complex public transport system ferried people quickly around the city in a sparklingly clean environment.

Beside her Marty and Davina also strolled, marvelling at the sights. "How do people hunt? Surely no game animals would live in a place like this."

Such was the nature of the city that it was likely that deer and other game animals did live in the parks and other open spaces, but An Kohli didn't want to embarrass the two clones by pointing this out. "They don't hunt." An Kohli told them. "If they are like the majority of inhabited planets the food that is needed will be mainly grown on farms. That includes any animals needed for meat. "

"But there are so many birds. Surely they eat birds."

"I'm not familiar with their diet, but I would guess that some birds have also been domesticated for food. You must have read about farming when you studied the PMDs left by your mother. Didn't you also farm?"

"Yes, but there were never more than one hundred and fifty of us; sometimes less. It's easy to farm for so few. Here there are thousands of people living in one place. If we are to believe what we read about this planet, while we were on board your ship, there are hundreds of places like this."

"Yes, but they have been living like this for centuries. It has allowed them to shape the land to meet their needs. Here farms won't be just a few rows of plants. They will be made up of several large fields, each with a different crop or a different animal in them. Actually, compared to many planets this one is very sparsely populated. The whole population is less than twenty million. For a planet the size of this that is hardly anything."

They had walked a rectangular route along one side of the river, across a bridge and back along the other side. Now they crossed a second bridge to take them back to their start point. Waiting for them was an Ecosian by the name of Filar Hup, who was acting as their host. An Kohli had expected massive media interest in the arrival of the two clones, but the media had been expertly managed and Marty and Davina had been allowed space as they tried to come to terms with what would become their new home.

"Did you enjoy that?" Filar asked as he rose from the bench upon which he had been sitting. He led them back towards the building where he worked.

"So many questions." An Kohli answered for them. "I'm afraid I didn't do a very good job of answering them."

"Of course. So much of this is new to the two of you." Filar addressed Marty and Davina directly. "No matter, we have come to a solution to which we hope you will agree. A teacher has offered you a place in her home, as a temporary measure. She will help you to deal with the major cultural issues that you may be struggling with, such as the wearing of clothes." He stifled a smile. It had been a significant battle to persuade Marty and Davina of the need to dress modestly, in fact the need to dress at all. "We trust that you won't find it all too arduous. When you feel ready we will help you to find work. You have a wide choice available to you."

"Perhaps we could farm." Said Marty eagerly.

"If that is what you want, then we will see what we can do."

"What about the others, when they arrive?" An Kohli was anxious that her Marty and Davina wouldn't be accorded special treatment just because they were the first to reach the planet.

"Everything is in hand to welcome them." Filar assured her. "The arrival of these innocent victims has created much excitement and there is no shortage of people wishing to help them."

"Good. I'm pleased to hear it."

"Now, what about yourself and your crew? We hope you will avail yourself of the simple pleasures to be offered by our planet and in our modest city. Without you there would be nothing for us to celebrate."

An Kohli had planned to just drop Marty and Davina off and then carry on with their mission, but the Ecosians had made it clear that they expected more of them. They at least expected to be allowed to make a fuss of them for a while.

"Perhaps we might rest for a few days before we leave. It would be nice to see some of your very pleasant planet."

"Good. We have found you hotel rooms which we hope will suit, and have assigned someone to help you with whatever you need, day or night. Please don't be shy about asking. We are grateful for you bringing our people home. We would like to demonstrate that gratitude in some small way."

"Again, thank you. However, no thanks are needed. We only did what any responsible space traveller would do. In fact, I wasn't even involved. All the thanks are due to my co-pilot, Gala Sur."

"As you have told us many times. Right now your co-pilot is meeting our President and he, personally, is thanking her and she will be his guest at a banquet this evening, along with Marty and Davina. Will you be joining them?"

An Kohli could think of nothing she would enjoy less than such a diplomatic bun fight. "Perhaps you would express my regrets to the President. I think I need to rest. Life has been very full over the last few months."

"Of course. Even here on Ecos we are aware of your achievements. They must exact quite a toll."

You wouldn't believe the half of it, An Kohli thought. She just gave a self-deprecating shrug. "I do what I'm paid to do, that's all."

"As do we all. What you do, however, seems somewhat more demanding."

They had reached the building where Filar had his office. "Can I get you a hover taxi to take you to your hotel?"

"No, thank you. The cramped confines of a spaceship don't allow much space for exercise, so I'll walk."

"Very well. You'll find the details concerning your hotel on your communicator, including a map. I'll take Marty and Davina on a little shopping trip, in preparation for tonight. I think they need something just a little bit more formal than they are currently wearing."

An Kohli suppressed a smile. It was true that the baggy sports wear that the two had chosen to clothe themselves in, the only thing they would consider wearing when they arrived, wouldn't look too good in the official photographs of the formal banquet. She wished them goodbye and headed off along the broad street.

One thing that Ecos had in common with Earth, despite the two human races never having had contact, was a love of beer. If anything the Ecosians had an even greater passion for it than the Earthlings, if that were possible. As soon as An Kohli had checked in she made her way to the bar to sample some of the speciality brews.

The barman recommended a particular label, the liquid glowing pale green with hints of gold floating in it. She took a seat on the terrace and sighed with contentment after taking an experimental sip. The barman had made a good choice. Stretching her long legs out in front of her An Kohli slid down in her comfortable seat so that her face was turned naturally towards the late afternoon sun.

"Is this seat taken?" A quiet voice asked her.

Opening her eyes An Kohli swept them across the almost empty terrace with its carefully arrayed tables and chairs. She was about to make a none too subtle response when she captured her first view of the voice's owner. He was tall and lean, slightly angular in his movements. His face was narrow but pleasant and the piercing blue of his eyes searched out her inner secrets. Why not? She asked herself. She deserved some R&R.

"Please, help yourself." She drawled, treating him to her Sunday Best smile.

He folded his long frame into a chair and placed a glass of beer on the table in front of himself.

"I hope I'm not intruding."

"Not at all. I was just enjoying a few moments in the sun. In my job I don't get many."

"What do you do?" he asked.

"I'm in law enforcement."

The corners of his mouth turned downwards into a mock grimace. "Should I be worried?"

"I don't know." She teased. "Should you?"

He let out a throaty chuckle which sent a shiver of anticipation down An Kohli's spine.

"Your face looks familiar. Have we met before?"

"It's just one of those faces, I think."

"No it isn't. I've seen your images today on the media. You're that female who found those two Ecosians on that planet in Sector One, aren't you."

It looked like there was little point in trying to protect her anonymity. "Right and also wrong. It was actually my co-pilot. I wasn't even there."

"You're too modest."

"No I'm not." An Kohli could live without the undeserved hero worship. She finished her beer and was about to leave.

"I'm sorry." The mystery male blurted out. "I'm making you uncomfortable." Well, at least he was perceptive. "Let me buy you another drink and we'll start again."

"No, it's OK. Let me buy you one. I'm a guest of the government at the moment, so we may as well both benefit from it." She punched a drinks order into the table's communicator.

"OK. So starting again, my name is Max, Max Wallfly."

"How do you do, Max. I'm An Kohli. Please don't shorten it." She warned.

"OK, An Kohli, I won't. So where's your co-pilot now?"

"She's with the President taking her well-deserved adulation. She'll be hating every minute of it." Which was true. If An Kolhi didn't much like the limelight, Gala positively hated it.

"In that case you must be at a loose end for dinner. Can I step into the breach?"

An Kohli considered the offer. Despite the gushiness of his initial approach he was rather good looking. Not as good looking as Veritan, perhaps, but Veritan was dead. Neither was he as good looking as Merkaloy but Merkaloy was with Laurel now. And, despite a tendency towards hero worship he did seem to be quite a nice being. Why not? She asked herself again. She hadn't been out with a male for anything other than business since… She realised that she couldn't even remember the last occasion. Bounty Hunter parties didn't count as dates, of course. They didn't even count as parties, more sort of controlled collapsing. She really had to stop the good ones slipping through her fingers. She might as well try and find out if he was one of the good ones.

"Got anywhere in mind?"

"There's a nice little place just around the corner. Smooth music, discrete service and excellent food."

"Sounds good. You'll have to take me as you find me though. This is the smartest clothing I've got with me." She swept her hand along the line of her body, covered in its hair thin layer of skin tight Superskin™ material.

"I think you'll be fine in that." He smiled appreciatively. "I'll meet you in the lobby in two hours." The service droid arrived with their drinks and they sat chatting for a few more minutes, then An Kohli made her excuses and returned to her room.

She gave her suit a rinse in the shower, knowing it would dry in plenty of time, then took a shower herself. While she waited for her suit to dry she got down to some serious work with a hairdryer and make-up.

* * *

As she woke, a number of thoughts went through the mind of An Kohli. The first was that her hair was plastered to her head by sweat and that was never a good look. The second was that she hadn't taken her make-up off the night before. Why was it, she wondered, that her species could travel the galaxy in complex ways, using science they barely understood, but they couldn't invent make-up that would survive a night in bed? Over the centuries it was a question that billions of females had asked.

As she patted the empty bed beside her she felt her heart sink with disappointment. She had thought that this one might be just a little bit different, but no, it appeared that he was just…. then her heart skipped a beat as she heard the high pitched whine of the body dryer start up in the bathroom.

Panic over, he was just taking a shower. As though to confirm her guess Max walked back into the luxurious bedroom wearing a smile, a dab of hotel supplied cologne and nothing else. He was more muscular than she had thought, his clothes disguising the sculpted form of his body. She took a moment to appreciate him.

"You could get arrested for walking around like that." An Kohli purred.

"So slap the cuffs on me." He grinned at her while offering her his wrists. "I hope you don't mind, but I've ordered breakfast."

As though waiting for its cue, a service droid announced its presence outside the door of the room and An Kohli gave it permission to enter. It pushed a trolley ahead of itself, layered with covered dishes and pots of steaming liquid. Uncoupling itself it rolled out the way it had come, the door swishing shut behind it.

Max strolled over to the trolley and moved it closer to the bed on An Kohli's side. Perching on the edge of the bed he removed the covers from the dishes, picked up an empty plate and looked at her expectantly. As she pointed to her favourite foods he piled the plate high with her selections.

An Kohli sat upright in the bed, grabbed the pillows from his side and made herself comfortable. The sheet slid down to her waste but she ignored it. There was nothing for him to see that she didn't take great pride in, though she would have to take care not spill her coffee. Besides, he had seen it all the previous evening, so it was a little bit late for modesty. Rather, she hoped the view might distract him from the wreckage of her hair and make-up.

They ate in companionable silence, exchanging the occasional smile. An Kohli was glad that he didn't feel the need to fill the silence with small talk. As she finished the last sumptuous morsel she handed him back the plate.

"What are your plans for today?" She asked him, tracing a line along his naked thigh with one razor sharp finger nail.

"I have a business meeting in a couple of hours' time. It will take most of the day."

"You had better leave time for another shower." She said, a suggestive smile playing around her lips.

"Why would I need another shower?" he asked, just as An Kohli pulled him backwards onto the bed. One of his feet clattered against the service trolley upsetting the coffee pot, which dripped quietly and unnoticed onto the floor.

* * *

Returning to the bedroom after her shower, An Kohli made her way to the vanity table to start drying her hair. Her communicator chirped to attract her attention. It was Gala.

"Where did you get to last night?" There were traces of anxiety in her voice. "I tried to contact you but you weren't in your room and you didn't answer your communicator."

"Sorry, I went out to dinner. Speaking of which, how was your banquet?"

"Far too long, far too many speeches and by the time the food was served it had gone cold. Marty and Davina seemed to enjoy it, though."

"Good. But I hope it doesn't raise their expectations too high. Pretty soon they'll be yesterday's news."

"So how was your dinner?"

An Kohli was deciding how to answer that question when her face gave her away.

"I know that look, missee. That's the look of a female who had a lot more than dinner last night."

"No, it was nothing like that…. Well maybe a little bit like that, but…"

"But nothing. I reckon it was a lot like that. Come on now, spill the beans. Who is he?"

"Just a guy I met on the hotel terrace. We went out for dinner. It was nice."

"Forget about dinner, I want to know what happened after dinner."

"That's nothing to do with you."

"It's everything to do with me. If he gives you the run around I'm the one that has to share the command deck of the Adastra with you for the next year while you moon over him."

"It's not that serious." Though An Kohli wasn't that sure she was telling the truth about that. "He was nice; we had a bit of fun; that's all."

"Well, I hope that is all. So what are you doing today?"

"We're guests of the government in a luxury hotel, I think a pampering day might be in order."

"Well, be careful, remember what happened on New Earth. Make sure whatever they rub onto your skin is compatible with our species." *(see New Earth)*

"Yeah, I don't want that again. What about you?"

"Depends on how long we're going to be here, which is why I'm calling. When do you want to leave?"

"Oh, I'm not in any rush. Maybe we'll stay a couple of more days."

"Now I am worried. An Kohli not in a rush to get on with a mission, that's as rare as an intelligent Jackon. I think you're more keen on this male than you're telling me."

An Kohli felt her skin flushing and she checked in the mirror. Yes, her skin was taking on a definite purple tinge. "Well, it won't do me any harm to have a nice guy paying me some attention for a change." She blustered, pretending not to grasp Gala's full meaning.

"OK, but you be careful." Lengthy experience had shown Gala that when it came to males, An Kohli's armour was as fragile as an egg shell. "Well, if you're going to spend the next few days mooning over some male then I'll go up to the Adastra and check out its systems. I'm still not happy about the way that circuit board and its back up both failed at the same time. That's not supposed to happen."

An Kohli didn't try to dissuade her co-pilot. Gala would be as happy crawling around the guts of the Adastra's engineering spaces as she would be being waited on hand and foot by half a dozen Aloisan males.

Gala's face had barely disappeared from the screen of An Kohli's communicator when Den's name appeared. With a sigh, An Kohli accepted the call. At least with the less perceptive Den she wouldn't have to discuss her sex life. She did a quick check to make sure her robe was secure, then Den's face appeared.

"How's life on Ecos?" He opened the conversation.

"Not bad. It's a nice place with nice people. I get the impression it's not the sort of place that has a lot of excitement, so I doubt it would suit you."

"How long before you join me at Aragan?"

"We're staying here a few more days, then it will take about a week to get there."

"Oh, I thought you were just going to drop Marty and Davina off and head straight over here."

"Well, the Ecosians are making a bit of a fuss over us. Gala actually had to attend a banquet last night with the President." It would do no harm for Den to believe that was the real reason for the delay. She just hoped that he didn't compare notes with Gala. "So, why the call?"

"Just to catch you up really. Aragan seems to be an undeveloped planet. It supports a lot of life but I've seen no signs of any sort of civilisation. There are no towns, not even a few mud huts so far as I've been able to find out."

"That accords with the available data. Any signs of anyone else taking an interest in it?"

"No. There's nothing in orbit, nor around any of the other planets. Look, I don't want to complain, but there's not a lot for me to do around here for a week and a half while you are being feted by the high and mighty on Ecos."

"Point taken. If you fancy a couple of days of planet leave then go ahead, but be back in time to meet up with us. I'm going to need you to help me search for the you-know-what."

"OK, message received. Let me know when you leave Ecos, so I know when I have to be back. In the meantime, give my regards to El Presidente."

The communication was cut at Den's end. Now that he had An Kohli's permission to skive off, he wasn't going to waste any more time. He interrogated the Pradua's computer to find out the location of the nearest planet that had a casino that employed Sutran croupiers.

* * *

Tiger stretched his long legs across the floor of comfortable lounge of the Starcruiser Shogun. He was enjoying imparting his news to them, but he had hoped for a greater degree of admiration than he was getting.

"Why didn't you just kill her while you had the chance." Spat Attila. "She would be dead and we would now be going about our normal business."

"Because, esteemed colleague, our objective is not just her death, it is also the recovery of the other Magi eggs. If we just kill her the Guild will just send more bounty hunters to find the eggs and they will be able to share in the accumulated knowledge that An Kohli has garnered. If we let her live then she will show us to the next egg, at least, and we can take that from her before killing her."

"She doesn't suspect anything?" Desire was more concerned for her own safety than arguments over their strategy. If pressed she would say she felt happier with An Kohli dead, but she also didn't want to answer questions from the Fell with regard to the recovery of the eggs.

"No. I used my not inconsiderable charm on her. While she slept I bugged her room and that has already proved its value. Her gofer Den is currently conducting a reconnaissance around the planet Aragan, which would lead me to believe that the next egg she is pursuing is located there.

"So why don't you just kill her now?" Attila asked.

Tiger suppressed his impulse to crush this stupid Dysac's head in his bare hands and instead pasted a smile across his face. "Because we don't know its precise location. Only An Kohli knows that. Once we have that detail and the egg is safely in our hands I will take the greatest of pleasure in killing her."

"I want to be there. In fact I want to do it, slowly, painfully." The Dysac seemed to drift off into a dream world of his own.

Desire managed to fight her own feelings of jealousy. She had hoped that she and Tiger might have... well, it was still possible. Once An Kohli was dead they would have time on the return journey for her to persuade him. Perhaps seeing An Kohli being disfigured in some inventive fashion might show him that she, herself, had some admirable qualities, and that it would not be a wise move to refuse her.

"Unfortunately I didn't have the right sort of bug to install in her communicator, so what she says outside of her hotel room won't be monitored, but as I plan to be there in person that shouldn't be a problem.

"Is she good." Attila hungered for salacious details with which to feed his imagination. "What is her body like. Did you…"

Tiger raised his hand to silence his colleague. "A refined being doesn't tell." He said and he did regard himself as a refined being. "What you do with her later is not my concern." He rose and strode towards the door of the lounge. "Now, I must return to Ecos. I can find out a lot during that time, which may be of use to us later."

* * *

The space around Ecos was starting to get a bit crowded, Gala realised. The descendants of the crew of the Namsat Able were due to arrive within the next couple of days and it was the galactic news event of the year, if not the decade. The media were descending on Ecos like a swarm of hungry locusts and they weren't too fussy about observing the protocols of orbital parking. They all wanted to be above the best point of entry into the planet's atmosphere to reach the city of Salvar, the planet's capital.

After her shuttle made the close acquaintance of a particularly pushy craft that was trying to force itself into a parking orbit, Gala decided that it would be prudent to move the Adastra a little higher to avoid the crowd.

The ship responded sweetly to her commands and the auxiliary jets fired a few short bursts to push the Adastra upwards a thousand li as she increased power on the main engines just a fraction to gain the velocity to maintain their geostationary orbit. Satisfied, she closed down the auxiliary jets and reduced power once again as she locked the ship's new position into the navi-com. That would make sure that it hardly deviated in its orbit by a sim until she entered her next set of commands, which probably wouldn't be until they departed.

She did a quick visual exterior scan to make sure the Adastra wasn't encroaching on the space of any other ship. A movement on one of the external viewing screens attracted her eye and she realised that it was a shuttle departing from one of the ships that were now below her. Normally she would barely give such an event a second glance but there was something about the ship that tickled a memory.

She zoomed in on it. There was nothing remarkable about it, just a run of the mill Starcruiser, like a hundred others she had seen before. A rich being's plaything, big enough to hold a family and a few dozen guests for a space born cocktail party. It was capable of inter stellar travel but she wouldn't want to rely on its acceleration to get away from something that was chasing her.

She was just about to dismiss it from her mind when it occurred to her to check its identity. She zoomed the camera in closer and searched until she found the name emblazoned along the side of its curving nose: Shogun.

She sat back in her chair. It could just be a coincidence, but… no, she didn't believe in coincidences. The last member of the Fell who had come after them was called Shogun and he had used a Starcruiser. She hadn't checked its name. There hadn't seemed to be any point, but she would bet her life that the one she had seen in orbit around The Hideaway *(see New Earth)* had been called Shogun, after its owner.

"Lazarus. Identify the ship from the image on camera twelve and search for registration details." She instructed.

"The ship is the Shogun, registered to a company called Benefit Enterprises Incorporated." The computer answered almost at once. "And before you ask, there is nothing of note in my databanks or the Galacticnet regarding that corporation. It is registered on Falcona but I can't find anything else relating to it."

Falcona, she knew, was a planet that provided 'brass plate' registrations for companies across the galaxy, a lucrative business with very few overheads. The planet acted as the place of registration for a company without the lawyers who ran the offices having any knowledge of the company itself, and what little they did know they kept strictly to themselves under the rules of client confidentiality. Whoever, or wherever, Benefit Enterprises were she wouldn't find out much from Falcona.

"Thank you Lazarus." Gala felt sure that the presence of the Shogun in orbit around Ecos was neither good news nor a coincidence. She could almost smell the presence of the Fell. Well, time to look into that mystery later. First off she had some engineering investigations to complete which were of a far higher priority.

Glossary

Gofer - Slang, derogatory. A person who is seen as being akin to a servant and who may therefore be instructed to "go for this".

R&R - Rest and Recreation. Can mean anything from a few hours spent in idleness to several weeks spent in idleness. The recreation part is dependent on individual preferences. It's amazing what some beings regard as recreation.

Sutra - A planet in the Flage system that is purported to be the home of the most beautiful women in the galaxy. Like the Gau they have the ability to shape shift to appeal to the different subjective opinions of what constitutes beauty.

9 – A Reluctant Farewell

"Got a few minutes for a coffee and cake with your co-pilot?" Gala asked over the communicator.

"Always. Any particular reason."

"Not over an insecure line." Gala said, mysteriously. "There's a coffee shop in the hotel lobby. I'll meet you there in five."

An Kohli was intrigued. Gala wasn't the coffee and cake sort, more beer and crisps. She made her way to the coffee shop and found Gala waiting. There was a mug of frothy coffee in front of her with another in front of the vacant seat opposite. Between the two mugs sat a gooey looking confection and two empty plates.

"So, why the sudden urgency and why here? Why not my room?"

"I wanted to speak to you before you went out with your mystery male tonight and I wanted to make sure we weren't overheard. I think you should be careful?"

"Look, Gala, you haven't even met him yet, so…."

"No, it's not him I'm bothered about. I think there are Fell lurking about. They may even have gained access to your room and bugged it." Gala gave her employer a quick rundown on what she had discovered. "I asked the staff at the shuttle port what the being that arrived in the Shogun's shuttle looked like but they were rushed off their feet trying to park over a hundred shuttles in a space designed for fifty. They're trying to get the passengers to return their shuttles to the ships in orbit but they all claim they have an urgent need for them to be parked in the spaceport. The staff are practically tearing their hair out."

"So, no images or descriptions?"

"No. All I could get out of them was that the passenger arrived alone. Whoever he or she is they're probably just on a scouting mission, trying to track us down."

An Kohli chewed at the inside of her cheek. "What would you recommend?"

"You're not going to like it."

"Well, tell me anyway."

"I think we should leave. They'll know we're here, of course. We're all over the galacticnet right now. They'll also have seen the Adastra. But if we make a break for it we can be inside a wormhole before they even have time to leave orbit. There's no way they can follow us."

An Kohli knew it made sense. She really didn't want to have to deal with more of the Fell right now. She had been lucky up to that point, but the next time… who knew? It would only take one lucky pulsar shot and Gala would have to open the message she left on the Adastra's computer giving instructions for her funeral.

"You're right, of course, but…"

"But lover boy is too good to leave in such a hurry."

"I wouldn't put it quite like that, but yes."

"OK. Compromise. Do whatever it is that you're going to do with him tonight, then we leave before dawn in the morning. He'll be in the land of nod and the Fell won't be expecting it. The rest of the clones arrive tomorrow and they'll expect you and me to be there to greet them. Especially me."

It hadn't been part of their plan to be present when the clones arrived, but their continued presence on Ecos would be interpreted as being for that purpose. It did provide a cover for their escape.

"OK. Well, he's taking me for dinner again."

"That won't take all night, will it?"

"No, but …."

"No need to draw me a picture. I'll watch your back while you're at dinner and then I'll keep your room under observation."

"Is that strictly necessary?" An Kohli didn't like the idea of her best friend being just outside her door while she was… well, while she was inside.

"It's either me or Hotel Security. You choose."

* * *

An Kohli lay on her side, her hand on Max's chest. "You don't have any hair on your chest. She observed, for the want of something to say.

"Our species hasn't. We don't have any body hair, or facial hair either."

She wanted to ask what species he was, but that wasn't a polite thing to do. He would tell her if he wanted to. If not, then did it really matter? Physically they were compatible and that was what was important. "Must save a fortune on laser shaves." She cooed, running a finger along his smooth jawline. While outwardly she seemed calm, inside her stomach was churning at the thought of what she had to say to him. She tried to think of some more small talk to delay the moment, but nothing would come.

"There's something on your mind, isn't there. I can tell."

An Kohli was taken by surprise. In her experience males weren't normally so perceptive, especially after sex. Normally all they wanted to do was go to sleep.

"Yes, you're right. Look, there's no easy way to say this, but I have to go."

"Well, it's just through there." Smilingly he pointed at the bathroom door.

"Fool." She slapped him playfully on the chest. "No, I mean I have to leave."

"When?" He sounded genuinely disappointed.

An Kohli considered telling him the truth but realised that it would complicate matters to tell him she was sneaking off in the middle of the night.

"Tomorrow, after the welcoming ceremony." She lied, hating herself for doing it.

"Will I see you again?"

"Do you want to?"

"Of course I do. Look, I know we've only known each other for a short time but…"

She laid a finger on his lips to silence him. "No declarations of love, please. We've had fun and, yes, I would like to see you again, but let's take it one step at a time."

"OK, but only if you tell me where and when."

"I can't tell you when. My plans don't allow me to make those sorts of commitments, but I can tell you where. Right here in Salvar. I'll send you a message when I can get here and we'll meet downstairs in the lobby." Knowing that she wouldn't pay the prices charged by the hotel she didn't want to admit she would find somewhere cheaper to stay.

"OK, well, you've got my number. Can you tell me where you're going?"

Again An Kohli was torn between wanting to put her total trust in this male and the need to keep her movements secret. It was for his good as much as hers. What he didn't know he couldn't inadvertently betray. "No. In my business it's better for people not to know what I'm doing. What you don't know can't hurt you."

She checked the time on the big media screen opposite the bed. Two more hours before she had arranged to meet Gala. Well, she wanted to make sure he was asleep when she left, so the best thing she could do was make sure he was really, really tired.

"Now, as my way of saying sorry for having to leave, how about I..." and she whispered something in his ear that made him growl with anticipation.

Later she quietly wriggled into her Superskin suit and gathered her few possessions together. She had to struggle a little with her boots and was worried she might wake him, but he showed no signs of stirring. Carefully she tip-toed out of the room, grateful that a top of the range hotel such as this, made sure its doors were the most silent type available.

No sooner had the door hissed shut than Max Wallfly rolled onto his back, picked up his communicator from the night stand and sent a pre-prepared message.

He didn't consider himself to be a bad man. It was all just business to him. An Kohli was an inconvenience to his business and she had to be dealt with and after spending two nights with her he would rather not deal with her by killing her, but what she did would rather decide matters. His colleagues, of course, had a different agenda. As far as they were concerned An Kohli had to die. Would he intervene? That would rather depend. There was no point in being in business if he had to die protecting someone else.

Of course, Max Wallfly wasn't his real name; that was Castor Macati. He had committed his first crime when he was just a youngling and never really looked back. He had spent just one short spell in prison, an experience he had no desire to repeat.

He had been born on the planet Karakara in the Faron system, the son of two miners. Everyone on Karakara was a miner, or worked for the mining companies or for the companies that supplied the mining companies. Karakara had little else going for it other than mining and when the mining companies had run out of bits of Karakara to ship off to nicer planets it would be left alone with a lot of big holes in the ground and nothing else. Castor Macati had decided early on that he wasn't going to wait for the day when that happened.

The miners were well paid, there was always a roof over their heads and food on the table with some money left over so that vacations could be taken in places where there wasn't a constant pall of dust overhead.

But when the mining companies went there would be no more paydays. Everyone else said it would be centuries before that happened, but Castor Macati didn't believe them. Every year there were fewer mining vessels in orbit and another mine finally shut its gates. Fortunately, labour was in short supply and most of the miners that lost their jobs in one mine were able to find work elsewhere, but Castor Macati knew that couldn't last forever.

From petty crime, mugging drunken mining ship crew members for whatever was left in their pockets, he graduated to stealing mining equipment for the burgeoning black market, but that was risky, so he switched to good old sex and drugs, supplying the miners and the ships' crews with whatever they needed to make their leisure time go with a bang. Finally he had enough saved to get him away from Karakara, where he found a whole galaxy waiting for his talents.

He had run into Roselee, whom the galaxy would come to know as Gypsy *(see The Magi)*, when he had only been away from Karakara for a few months. She had taken him under her wing and he had thrived. But they had never had a close bond. There was a ruthless, even callous streak about her that the young Castor couldn't like. However, she had been useful and later, when the Fell came into being, his mentor had provided the introduction that had gained him a place at the virtual table.

His presence on this mission was partly to fulfil a debt of honour he felt towards Gypsy. He didn't know what had happened to her, but he did know that An Kohli was involved in her disappearance. Through his contacts he had searched the jails across the galaxy seeking any news of Gypsy, but no one knew anything, and for the size of reward he was offering for information they would have sold their grannies if he had been buying.

But mainly he was doing this because the Magi were bad for business, at least bad for his business, and until they had been completely eliminated the Fell couldn't be sure of being allowed to continue with their businesses: legal, barely legal and completely illegal. He placed no faith in the elections that were to be held. Whatever government was elected it wouldn't be seen as legitimate so long as the Magi were still alive, even if it was only in the form of a data storage egg. An Kohli seemed to be the key to that and so it was better for her to be alive than dead; at least for the moment.

Would he stand by and watch her being killed? He couldn't be sure. He had always tried not to be violent if that was possible. He had never knowingly been responsible for the death of another being, but he wasn't going to go to prison and if An Kohli had to be killed to prevent that then killed she would be. Two nights of sex, even if it had been very good sex, wasn't going to change that. But if she could be saved?

No. he wasn't the sentimental type. The seduction of An Kohli had been a means to an end, that was all. Time to move on.

10 – Cargo Cult

"I knew you'd have a face like a smacked backside." Gala said as she entered the command deck of the Adastra for the start of her watch.

An Kohli was staring into the middle distance with a sorrowful frown on her face. She didn't respond to her friend's banter.

"I said Den's in your cabin trying on your clothes." Gala tried again.

"Eh, what?" Her words finally penetrated An Kohli's consciousness.

"You're away with the space goblins, aren't you? That bloke has had quite an effect on you."

"Sorry, yes I was rather remembering how his..."

Gala clapped her hands over her ears in mock protest. "Enough, I don't need to know!"

"How his smile crinkled the corners of his eyes, I was going to say."

"Oh. Look, I know I'm only the hired help, but I do think that you need to keep your mind on the job. If you're like that when you go down to the surface of Aragan who knows what sort of mess you might blunder into."

An Kohli knew her co-pilot was right. Being a bounty hunter was a dangerous enough business without her making it more dangerous by not maintaining her focus. "OK. Point taken. And you're not just the hired help. You're my best friend; my only true friend. Now, what do we know about this planet?"

"Not much more than Den told us, I'm afraid. It was first explored about ten years ago. It has quite a lot of wildlife but no traces of civilisation were found. That doesn't mean there's nothing there, as we know from other planets, but if there are they're good at hiding. Very bio-diverse in terms of its plant life and that supports a strong ecology amongst the animal life. There are minerals beneath the surface but they're pretty common ones: fossil fuels, iron ore, bauxite, copper, that sort of thing. Not much to attract the mining corporations. I'm surprised it hasn't been colonised though."

"It takes more than ten years to organise colonisation. The simulations alone take five years."

Gala looked puzzled. "What are simulations?"

"The would-be colonists go through a rigorous selection process to make sure they're the right sort of beings to undertake the role. Establishing a new colony is hard work and not everyone is suited to it. The final step in the selection process is a five year simulation. They put the colonists into a closed environment similar to the one they're going to have to live in and see how they manage. They're kept under round the clock observation and any that show signs of undue stress are removed. Maybe seventy five percent of the first draft don't make it. Then of course they have to introduce replacements who have to try to integrate with an established group so the whole process starts again."

"Sounds pretty tedious."

"Tedium is one of the challenges. Life in a new colony is often tedious and some people can't deal with it. The sort of beings that need constant stimulation probably aren't the sort to become colonists. Life is usually quite primitive. They take solar panels and other power generating equipment, but it's never enough to do more than maintain the basics of survival. There's no power surplus for entertainment systems and the like, so people have to make their own entertainment. Imagine that! No media streams to while away the night time hours. No galacticnet except for communication and information analysis, so no social networking. Do you think you could survive that way?"

Gala laughed. "No, I don't think I could."

"Anyway, I'm sure that the nearest neighbours have this place on their schedule for colonisation unless the hippies get here first. That usually ruins all the plans."

"Yeah, no one wants to live anywhere the hippies have been first. It gives the whole place a bad name."

"Did you ever hear the story of Marathon Beta?"

"Vaguely. Didn't all the colonists die?"

"Yes, but it was worse than just them dying. They resorted to cannibalism. They had plenty of food growing around them and plenty of wildlife, but somehow one being became dominant and forced the remainder into ever more bizarre behaviour. He was mad, of course, but he smashed the communications equipment so no one could call for help and he organised a bodyguard around himself and they enforced his edicts. The bodyguard got the pick of the females, so they stayed loyal. One of the edicts was that anyone that transgressed would be killed and their body eaten by the remainder, as a warning. Soon all traces of civilisation had just about vanished and they were informing on each other just to try to survive. Of course, anyone who was accused of a transgression became the next one on the list to be eaten. It all became highly ritualistic and there was evidence of some sort of religious motivation. Some beings escaped into the wilderness but were either hunted down or died of thirst and starvation. Eventually there was only a handful of them left and they seem to have killed each other in some kind of final shoot out."

"How come that behaviour didn't show up in the simulations?"

"Oh, they weren't colonists, they were peace loving hippies."

On that happy note An Kohli handed over the watch to Gala and made her way to her cabin to sleep.

* * *

"You didn't give me much time for planet leave." Den grumbled for the umpteenth time as the ramp of the Adastra's shuttle lowered itself and they stepped forward to take their first look at Aragan.

An Kohli was fed up with trying to apologise, but she decided to give it a final go. "Yes, I know and I'm sorry, but with the Fell hanging around it seemed prudent to leave. You weren't the only one to have your sex life interrupted, you know."

That last sentence was new information for Den and he turned to look at An Kohli in surprise. "You mean Gala pulled?"

For some reason, An Kohli felt offended, as though Den was insinuating that she was incapable of attracting male admirers. "Gala isn't the only one who has male friends, you know." She snapped at him.

"Er, sorry, I didn't mean… well, good for you." Den recovered. "Who is he?"

"His name is Max Wallfly and he's cute. That's all you need to know."

"What planet is he from?"

An Kohli was caught off guard by the question and realised that she didn't know the answer to it. "Erm.. I'm not sure."

"OK, what does he do?"

Again, An Kohli didn't know the answer. "Some sort of business." She answered, lamely.

"Wow, you really got to know him." Den scoffed. "He must be a real keeper."

"At least I didn't rent him by the hour." An Kohli snarled back, angry more with herself than with Den.

Den laughed, shrugging off the intended insult. When it came to his sex life Den was hard to embarrass. Despite that he tried to change the subject. "So where do we start looking for the egg?"

"Well, we know that Su Mali always leaves some sort of marker, so she could find the egg herself when she returned. The shuttle has put us within a couple of met of her original landing site, so we can't be far away." She surveyed the swaying grass of the plain in front of her. "She may not have made the marker very tall, perhaps she deliberately wanted the grass to conceal it from accidental discovery."

"So we're looking for a noodle in a hay field."

"The saying is 'haystack'."

"I know, but there isn't one of those, but there is plenty of grass, so hay field."

An Kohli decided that there was no point in pursuing that discussion; with an exaggerated sigh she started to walk around the shuttle to see what was behind it.

There was more grass spreading away into the distance, but also a small copse of tall thin trees away to one side

"OK, so you land on a strange planet; you might be being pursued, so you need to find your marker quickly. Do you (a) put it in the middle of a sea of grass, or do you (b) put it near the only other physical feature available to you, the trees."

"Trees every time." Den responded.

"That's what I thought." She started to walk towards them, the tall grass swishing against her thighs. As she got closer she could hear the sound of birdsong above the sighing of the breeze. The trees were providing a secure home for the local birdlife. The song sounded familiar and she wondered what sort of birds they were.

She found the marker at the edge of the small wood. A tree stump, cut off at about half a met in height so that it was hidden until she was right on top of it. She called Den across to her.

Bending down he examined it close up. "Cut by a saw, and from the marks I'd say some sort of mechanical one."

"A chainsaw?"

"Perhaps. See, the grooves are quite deep and regular, some of them are curved at the outer edge, near the bark, as though she was pulling and pushing the saw to stop it from jamming in the wood."

"Well, the tree certainly didn't come down because a beaver chewed through it and I think we can rule out a lightning strike."

"Erm, I don't want to appear picky, but where's the rest of the tree?" Den, a born survivor, was always on the lookout for signs of danger and right at that moment his thumbs were pricking. The lack of a tree trunk and branches didn't fit in with an uninhabited planet.

"Maybe she dragged it away for some reason."

"Look at the size of the trunk." She spread laid his palms on the stump, his thumbs barely touching at the centre, and spread his fingers. They didn't reach the bark covered circumference. "And see how tall its neighbours are. No, this tree would have been far too heavy for her to drag it away."

"Not if she cut it up. She did have a chainsaw, after all."

"But why would she do that? It would just be taking up more time. With the tree lying on the ground the grass would conceal it, except for maybe the branches. She might cut those off to make it harder to spot the marker, but cutting up the whole trunk? No, I don't buy it."

An Kohli new better than to challenge Den's instincts. They had saved them well on many previous occasions.

"OK, I'll go along with you, but who else could have removed it? You did the survey. You said there was no civilised life."

"No. I said the was 'no sign of' civilised life'. It doesn't mean there isn't any."

At that point the short hairs on the nape of An Kohli's neck began to rise and she rested her hand on the butt of her pulsar, as if to reassure herself that it was still there. "In that case we'd better find the egg quickly and get out of here."

"Well, the grass here is shorter and not so dense, as though it hasn't been growing for so long." He pointed to a patch close to An Kohli's feet. "I'll go back to the shuttle and get the spade."

As he trotted off, An Kohli scanned the horizon, seeking out any threat, but there was nothing to be seen but the heads of the grass stems waving in the gentle breeze. All she could hear was the gentle susurration of the wind through the leaves of the trees and the chiming of the bird song. So why did she feel as though she was being watched?

Auto-suggestion, she decided. The idea that the planet might be inhabited had led to the planting of the idea that she was now under observation. She shivered despite the warmth of the sun, then scolded herself for having too vivid an imagination.

Den returned with the spade and offered it to her. In return she gave him a look that said 'you're kidding me, right?' He took the hint and started digging.

It wasn't deep, just a few sim below the surface they found the polyviol bag that they had come to associate with the eggs. Den stopped digging in case he damaged the contents and gently brushed the soil aside. It was soon clear that the bag was empty; abandoned after its contents had been removed.

"Shit." An Kohli cursed.

"Indeed." Den replied, standing up and leaning on his shovel in true workbeing fashion. "So, another conundrum." He continued. "Did the beings that chopped up the tree also remove the egg?"

"And if they did, were they resident on the planet or did they follow Su Mali here?"

"Whoever removed the tree was definitely resident. Why do it otherwise? Here's my hypothesis, based on the available evidence. There is some form of intelligent life on this planet and some members of that life form observed Su Mali, probably from a distance and unseen by her, or she wouldn't have left the egg for them to find. After she left they came over to get the tree, because it's fuel and she had saved them the bother of having to cut the tree down themselves. They found the bare soil covering the hole she had dug, opened it up, took out the egg and decided to keep it. They probably don't even know what it is."

An Kohli nodded her head. She had to admit that the hypothesis fitted the known facts.

"Do you think those same life forms are watching us now?"

"I think it's probable. If they were close enough to see Su Mali, or at least close enough to see her shuttle landing, then they're close enough to see us and/or our shuttle."

An Kohli swept her gaze across the ocean of grass again but could see no signs of any beings. The only tracks through the grass were the ones they had made and they would soon disappear. "I suggest we get back to the shuttle and get out of here. We can think about this some more when we're safely on board the Adastra."

"I concur." Den was turning and heading back towards the shuttle before he had even finished speaking.

They had almost reached the safety of the shuttle when the sea of grass seemed to erupt in front of them. Humanoid figures rose out of the ground to stand across their path. An Kohli's brain tried to count but it was an impossible task.

"Where the fuck did they come from?" was all Den managed to say.

Instinctively An Kohli's hand went to the big Menafield pulsar at her hip but an arrow zipped past, grazing her skin. She quickly withdrew the hand, the warning heeded. All hope of flight was dismissed as the outermost figures in the group moved around behind them, cutting off any possibility of retreat.

The figures were tall and well-muscled, their skin tanned by the sun. They wore their hair braided in fanciful designs or just in plaits hanging down over their shoulders. Some sported tattoos but others relied on paint to make themselves appear more threatening. Den concluded that the paint was unnecessary. The array of bows, spears, clubs and knives more than made up for any lack of fearsomeness that they might have had without the paint.

An Kohli noticed that they were all male; her conclusion was inescapable given their lack of clothing. They wore only a breach clout and that was probably only to protect the most sensitive parts of their body from the abrasive grass. The lack of females wasn't unusual. Primitive societies were often male dominated. She thrust the anthropology lesson to the back of her mind as she struggled to deal with this fresh set back. Feigning a movement to appease the … well... warriors, she guessed she should call them, she passed one hand over the buckle of her belt and gave the metal a covert twist, sending a distress call out to the Adastra. Gala would immediately select a high definition camera and zoom it in on their position to identify the nature of the problem. What she decided to do after that was another matter entirely. A one female rescue party was out of the question.

The biggest warrior, the one in the centre of the group, shouted something incomprehensible. An Kohli suspected that it was some sort of challenge.

"We mean you no harm." She replied in Common Tongue.

The warrior shouted again, seeming to get angry that his question, or challenge, wasn't being answered.

Den tired his own language. It was a vain hope and got no better reaction than An Kohli's response. He then tried English, which had some popularity in the galaxy. Again, no joy, just more shouting.

The apparent leader stood to one side and pointed. To reinforce the message An Kohli felt the prick of a spear tip in one buttock. She took the hint and started walking in the direction indicated. As she passed the leader she saw that the grass had been parted at ground level to form a sort tunnel, leaving the tops of the long stems apparently undamaged. So that was how they had approached unnoticed. But they had been so fast. Surely it was no more than thirty standard minutes since they had landed. She soon found out how they had managed to get so close without being observed. A few paces beyond the shuttle the ground fell steeply away into a valley before rising again on the other side.

Dead ground it was called. The grass gave the illusion of being on an unbroken level plain as far as the eye could see, whereas the ground was actually undulating, rising and falling through hidden valleys. At the bottom of the shallow valley the grass had been flattened by the passage of many feet before the trail stopped just below the brow of the slope to be replaced by the tunnel through which the warriors had crawled in single file. Neat.

The warrior in the lead turned onto the trampled path which stretched away in front of them. An Kohli knew that they wouldn't have far to go. The warriors had to live close by to have reached them so quickly.

The trail came to an abrupt end and An Kohli wondered how the beings could possibly have arrived at that point without leaving any trace. She soon found out. Two of the big males knelt down and felt around in the grass. With a brief exchange of words that sounded like counting they heaved upwards, revealing a trap door made of branches woven into a lattice with the living turf laid on top to conceal it.

Beneath the trap door a flight of crudely cut steps led downwards. A warrior took the lead and then An Kohli and Den were prodded to follow.

The descent, An Kohli estimated, was about five met. They found themselves in a tunnel, the roof supported by stout beams. The amount of wood needed must have been considerable. Well, thought An Kohli, that accounts for the lack of trees in this area. The finding of the tree cut by Su Mali must have been a pleasing gift for them and perhaps accounted for why Su Mali hadn't been given the same treatment as they were getting.

The tunnel ran almost straight for a long way. She lost track of how long they walked in the darkness. These beings clearly had no problem seeing in the dark, as they made no effort to light their way. At last a glow appeared ahead of them.

The tunnel opened out into a communal living area perhaps twenty li across. There was a large hole in the roof, half to provide light and half to allow the escape of smoke from cooking fires. Around the wall crude torches were planted in niches, giving out a thin glow. No doubt they were more effective at night. Younglings ran to greet their fathers. After their joyous greetings the younglings cast serious, solemn stares in their direction as they inspected the newcomers.

Following at a more sedate pace came the females. They were naked, not even bothering with the minimal covering that the males adopted. They obviously didn't venture outside very often. That feeling was reinforced by the pallor of their skin. Unlike the males they didn't bother to dress their hair, preferring to let it hang in glossy swathes over their shoulders.

The females dutifully stood to one side to allow the males to proceed across the floor of the vast area. An Kohli estimated that there must be a hundred beings living there and the space was barely half occupied. They were led to an opening in the wall. The warrior stepped forward, speaking to them once again. There was a difference this time, however. His voice was hushed, almost reverent. He pointed and An Kohli looked at whatever he was trying to explain to her. She stuck her head through the gap and into a small space, barely large enough to hold a single person. There, in a niche in the wall opposite the entrance, was the egg, the one they had come to find. Flanking it were torches to make sure it was visible at all times.

She withdrew her head and indicated to Den that he should take a look.

"Cargo Cult." He muttered.

Yes, thought An Kohli. She had heard of them. Primitive peoples who found the flotsam and jetsam left behind by more advanced species and worshiped it as though it held magical powers, waiting for the day when the people who had discarded it would come back to claim it and…. and what? She wondered. In her experience they returned to steal the wealth and spread diseases for which the native population had no natural resistance.

And then she realised; they had arrived. Their arrival wouldn't just be viewed as some mysterious happening. It would be imbued with a much greater meaning. These people probably believed they had come for some purpose connected to them, not just connected to the egg that they had salvaged.

The question was, what would these people do when they discovered that An Kohli and Den Gau had nothing to offer them?

Glossary

Hippies - A word used to describe people with long hair, from the initials HP, meaning hairy people. They tend to wear natural fibres, eat only organic vegetables which they grow themselves, they eschew violence and avoid soap and water. They can usually be recognised by the fact that they are pale, look hungry, smell bad and have difficulty lifting even the lightest of burdens. They use words like holistic, spiritual and mystic without any trace of irony. Often seen in the company of large groups of children, some of which might actually be their own but they aren't too sure. They are always seeking places where they can live without rules and without interference 'from the man' and so seek to colonise uninhabited planets. This allows them to take drugs without being arrested, but they won't admit that this is the main reason that they do it. After colonisation there will usually be a schism over some minor infringement of the communal living agreement, with one faction accusing the other of behaving like fascists. The smaller faction will then leave to colonise another unsuspecting planet and so the cycle continues. Older hippies live on canal boats or in caravans that are supported by bricks and the state benefit system. They will always travel in the most environmentally unfriendly vehicle available.

Menafield - The Menafield Arms Corporation (part of the Gargantua Enterprises Corporation) produces a wide range of pulsar and projectile weapons for military, business and family use. The Menafield Pulsar, as used by An Kohli, is reputed to be the most powerful hand held weapon in the galaxy and can punch a hole through ¼ inch steel plate.

Polyviol - A material similar to plastic but which is wholly biodegradable. Its use to protect the egg suggests that Su Mali hadn't intended to leave it in the ground for long.

11 – The Village

"Ships detected entering star system." Lazarus informed Gala, almost languidly.

"How many?"

"Three."

"Have they detected us yet?"

"Negative. Their systems are still powering up. You have an estimated twenty three seconds before detection."

"Can you get us out of here undetected?"

"Of course." Lazarus made it sound as though nothing could be simpler.

"Then do it."

"Done."

The Adastra plunged towards Aragan's surface and skimmed along just above the fringes of its atmosphere before rising again to soar towards the planet's moon, where it took up a station behind it, screened from any detection systems. Gala realised that the manoeuvre had kept the glow of the star behind them, preventing detection by either visual or infra-red equipment. Slick!

"Great. Now I can't see anything." Gala grumbled.

"Your instructions didn't include any requirement to be able to detect the other ships. On the other hand there is no location within the star system where you can position this ship so it can detect the new arrivals without itself being detected."

The computer had adopted 'smug mode' again and Gala found it infuriating. "Smart arse." She muttered. Out loud she said "Can you identify the ships?"

"Negative. They were too distant."

"Were any of them large enough to be a Starcruiser?"

"Affirmative. However, it should not be assumed that any of them were actually Starcruisers."

"Don't worry, Lazarus, I won't make any erroneous assumptions based on what you have told me."

Gala thought she might have heard the computer say "Good" but she wasn't sure.

An alarm bleeped.

"Distress call received." Lazarus confirmed for her. "Identified as ship's owner, An Kohli."

"Location?"

"Twelve met from the shuttle craft."

"Can you track it?"

"Of course. Do you want me to?"

"Of course." Why did it make Gala feel so superior to be able to out smug the computer? She wondered.

* * *

"Where is the Adastra. Tiger said that the Adastra would be here." Desire fumed.

"I have located the Pradua, but it appears to be unoccupied." The Captain of the Shogun reported.

"That is no help to us."

"She may be hiding. There are several other planets, moons, asteroids etc where a ship could be concealed."

"We have no time to go hunting for it." Attila snarled.

Desire wondered what his hurry was. To the best of her knowledge they weren't working to a specific deadline. They could afford to wait for the Adastra to come to them. If the Pradua was still present then it suggested that she would. "I'll send the two pirate ships off to scout around."

"Make sure they don't kill An Kohli. I want that pleasure all to myself." The Dysac's voice took on a dreamy tone as he entered into the fantasy where he inflicted great amounts of pain to An Kohli's vulnerable body.

"They will do what they have to do. An Kohli dead is less dangerous than An Kohli alive. We'll worry about the Magi eggs if and when we are able to locate her and her ship."

"Excuse me, Ma'am." The Captain intruded into their conversation. "I have located a shuttle craft on the planet's surface."

"Show me."

The Captain indicated the sensor array that showed the unmistakable trace of an ion powered engine on the planet's surface. He selected a camera, locked in the co-ordinates and waited while the powerful lens zoomed in to provide an image.

"It's too big to be the shuttle from the Pradua. It must be from the Adastra." Desire muttered almost to herself. Louder she said "Any trace of life forms near it?"

The Captain zoomed the camera out so that he could scan the ground around the shuttle. "There is a beacon flashing on the shuttle, probably a distress signal of some sort. I have tracks leaving the area." He announced. "Quite a lot of tracks, but no sign of what made them. Now…. that's odd."

"What's odd?"

"The tracks end in the middle of nowhere. It's as though they sprouted wings and flew away."

"Or went underground." Desire concluded. As someone who spent most of her life in a secure bunker, as protection from detection and attack, she knew the signs of an underground hiding place when she saw one.

"Prepare a landing party? All twelve of the security personnel."

"Who will lead them Ma'am?"

A good question. Desire was not used to exposing herself to danger and she wasn't about to start. "Attila, you shall have the honour."

The Dysac blanched. Personal danger wasn't something he had signed up for. But at the same time he couldn't appear afraid in front this… this female; his ancestors would turn in their graves, especially his brother.

"Very well. Tell me all I need to know."

* * *

"So what do you think will happen now?" Den asked. A fair question, considering the circumstances and one to which An Kohli didn't have an answer.

She chewed on a bit of charred meat while she considered. "Well, they've fed us, which is a good sign. You don't usually waste good food on beings that you're just about to kill."

Den accepted that answer with a visible look of relief.

After being shown the egg in its small shrine they had been herded into a corner area, almost a cave in its own right. Two guards stood within easy spear stabbing distance, but not too close so as to invade their personal space. The food had arrived about thirty minutes later along with a large bowl of milky looking liquid that had quite a pleasant taste.

"There's a lot of weapons sharpening going on." Den observed.

"Yes. I noticed that. Maybe they're going hunting."

"I doubt it. A hunting party that big would scare all the game away. Nope. I reckon they're getting ready for a fight."

"But with whom?"

"I'm guessing here, but if you look at the evidence it isn't too hard to come up with a workable theory."

"OK, I've got nothing better to do right now."

Den ignored the sarcasm. "So, they live in a cave which has obviously been hand carved out of the ground. It's much easier to build above ground, so there has to be a reason for digging. Then there's the tunnel we came down. I don't know how long it is, but it took ages to get here. I reckon it must be several thousands of met long. You only dig a tunnel that long if you're trying to disguise where the other end is; this end. Now, see that smoke hole?" Den jerked his head upwards. "I'm thinking that's screened by trees or maybe rocks, so by the time the smoke rises high enough it will have dissipated so much it won't be visible. If there's also an updraft, as there often is up the sides of hills, then it will be carried so high it won't even be possible to smell it, not with enough accuracy to track down where it has come from. Conclusion, these people are hiding from someone or something."

"There must be seventy or eighty warriors in here. That's quite a formidable force."

"Which means that whatever or whoever they're hiding from is bigger and stronger. It must be another tribe."

"So why all the weapons sharpening now?"

"They've got an ace up their sleeve they've never had before. Our pulsars."

"Do they even know what they are?"

"Probably. They may be primitive but that doesn't make them stupid. When beings live by the spear point then they will usually assume that everyone lives by the spear point and they are intelligent enough to recognise that the only artefacts that we were carrying that are big enough to be metaphorical spear points are our pulsars. They saw Su Mali take down a tree in a few minutes which it would have taken them an hour or more to hack down with their flint headed axes. So they now equate our technology with power."

"But they don't know how to use them. They wouldn't know a safety catch from a hole in the ground."

"They don't have to. They have us. We use the pulsars and that pays the price for our lives."

"So we're guns for hire." An Kohli summarised.

"Not even for hire. Weapons to be pointed and used at will is what we are."

As they had been speaking darkness had started to fall. An Kohli looked upwards to see that the sky above the smoke hole was now a dark blue and the first stars were just starting to peep through. Her eye was attracted to movement and she saw the big warrior, the one she suspected was the chief of the tribe, stride into the middle of the village to stand directly beneath the centre of the smoke hole.

He raised his voice in a shout. The male warriors stopped what they were doing and paid attention. He shouted some more and the warriors started to drift towards him, forming a loose ring. He harangued them for a few more minutes and An Kohli could hear rumbles of agreement from them. Someone shouted, whether it was in protest or agreement she couldn't tell, but there were answering shouts. The chief harangued them again for several minutes then a rhythmic chanting started. Spears were brandished in time to the beat. The chief strode round the edge of the ring and An Kohli noticed for the first time that he was holding their pulsars. Now he raised them above his head, pumping his arms up and down in time to the beat while shouting the chant into the air.

"If that isn't a call to arms I've never heard one." An Kohli had to almost shout to make herself heard above the chanting.

The females of the tribe started to gather, forming a circle around their males. They too joined in the chanting, their higher pitched voices adding a counterpoint, before starting to dance in a circle around the outside of the ring. One by one the males turned outwards to face the females, their loose ring becoming an identifiable circle. They too started to dance, moving in the opposite direction to the females. From the shadows the younglings watched with big, curious eyes.

The circles moved faster as the chant increased its cadence. The males leapt into the air, stabbing downwards with their spears, no doubt mimicking the moves they planned to make in the coming battle. As the males leapt the women ducked, sliding under the flying legs to rise again in front of a new dance partner before repeating the manoeuvre and moving along. A male grabbed a female as she passed, seemingly at random and together they hurried to a shadowed area of the cave. His lack of clothing left no doubt as to his intentions. Another warrior grabbed at a passing arm, then another and soon only the chief was left in the centre of the village. The significance of the dance was obvious. The males knew that some of them might not return and they were going to have one last glorious night, perhaps even planting the seed for the generation that would replace them.

A female, young and very pretty, made her way tentatively to the centre of the village and bowed her head shyly in front of the chief. Keeping her eyes on the ground she offered her hand. The chief took it and led her away, out of sight of An Kohli and Den's corner.

"The guards haven't moved." She whispered to Den. "That's good discipline."

"Or maybe just a low sex drive." He chuckled, then made a show of settling himself down for the night.

Typical Den, An Kohli thought. Making a joke to mask his fear. It was now full dark above the smoke hole and a thin sliver of moon was starting to show. She longed to take her communicator out from its place of concealment behind her belt and make a call to Gala to try to find out what she was planning, but she dare not. If the guards saw it they would no doubt confiscate it and she was certain that if they got out of this mess she was going to need the device.

An Kohli looked at Den's recumbent back as he pretended to sleep. Poor Den, she thought, the scrapes I get you into. She gave a deep sigh and searched around for a stone free area on which to stretch out and maybe try to get some sleep herself. She laid her head on the crook of her arm and closed her eyes.

* * *

She must have succeeded in finding sleep at some point during the night because she was woken by a toe jabbing her repeatedly in the ribs. She was about to lash out at it when she remembered that the toe was attached to a being that had a spear in its hand. She sat up and rubbed the sleep from her eyes. Den, too, had been roused and was looking around him, bleary eyed and confused.

"Looks like it's party time." She muttered, just loud enough for him to hear. She had no idea why she was keeping her voice so low. The guards didn't understand a word they said, but it seemed somehow appropriate.

The chief appeared in the middle of the village once again, a guttering torch in his hand. Above him the sky was still the deep black of night, a trail of stars forming a twinkling blanket. The moon had moved out of vision while she had slept.

The chief shouted a command. Bare feet pattered across the packed earth floor as the warriors gathered, bristling with bows, quivers full of arrows, spears, flint headed axes, clubs and flint knives. He shouted again, this time getting a full throated roar in reply. He turned and they headed towards a tunnel. An Kohli noticed that it wasn't the one by which they had entered, but a different one that seemed to lead off at right angles.

The guard shouted at them and pointed, making it clear they were supposed to follow the crowd. They did as they were bid; there was nothing else they could do without risking ending up on the point of a spear. They were bustled along until they caught up with the back of the column of warriors. Younglings were scampering around them, no doubt following their fathers or maybe their older brothers, but after a while only the boldest remained, and even they were eventually sent home. They stood in the dark watching the warriors depart. For all An Kohli knew they would still be there when the survivors eventually returned.

The tunnel was nowhere near as long as the one through which they had arrived. They had only been walking for about twenty minutes when the column came to a halt while a couple of warriors wrestled a latticed screen away from the exit. They passed through and An Kohli turned in time to see the screen replaced. So perfectly did it merge into the background scrub and vegetation that had she not known where the tunnel entrance was she might have walked straight past it in broad daylight.

The exit had led them out onto a heavily forested slope. A path curved around the side of the hill. Other than an open patch directly in front of them, as the slope continued downwards, they were surrounded by ancient trees. She could tell by the lack of ground cover that even in day time little light penetrated. The path was, however, well worn by many feet. The silence was all pervading, with only the soft slap of feet to be heard and the heavier tread of An Kohli's and Den's boots.

The warriors set a brisk pace. Den puffed along beside her as though he was struggling to keep up. They seemed to walk for hours, but it was impossible to tell with only the briefest glimpses of the stars and the pale sickle moon above their heads.

At last the tribe slowed its pace and then stopped. An Kohli and Den were hustled to the front. An Kohli quickly realised that they were at the very edge of the forest, with trees on three sides but none in front. Along the distant horizon there was the faintest hint of light as dawn approached.

Directly in front the ground sloped downwards into a valley, the bottom of which was deep in shadow, almost totally black; almost, but not quite totally black. Dotted along the bottom of the valley were a number of red smudges. Cooking fires, An Kohli concluded, allowed to burn down overnight but still with enough life left to be re-kindled in the morning. They had reached their destination.

The chief handed each of them a pulsar, giving the larger one to Den. An Kohli pointedly swapped them before sliding the Menafield into its holster. The chief started on a rambling set of instructions which were meaningless to her. But she didn't need to be told what to do. Go down to the village and start shooting, or whatever it is those things do. When we think it's safe we'll come in and finish the job.

"Come on Den." An Kohli muttered. "Let's go and start a war."

They started down the hill and could feel, rather than hear, the throng following.

"So what's the plan. We're not really going to kill anyone, are we? I know your feelings on needless loss of life."

"What is it that you're best at doing?" An Kohli said by way of reply.

Den bit back on the sarcastic reply he was about to make. This was An Kohli and this was An Kohli's way of explaining a plan. He played along. "Running away. I've got prizes for it, or at least I would have if anyone could catch up with me for long enough to give them to me."

"Precisely, and that's just what we're going to do."

"Are you mad. This lot will be on us in a trice."

"No, not while they're with us. My guess is that they'll stop short of the village and let us go ahead. So that's what we'll do. We'll fire off a few pulsar blasts, wake everyone up then find a back door to slip out of. The two sides will start tearing lumps off each other and we'll circle back, go and collect the egg from the cave then get the flock off this planet."

"Just like that." Den's voice was now heavy laden with sarcasm.

"Well, I hope so. Look, just stick with me. If it works it works and if it doesn't we're no worse off than we are right now."

"Well, that's true enough. Unless…"

"Come on, spit it out."

"Unless the other side catch us. I doubt they'll be too pleased with us."

"We'll just have to make sure that doesn't happen then, won't we. Now, dawn can't be far away and we need the dark if we're going to slip away without being noticed, so I'm going to up the pace."

With her long legs she started to stride out, then broke into a trot. The warriors must have taken her speed for eagerness and they matched her stride for stride. Den huffed and puffed alongside her, just managing to keep up. They felt, rather than saw, the warriors come to a stop. One moment they were there and the next they weren't. A quick glance back confirmed her feelings and she saw them start to spread out in a long line, ready to sweep down into the village when the time was right.

"We're on our own." She panted.

Too busy trying to breath, Den didn't attempt an answer.

They reached the first hut and came to a stop in its shadow. It was old, its thatch rotten. The home of a widow, thought An Kohli in passing, with no one to help her maintain her dwelling. She heard the sound of snoring and saw a sentry asleep on his feet, his body angled against the wall of a neighbouring hut. Den crept over and lightly lifted his spear out of his unprotesting fingers and took it with him. No point in leaving an armed warrior behind their backs.

An Kohli saw what she was looking for. In a pen some animals were milling around, a species similar to agravargs, she thought, grubbing in the dirt with their snouts. She pulled out her pulsar and fired a single blast. The crack-zap of the pulsar split the silence of the night. An animal fell dead and the others started to squeal in panic, charging from side to side looking for an escape route. Voices started to call out, wondering what was going on. They didn't yet sound too alarmed.

An Kohli fired again, this time at the thatch of the ramshackle shelter at the far end of the pen, which burst into flame and the animals went wild with fear. They massed along one fence and their combined weight collapsed it. A tidal wave of panicked animals swept through the village. One collided with a hut which started to lean over drunkenly before finally giving up the fight and collapsing gracefully into the dirt. There were some screams from inside, followed by a male voice shouting angrily.

Den fired at the roof of another hut and it too burst into flames.

"Careful Den. We don't want to kill anyone." Her protest was at once rendered moot as she was charged by a spear brandishing warrior, probably another sentry.

She tried to dodge out of his way but he was fast and came straight back at her. She stared into his eyes and saw them narrow as he prepared to strike. His rear foot braced, ready to put more power into the spear thrust. As he lunged An Kohli swayed out of his path, but felt the tip of his spear snag on the thin fabric of her suit, tearing a hole. As his momentum carried him forward she swing her pulsar and the butt connected with his temple with a sickening thunk.

He dropped at her feet, out cold. Picking up the spear she threw it out of easy reach and hurried on. There was a pile of grass standing next to a half finished hut, so she set fire to it with another shot from her pulsar before turning to seek out Den.

The village was now in an uproar. Den had set fire to another roof and panicked figures ran back and forth, no one knowing which was the way to safety.

"This way Den." She called, pointing to a gap between two huts that was less than half a met wide. Their shoulders clashed in the middle and they burst out the other side like a cork from a bottle. An Kohli turned and fired into the sides of the huts, which burst into flames. No one would follow by that route. People charged past them, bumping into them, tripping, falling then scrambling to their feet and running on. No one tried to fight them. In the dark no one knew who was who, so the only difference between friend and foe was if someone was brandishing a weapon. An Kohli and Den lowered their weapons so they wouldn't appear threatening and therefore no one challenged them.

They passed the last hut on their side of the village and were soon once again up to their wastes in grass. They heard a chant break out from the side of the hill as the war band prepared to charge. Good. Any would-be defenders would head in that direction in order to face the threat. They could fight it out between them and good riddance, thought An Kohli.

She signalled to Den to drop to his knees and she did the same. They crawled away up the side of the hill. An Kohli felt the first warmth of the sun reach her shoulders and realised they must now be well up the side of the valley. Carefully she raised herself, her hands and knees almost sighing with relief as her feet once again took her weight.

The village was still in shadow, lit only by the fires. There were more now and in parts of the village she and Den hadn't been in. They must either have been lit by drifting embers or by someone else.

As she watched a warrior came running from the village pursued by two others. One of the pursuers thrust a spear into his back and he fell. They were quickly on him, hacking and bludgeoning until he was nothing but a bloody mess. Which side he had been on she had no idea. The two assailants gave their victim a parting stab with their spears then trotted back into the maze of burning huts.

"Come, on. Let's get out of here." An Kohli said flatly.

"Who do you think is winning?" Den asked.

"I don't care." She felt ashamed at her part in the killing, even though they had been under duress.

She set a crippling pace back up the slope and into the forest. She found the path easily enough and they trotted along. Den struggled hard but maintained the pace as best he could. At last he had to stop.

He bent double, his hands on his knees, dragging in huge gulps of air.

"I thought running away was what you were good at." She mocked him gently. She was gasping for breath herself.

"I'm getting too old for this." He panted at last. "When will you start paying me my pension."

"What pension?" She panted back.

"Oh yeah, I forgot. Bounty hunting doesn't have a pension plan."

"Actually it does, a very good one, though very few ever live to draw it. Their next of kin tend to benefit most." She straightened up and started walking. "Of course you have to pay in first and you have to be a Guild member."

"Well, that's why I'm here. Are you ready to recommend me yet?"

"Let's wait until we're off the planet before we discuss that."

"Do you think they won? Our lot I mean."

"No idea. If they did they'll probably spend the day celebrating. Spoils of war and all that. If not then they'll be hunted until they're caught. Some survivors might make it back to the tunnel, eventually."

She broke into a trot once more, but a more gentle one than previously. Den was able to keep up more easily. The gloomy forest slipped past them, one bit looking much like another.

"I think we've passed it." Den announced, stopping for a breather.

"Not yet, I don't think. The entrance was on a bend in the track with a gap in the trees directly opposite and I don't think we've reached that yet." The path they were on did seem to run almost dead straight both behind and ahead of them. Having never seen the path in daylight she was only guessing. Maybe they had passed the tunnel without even knowing it.

They walked in silence for another twenty minutes and the path started to take a gentle bend as the ground on their left rose steeply to form the side of a hill. A gap in the trees opened out on the right hand side.

"This is it, I think, somewhere around here." She slowed her pace further as she examined the side of the hill, looking for any trace of the latticed screen. In the end it was her hearing that found it for them, not her sight.

"Hear that?" she asked Den.

"What?"

"Someone's crying, I'm sure of it."

Then Den heard it as well. Not so much crying as sobbing. He moved along the face of the hill a few more met and pointed, mouthing the word 'here'.

An Kohli crept forward to join him. There was no doubt, someone was sobbing. Then a youngling whimpered and was shushed.

12 – The Dysac

Den grasped the edge of the lattice screen and heaved. It came away from the edge of the tunnel and An Kohli stepped into the opening, her pulsar levelled to face whatever threat was behind it.

A female cringed back, one hand covering her eyes against the sudden light while the other struggled to push a youngling to safety behind her. The youngling cried out in protest, or perhaps it was fear.

The female was bleeding, her arms and body scratched and her face battered and bruised. There could be little doubt that she had been beaten. Tears streaked her filthy face and her hair was matted with sweat and soil. Holstering her pulsar so that she appeared less threatening, An Kohli raised her hands in a pacifying gesture, murmuring what she hoped were soothing words.

"There, there. It's going to be alright. There's nothing to be afraid of."

The female obviously disagreed. As An Kohli stepped towards her she cringed away from her, forcing her protesting infant between her and the tunnel wall in order to protect it. An Kohli got the message and took a step backwards. The female still cowered from her, but had stopped trying to hide the child, which meant she was doing it less harm.

"Something very bad has happened here." An Kohli told Den.

"Yeah, I'd sort of worked that out. There's blood on her thighs."

For the first time An Kohli noticed it. This female hadn't just been beaten, she'd also been raped.

"How many males were still in the village when we left?" An Kohli asked.

"I didn't see any. I thought they all went with us."

"That's what I thought as well. So who did this? If there were only females and younglings left behind…"

"Someone else must have attacked while we were away."

"Time to break radio silence, I think."

An Kohli pulled her communicator from its hiding place and walked out of the tunnel so that she could get a signal.

"Gala, what's going on up there."

"Oh, you've finally woken up. What was the distress signal for? They hadn't even gone down to the planet when you sent it."

"Who is 'they'?"

"Whoever is on that Starcruiser. Ah, so you didn't know about that. In that case why did you send the distress signal and are you OK now?"

"Right, in the order of your gabbling, no we didn't know about the Starcruiser, I sent the distress signal because we'd been taken captive by some sort of stone age tribe and yes, we're OK now, depending on your definition of OK. Let's say we're alive, for the moment and we're no longer captives."

"Right. Well, I'm hiding between a couple of asteroids right now, thanks for asking. If one of them gets nudged out of orbit I'm going to be squashed so flat you could slide me under the belly of a snake. There are what looks to be a couple of pirate ships hunting me, so I'm dodging around a bit. I have to say Lazarus is doing a good job of keeping one step ahead of them." An Kohli thought she heard a self-satisfied sigh come through the communications channel but she couldn't be sure.

"Have any shuttles left the Starcruiser?"

"Yes. Three of them. They went down just before dawn this morning."

About the same time as she and Den had been descending towards the village. She was surprised they hadn't seen them, then realised that the bulk of the hill was probably between them and the shuttles' landing site.

Three shuttles; if she recalled correctly from her encounter with Shogun at The Hideaway *(see New Earth)* the Starcruiser's shuttle held a maximum of six passengers. That meant between twelve and eighteen beings. More than enough to overpower the village if the males were absent.

"Thanks Gala. Looks like we're going to have a bit of trouble getting off this planet, but we'll take care of that. You just keep out of reach of those pirates. If necessary make a run for it and go and get help."

"I'm not leaving you behind."

"Yes you are. No arguments, got it? We can't go anywhere if the Adastra is lost, so that's your first priority. Now I'm off to find out what's going on down here." An Kohli cut the communication off before Gala could argue any further. Gala would do as she was told. Reluctantly, perhaps, but she would obey her orders.

She stepped back inside the tunnel to where Den was waiting. "We've got some serious opposition ahead of us, I think. A minimum of twelve pulsars to our two."

"So we'll be heading back to the Adastra then." Den stepped towards the exit.

"That wasn't my plan."

Den crouched down and started to draw a sketch in the dirt with his finger. "Look, here's the village." He drew a circle, "and here we are." A short line represented their tunnel. "Here's the tunnel we were brought in by." A longer line represented that. He joined the two tunnel mouths with a hypotenuse. "That route takes us round the hill then it's second star to the right and straight on till morning.* We disable their shuttles, get to ours and when we get to the Adastra we call for help and come back later to deal with the Fell and recover the egg."

"Sorry Den. It isn't just about the egg any more. A female's greatest fear, greater even than death, is to be raped. We're too late to stop it happening to this poor wretch." She pointed to the female still cowering against the tunnel wall, "but there are about seventy females down there and whoever is there can't have worked their way through all of them yet. We… I can still help them. Look, I can't ask this of you. If you want to go back to the shuttle I won't hold it against you. This is my fight. You go to the Adastra and call for back up like you said. If I get out of here I'll call when I want you to collect me."

Den gave her a long look. "OK, An Kohli, if that's what you want. You were never one to run from fight and I respect you for that, but running from fights is what I do. You've always known that. You take care now."

Den pushed the screen further to one aside and left the tunnel. When he got out into the open An Kohli saw him stop, as though not sure which way to go. He looked up towards the sky as though seeking inspiration. Then he swore. He swore loudly and repeatedly.

Turning on his heel he came back into the tunnel, storming past An Kohli and heading for the subterranean village.

"Fuck you An Kohli."

"Only in your dreams, Den." She countered before following him. "Only ever in your dreams."

"You owe me big time. If you don't recommend me for the Guild after this then we're through, you understand." He was gesturing wildly as he walked.

"Better keep your voice down. Sound travels a long way in tunnels." An Kohli advised.

Den's voice dropped to a whisper but he continued his rant. "I'm telling you, An Kohli, this is the last time. If you don't recommend me for the Guild I swear you'll never see me again, ever."

"OK Den, message received. But it would be a good idea if we got out of here in one piece, so I suggest we don't just go barging into the village."

* * *

They crept towards the tunnel mouth, the light hurting their eyes after the darkness. An Kohli hugged one wall while Den pressed himself against the other. An Kohli had to stifle a gasp as she saw the carnage in the centre of the village.

Bodies lay everywhere, singly, in pairs and in family groups, females and younglings entwined in final embraces. Several lay spread-eagled like star fish, evidence of what had been done to them before they had been callously killed for no other reason than the pleasure of it. A group of sobbing females sat under the watchful, or perhaps lustful gaze, of a guard. Armour clad figures wandered around the perimeter, rummaging in the piles of skins that served as bedding, overturning cooking utensils and breaking anything that was breakable.

An Kohli recognised the armour from The Hideaway. It was useless against a pulsar but would provide an excellent defence against arrows or spears. The helmets were different, she noticed. At the Hideaway Shogun's bodyguards had worn helmets with a half face visor, so their noses, mouths and jaws were visible. Now they wore full helmets that left only a tiny gap between their shoulders and the bottom of the helmet. The surfaces were also emblazoned with nicknames of some sort, across both the front and the back. No doubt an aid to recognition. From where she stood she could see a 'Zombie', a 'Killer', an 'Ace' and a 'Nutter'.

An armoured figure appeared from a point just out of their line of vision, adjusting his clothing and re-arranging the groin protection of his armour. She thought perhaps he had been answering a call of nature, until he turned back, raised his pulsar and fired, ending the life of someone that she couldn't see; no doubt another poor female. A cold fury rose in her. She hissed at Den and nodded in the direction of the being, who had the legend 'Jumbo' inscribed on his helmet.

Den picked up a pebble and threw it at the figure. It rattled off the back of his armour, causing him to stop and turn. Den extended an arm and beckoned. With his face covered in reflective plexi-glass it wasn't possible to make out his expression, but he was definitely puzzled. He was also curious. He stepped forward hesitantly, his pulsar at the ready.

Den beckoned again and then retreated down the tunnel, seeking out a patch of deep shadow in which to hide. The figure entered the tunnel, passing An Kohli without seeing her; the disadvantage of wearing a visor that restricted peripheral vision. As he continued along, looking for Den, An Kohli stepped up behind him and grabbed him around the neck.

His actions were instinctive, dropping his pulsar he grappled with An Kohli's arm as she forced it across his windpipe, cutting off his air supply. His thick gauntlets prevented him from getting a proper hold and without finger nails he wasn't able to inflict any sort of injury that might loosen her grip. He struggled for a few more seconds and then lack of air made him faint, becoming a dead weight in An Kohli's arms. She lowered him none to gently to the ground. "Curiosity killed the cat." She muttered as she started to remove his armour. Den arrived to help her.

Hidden in the top of his boot was a wicked looking combat knife, the blade about ten sim in length, the back notched with a savage series of serrations and the cutting edge gleaming sharp in the thin light. Den started to cut strips off the clothing under the armour, which he used to bind and gag the prisoner.

As Den laid the knife in the ground they felt a sudden rush of movement and a naked female form grabbed at the wicked blade and stabbed at the recumbent thug. An Kohli just managed to grab the female's arm before the blow was struck, preventing her from killing her intended victim.

An Kohli shook her head in a clear negative motion. She pointed back along the tunnel then used her fingers to mime running figures, hoping that the female would get the idea that she should await the return of the warriors. Then she pointed at the armour clad figures roaming the village and mimed stabbing each of them.

A malicious grin spread across the female's face as she nodded her head in understanding. Why kill just one? Wait for the males to return and then they can all be killed. With a shudder An Kohli realised that death might actually be a blessing for any of the intruders that were caught.

Den dressed himself in the armour and pulled the helmet over his head. There was nothing now that could distinguish him from the other figures still prowling the village.

An Kohli saw one of the figures come closer to the mouth of the tunnel. Emblazoned on the helmet was the legend 'Bitch Queen'. Perhaps she had seen her comrade enter and wondered where he was.

"Female, I think." An Kohli hissed in Den's ear. "Her armour will fit me better." Den nodded silently and slipped out of the cave mouth. He swaggered over to the figure and engaged her in a short conversation. An Kohli had no idea what Den had said but it did the trick and Bitch Queen followed Den, aka 'Jumbo' according to his helmet, into the tunnel. She didn't fare any better than her colleague and An Kohli was soon putting on her armour as the native female took great delight in cutting up her clothing and binding her, pulling the knots tighter than was strictly necessary.

Damn, thought An Kohli. The Bitch Queen was a Lupine. Her lack of an elongated jaw and high mounted ears would be a dead giveaway if An Kohli had to remove her helmet. Never mind. Too late now, they would cross that street when the lights changed.

An Kohli couldn't bear to be parted from her Menafield Pulsar, but it would look out of place amongst the more utilitarian weapons used by the armoured raiders. She forced it under her chest armour, its hard surfaces digging into her ribs. She would live with the discomfort, she decided.

A shout went up and one of the figures strode across the village holding something aloft, like a trophy. An Kohli recognised the small shape of the Magus egg. For the first time she noticed the diminutive figure of a Dysac, easily recognised by the explosion of hair around his head. The Dysac had also put on some armour, but it was oversized and seemed to be getting in his way. He hadn't bothered with a helmet. No Dysac would ever do anything to harm his crowning glory.

The Dysac smiled in triumph. It was clearly what they had been looking for as he now put an end to the search. The armoured figures gathered around as An Kohli did a quick count. Ten of them plus the Dysac. Not good odds, but then again she didn't need to fight them if she could out think them.

The figures started inspecting the females huddled in the centre of the village. They must have been promised them as a reward when the search for the egg was concluded. An Kohli had to act fast if she wanted to save them.

Jerking her head towards the Dysac to indicate to Den that he was to follow her lead, she stepped forward. They made their way across the cave, stepping over the dead, until they were within a couple of met of the leader.

"Boss, me and Jumbo here found a female hiding in the tunnel."

"How nice for you." Drawled Attila, not interested in this minor event. He continued his close inspection of the egg, as though he had never seen such a thing before.

"We thought she was going for help, so we interrogated her. She told us that the male folk weren't far away and would be back soon."

"So what. You're not afraid of a few bows and arrows, are you?" Attila didn't bother to hide the contempt in his voice.

"It's not that, Boss!" An Kohli mock protested. "She said they would pull down the roofs of the tunnels, trapping us in here and leave us to starve to death. That way our pulsars would be useless against them."

Bullshit baffles brains, she had often heard it said, and this occasion was no different. The Dysac went pale and became quite agitated. So agitated that it didn't occur to him to ask what language had been used to conduct the interrogation. Or maybe he just couldn't comprehend that these simple natives might not speak Common Tongue.

"OK, all of you, get formed up. We're leaving."

Not waiting to see if his little army would follow he stretched his short legs to their maximum and hurried towards the long tunnel that led to their shuttles. If he could have run without ruining his credibility, she felt, he would have done so.

An Kohli and Den hung back, pretending to act as a rear guard, but really so that they could consult without being overheard. She heard a crackling in her helmet and realised it was fitted with communications equipment. She wondered if it was voice activated. "Anyone got anything to eat?" She asked. It wasn't just a test of the comms equipment, she was genuinely hungry. They hadn't eaten since the previous evening. No one reacted so she assumed that they hadn't heard. Therefore there must be a switch to operate the microphone. She daren't remove her helmet to inspect it so she took a closer look at Den's as they walked. There they were; a small press button just below the bottom of the visor on either side of the jawline of the helmet, but coloured the same so as not to be visible. Providing two of them meant that they could be activated with either hand without having to stretch.

An Kohli raised her gauntleted hand and touched one of the buttons. "Boss, I can hear voices coming from the other tunnel. Lots of them." The pace was increased until they were trotting and it didn't decrease until they were a long way into the long tunnel.

* * *

With the fast pace and their already tired state, An Kohli and Den started to lag behind the raiders, which suited them. An Kohli's stomach gave another attention grabbing growl.

"How come you're not as hungry as me?" She asked.

"My body has learnt to prioritise. Find a safe haven first, then worry about food. At the risk of sounding repetitive, what's the plan now?"

"I'll let you know as soon as I have one."

"I was worried that you might say that."

By the time they had wearily climbed the steps into the open it had grown dark once again. Half the raiders were sat on the ground, tucking into dried rations, while the other half patrolled a perimeter around the three shuttles that stood in a triangle with the tunnel entrance at the centre of its base. Work lights shone from the shuttles providing some illumination, though they also served to provide pools of deep shadow.

Across the valley they could see the steady throb of the Adastra's distress beacon, activated as soon as An Kohli had sent her distress signal. So near yet so far away.

"There's no sign of the Dysac." Den observed.

"No, he'll be in one of the shuttles, probably checking in to get fresh orders."

"They have the egg, why not just go?"

"Because they also want me."

"It must be nice to be loved."

With that Attila appeared at the head of the ramp leading into the centre shuttle. "You two! Where the hell have you been?"

"Sorry boss. We stayed behind to make sure no one was following."

The explanation seemed to satisfy him. "Oh. OK, well done. Get yourself some food and then you can relieve two of the others so they can eat."

"I would seriously love to eat." An Kohl muttered just loud enough for Den to here.

"Yes, you are rather recognisable if you take that helmet off."

"Tell you what. You change into the one we caught first, have something to eat and smuggle some for me. Once we're out on the perimeter, in the dark, I'll be able to eat it."

"Or we could just wander out into the dark and make a dash for our own shuttle."

"Not without that egg. If he gets it off the surface of this planet we've lost it for good. Just grab us some food."

Unfortunately, they didn't have time to put that plan into practice. "Bitch Queen." The Dysac called. "Come over here a moment."

An Kohli trotted to obey, just as a good minion should. She stood in front of the Dysac, towering over him. "That female you interrogated, tell me what she said again."

"She said that the males would be returning soon and…."

An Kohli noticed the expression on the Dysac's face, at once triumphant and also angry. An Kohli realised that she hadn't peppered her speech with the small growls and yips with which the Lupines accompanied anything they said in Common Tongue.

The Dysac drew his pulsar from its holster. It would be a small weapon in the hand of anyone else, but in his tiny fist it appeared enormous. He struggled to raise it and point it at her chest. "Drop your weapon and then take off your helmet."

"I'm sorry, I don't understand. What have I done wrong?" she blustered.

"Don't treat me like a fool. Drop your weapon now. I won't tell you again."

An Kohli gently laid her borrowed pulsar on the ground at her feet.

"Now the helmet." Attila jerked the pulsar upwards to emphasise his demand. Around the landing site those not on guard duty realised that something was going on and stopped what they were doing to watch.

Slowly, reluctantly, An Kohli drew the helmet over her head. Once it was clear she shook her head to free the waves of deep purple hair to fall in place and perfectly frame her face. The effect was spoiled somewhat by the fact that her hair was slicked to her skull by sweat and refused to bounce the way the manufacturer of her shampoo promised it would.

"Well, well, well. Who do we have here? If it isn't An Kohli herself. That is convenient. I have just been discussing you with my colleague and she was insisting that I stayed down here until I found you. It seems that you have found me instead."

"You." He pointed at the nearest armoured figure. "Restrain her. I want none of the problems that my predecessors had with this bitch." He turned back and addressed her directly. "The name on the helmet is apt. You are the Queen Bitch. I assume the original owner of that armour is now dead. Oh, well, it won't be long until you follow her."

The figure stepped forward and it was only as it pressed the snout of its pulsar into his neck that Attila realised that it was the same one as had been with An Kohli every time he had seen her since she had appeared in the cave.

"And I'm guessing that you are Den Gau." Attila said in a defeated sort of voice.

Behind her An Kohli heard the sound of weapons being drawn and she didn't have to have much of an imagination to know that there were now at least five pulsars aimed at her back and that didn't include the ones of the beings that were on guard.

"They really shouldn't have done that. Den will shoot if they don't put their weapons down."

The Dysac rewarded her with a grim smile. "There's no warrant out on me, An Kohli. Legally you can't do a damned thing and I know you won't kill me in cold blood. You play by the rules. It's your great weakness."

"Exactly. And I'm playing by the rules when I tell you that I am arresting you on multiple counts of rape and murder. You don't have to have a warrant out on you if I have reason to believe that you have committed an arrestable crime… and after what I saw in that cave there can be very little doubt. So, put down your weapon then tell your thugs to put down their weapons and I won't tell Den to shoot you."

"You're bluffing. You won't do it."

An Kohli pushed her hand under the chest piece of her armour and withdrew the hidden Menafield. The relief from the pain was instantaneous; she almost let out a sigh of pleasure. She levelled the pulsar at the Dysac's head.

"After what I saw down there, you really don't want to put me to the test. Now, give the orders or you will be dead before you even know I've pulled the trigger. And no, I won't be repeating the warning either."

The piercing look in An Kohli's eyes told the Dysac all he needed to know about her willingness, almost her desire, to pull the trigger. He let his pulsar fall from his fingers. "Drop your weapons." He shouted.

"Have they done it?" She asked Den.

"No."

"I'll count to three. If any of those goons are still holding weapons when I've finished you're dead. One…. Two…."

"For galaxy's sake drop your weapons." The Dysac screamed. An Kohli heard first one weapon hit the floor, then a second, then a veritable drum roll as the remainder were thrown down.

An Kohli turned and swept the Menafield through an arc, counting as she went. Ten. Good, that was them all. She remembered the wicked looking knife on the first of the thugs that they had caught. Of course they had only dropped the weapons they had held in their hands. Who knew what else they might have hidden.

"Form a line." Ashe called. "I'm going to call you forward one at a time to be searched. If I find any of you with a weapon I'm going to leave you here for the natives to deal with."

The threat worked like magic and soon a heap of knives, small pulsars and coshes was lying alongside the larger pulsars.

"Now, strip off your armour and those of you wearing helmets remove them as well." Her instructions were quickly obeyed. Beneath the armour they wore a sort of uniform of blue trousers, yellow shirts and black boots, though they were obviously made by different manufacturers. Some of the shirts bore logos and slogans.

Satisfied that there was now no visible threat she did as she had said and called the thugs over one by one to be searched. They appeared a lot less threatening without their armour, helmets and reflective visors.

One of the thugs was detailed to collect all the weaponry and armour together and deposit it inside one of the shuttles where it couldn't be accessed quickly by more than two of them at a time.

An Kohli returned her attention to the Dysac. "You have the advantage of me. You know my name but I don't know yours."

"Go to Hell."

"Maybe I will, one day, but not just yet. Your name."

"I'm called Attila."

"No you aren't. You call yourself Attila, but at least that confirms my suspicion that you're a member of the Fell. Now, what's your name?"

"Fuck you."

"OK, Den, you have my permission to hurt him."

The Dysac yelled in fear. "No, I'll tell you. My name is Lessar Fro."

"Any relation to Biggar Fro"

"He was my brother and you killed him."

"Actually I didn't. He was stupid and managed to get himself killed, but I have to admit he was in my custody at the time."

"So, as I said: you killed him. I'll see you dead for that alone, but for myself I'll see you suffer first. What we did to those females back there will be as nothing compared to what my bodyguards will do to you. But not until after I've finished with you first, of course."

"Oh no. Not more threats. Why do they always threaten us Den?"

"A total lack of imagination, An Kohli."

"Right, here's the deal. I'm going to disable two of the shuttles and the third will take us back to our shuttle. My colleague will take control of that and all three of us will go up to that Starcruiser of yours and you can introduce me to the colleague that you referred to earlier."

"But you told my guards you wouldn't leave them here if they co-operated."

"I lied. What can I tell you? It's the times we live in." An Kohli felt that justice would best be served if the natives were allowed to serve it.

Behind them some of the closest guards must have heard what was said because there were shouts of protest. Some got to their feet and started towards the shuttle that held the weapons. Den shot a warning pulsar blast into the grass at their feet, which was enough to make them stop, but only for a moment.

One of them was bolder and decided that he had nothing to lose. Staring fixedly into Den's eyes, daring him to shoot, he took another step forward and then another. Den raised his pulsar and took a steady aim, but still the being went forward.

The male arced his back and let out a scream. An Kohli shot an accusing glance at Den but then realised that he hadn't fired. The thug collapsed face down in the grass, an arrow standing erect in the middle of his back.

Out of the darkness war cries screeched out their challenge. The bodyguards scattered, some making for the dubious protection of the deeper shadows while others made a more determined attempt to reach the shuttles.

"Get him inside the shuttle and strap him down." An Kohli commanded Den, before taking aim towards the shuttle to her right.

She fired a blast and then another. Bits flew from around the shuttle's doorway. She cursed herself for forgetting how powerful her weapon was. This was no time for finesse. She aimed at the middle of the broad side of the shuttle and fired once more. A fist sized hole appeared in the shuttle's skin, through which she caught a glimpse of the interior. Swinging her pulsar through an arc of sixty degrees she repeated the shot on the other shuttle. Neither would ever travel into space again. The fate of their erstwhile occupants she left in the hands of the natives. Arrows zipped across the open space, one passing close to her nose. Dressed in body armour she could expect no special treatment from the natives, she realised. It was time to go.

Turning on her heel An Kohli stepped inside the shuttle and reached for the emergency take off button, slamming her hand hard down on it. The inner door slid into place with an efficient swish then she heard the whining sound of the ramp lifting itself, the noise cutting off with the final thunk. Then she was thrown across the cabin as the shuttle propelled itself skyward. The G force kept her pinned to the floor until the shuttle reached an altitude of one thousand Li, where it stopped and hovered, obeying its programming to wait for its next command. If none were to come it would lock onto the homing signal of the Starcruiser and take itself home, but for the moment it waited for its crew to decided what to do now that the immediate danger was past.

An Kohli picked herself up off the cabin floor, stepped over the feet of Den and the Dysac, Attila, and settled herself into the command chair. She switched on the external cameras and located the flashing light of the Adastra's shuttle and locked the computer onto it. It obediently tracked across the sky, descending as it went.

Something was nagging at the back of An Kohli's mind and she was wondering what it was. It was something important, she was sure. Of course, the Magus egg. She stood up again and crossed to Attila and quickly gave him a pat down search. When she didn't find it he smiled smugly at her but said nothing. An Kohli cast her eyes around the room and spotted it, sitting snugly in a cup holder next to the command chair. She picked it out and examined it, looking for any signs of damage but it appeared to be pristine apart from a couple of flecks of soil on its base from where it had sat in its underground niche.

As she replaced the egg the shuttle gently settled into the grass about ten met from its target.

"OK, Den. Be quick, get across to our shuttle and follow me up to the Starcruiser. I have no idea what we'll find when we get there, but don't be a hero. Surrender if you have to."

"Gee, you make it sound such an appealing prospect I can hardly wait." Den opened the inner door, waited for the ramp to finish lowering itself and hurried into the dark.

Left on her own with Attila, An Kohli closed the shuttle up and locked it onto the homing signal from its mother ship.

As the shuttle took off once again An Kohli caught a glimpse of the other two shuttles on the other side of the valley, sitting in their pools of light. Smoke poured from one. A figure flitted across a brighter patch, followed closely by another, but she couldn't tell if it was the natives or the bodyguards, one of each or which was which.

With one lot of barbaric killers intent on ending the lives of another lot of barbaric killers, she didn't have much sympathy for either side.

* J. M. Barrie; Peter Pan.

13 - The Good Ship Shogun

As the airlock door slid open she had expected the Dysac to be cheerful. After all, he was safely back on board the Starcruiser and there were friends close by who could rescue him, but instead he appeared downcast. Warily An Kohli stepped into the corridor, her pulsar raised and ready, but there was no one there to greet them. The floor, she noted, was bare painted metal. This wasn't an area where the ship's guests frequented except when boarding or leaving the ship. In front of her was a flight of stairs leading upwards. Just before they disappeared An Kohli caught a glimpse of deep carpet. Clearly the demarcation point between passengers and crew.

The neighbouring airlock door slid open and the muzzle of a pulsar appeared, followed slowly by an arm and then by the arm's owner, Den.

"We appear to be alone." An Kohli told him, to his visible relief.

"You get Attila. I'll take point."

Den ducked into the shuttle she had vacated and released the prisoner while An Kohli tentatively made her way up the stairs. She was greeted by the startled gaze of a white uniformed steward holding a tray on which stood a single glass containing a sparkling golden liquid. As the steward took in An Kohli's pulsar the tray started to chatter as the glass rattled. An Kohli reached forward to take the glass and silence the noise.

The steward's expression relaxed for a moment as he spotted Attila ascending the stairs and then turned to alarm once again as he saw Den close behind, pulsar in hand.

Beside the steward stood a table covered with a snowy white cloth and laden with more glasses filled with the bubbling liquid. A quick count revealed there to be twelve of them.

An Kohli took a sip from the glass, paused appreciatively and then drank half the remainder. She passed the glass to Den who committed sacrilege by downing the contents in a single gulp. He placed the glass back on the tray and the frantic rattling started once again.

"May I suggest that you put the tray down before you break the glass." As the steward obeyed, Den reached past him and picked up one of the full glasses, once again emptying it in double quick time.

"That's enough for the moment Den. You may need to shoot straight later." To the steward she said, in a kindly tone, "You have nothing to fear from us if you do as we say. Tell the truth and all will be well."

"Thank you Madam." He managed to stutter. He wasn't at all reassured by her. Perhaps it was the pulsar, she thought. It tended to have that effect on people who didn't have much contact with violence.

"First off, don't call me Madam, my name is An Kohli. Second off, where is the command deck?"

"Command Deck? Erm, oh you mean the Bridge. If you'll allow me Mad…. An Kohli, I'll show you." He started to lead the way along a long corridor, lined with reproduction wood, genuine expensive paintings, high quality paintwork and elegant light fittings. They passed numbered doors as they went.

"Who occupies these rooms?" An Kohli asked.

"The bodyguards M… An Kohli."

"How many of them?"

"Just twelve. There were more but a couple got killed a while back. Will they be returning? If so they'll want their champagne."

"I don't think they'll be coming back." This seemed to cheer the young steward up. An Kohli guessed that the hard-bitten bodyguards didn't have much truck with stewards. "Are there any more armed personnel on board?"

"Not that I know. Mr Attila was armed when he left here, but I'm not sure about Madam Desire."

They had reached a circular area with four doors set in the circumference like the points of a compass, each with a letter of the alphabet on it. An Kohli brought them to a halt.

"These look like suites. Are they?"

"Yes. That one." He pointed, "Belonged to Mr Shogun but he's dead now. His things are still inside. We didn't know what to do with them. Then there's Mr Attila, Mr Tiger and Madam Desire." His arm swept around the circle stopping at each door as he named the occupants.

"Tell me about Mr Tiger."

"He's not on board right now. He left the ship at Ecos and didn't come back. I've been told to keep his suite ready for him."

"OK, now, where are the crew quarters."

"Right below us. It's a similar layout, though everything is smaller because the store rooms are down there as well, and the laundry and the kitchens and…"

"OK, I get the picture. What about the crew. How many?"

The steward started counting off on his fingers. "There's Captain Sawyer, the First Officer, Second Officer, Chief Engineer and the Second Engineer. Then there's the Chief Steward and three ordinary stewards, I'm one of them, of course. Then there's the Head Chef, Sous Chef, Pastry Chef and two kitchen hands."

It told An Kohli a lot about the priorities on board the Starcruiser that the catering department was the largest. As if triggered by the thought of catering her stomach gave another rumble.

"Has anyone got access to weapons?"

"I guess Captain Sawyer has, you know, just in case we get attacked or anything, but if he has then I've never seen them."

"Madam Desire, where is she now?"

"Oh, she's on the Bridge with the Captain."

"Now, what's along that corridor?" She pointed to the only other exit from the circle.

"Well, at the end is the Bridge, but on the left is the passengers' lounge and bar and on the right is the passengers dining room."

"Very good. You did very well. I think that's all for now."

The steward looked extremely relieved, but his training kicked in once again. "Is there anything else I can get M… you before I go?"

"Actually there is. Bring me some food, enough to feed two." A thought occurred to her. "Oh, Den, do you want anything to eat?"

Den gave her a disgusted look for having been overlooked. "Yes, food for me as well. Oh, and make sure that none of the cutlery can be used as weapons."

"Well done Den. I'd never have thought of that. Now," she addressed the steward again, "you run along and sort out that food.

Leading the way she, Den and a very reluctant Attila made their way along the corridor to the Bridge.

As the door to the Bridge swished open, An Kohli propelled Attila through it to land in a heap in the middle of the generously sized room. The Adastra's command deck looked like a broom cupboard by comparison. It was as sumptuously appointed as the rest of the ship through the mass of technology tended to diminish the interior designer's vision of an old fashioned sailing clipper.

A short, stocky female turned to protest at the sudden intrusion but merely stood with her mouth hanging open when her eyes lighted on the pulsars pointed in her general direction. Behind her stood a tall, distinguished looking being, dressed in a smart uniform bearing four gold stripes on the shoulders.

"At the risk of sounding corny, nobody move." An Kohli said as she walked onto the Bridge and stood over the form of the Dysac, now struggling to get to his feet without the aid of his bound hands. "Now, I assume that you are Captain Sawyer." She addressed the distinguished looking being before turning her attention on the female. "Which makes you Desire."

The Captain was the first to regain his composure. "What is the meaning of this. How dare you enter my Bridge with weapons drawn."

An Kohli gave him a warm, reassuring smile. "The meaning is that as I am the person holding one of the weapons you will now take your orders from me. Or would you prefer it if I locked you up and put your First Officer in charge?"

"No, that won't be necessary." The Captain said quickly, his proforma protest having been made. "I'm not in the habit of disputing matters with beings armed with pulsars. I will follow your instructions."

"Very sensible, Captain." An Kohli decided that things would go more smoothly if she respected the Captain's rank and position. "Den, secure the female if you would."

Den crossed the Bridge and prodded the reluctant Desire into one of the many padded chairs that were dotted around the Bridge.

"You won't get away with this." Desire protested weakly.

"I have been told that before, and I usually do get away with it." An Kohli replied as if it was a matter of fact, which it was.

"Captain, do you have anything I can use to secure these prisoners?" Den asked.

"There is a selection of cables in the drawer to your left. We have to sometimes interface guests technology for them." He explained.

"Now, Captain." An Kohli attempted to get matters back on track after Den's interruption. "How are orders communicated to the pirates? Can you give them or must she?" She pointed her pulsar at the now securely bound Desire.

The Captain's mouth turned downwards with a disapproving look. Clearly he had no wish to be associated with pirates. "Madam Desire issues the orders, then I communicate them. There is a code word that has to be added to each message, but it's the same one each time so I know it."

"Very well. In that case send this message to the pirates: An Kohli is captured and the operation on Aragan is concluded. Proceed to Rigel to await further instructions."

A few moments later the Captain read An Kohli their reply. "They're refusing to go. Apparently the ship they are hunting was promised to them as part of their reward, as was the female member of crew on board it."

"Tell them that is in hand and the ship and its crew member will be sent to them at Rigel under command of a prize crew." An Kohli gave Desire a ferocious look, suggesting there would be consequences for offering up her friend as a reward to pirates. Desire looked away hurriedly, not wanting to meet her captor's eyes.

The reply came back quickly. "They have acknowledged."

At that moment two stewards arrived bearing trays of food. One was placed within easy reach of An Kohli and the other close to Den. "The Chef sends his apologies, but all the cutlery can be used as weapons so he has sent food that doesn't need cutlery."

"Please thank the Chef. Now, there's one more little thing I would like you to do."

"Anything you ask Ma… I mean An Kohli."

"Would you ask the rest of the crew to assemble in the passengers' lounge."

"The crew aren't allowed in there, except for the stewards of course, and then only to serve the passengers. It's against orders."

"I think obedience to orders went out the window when I started waving my pulsar around, don't you? Just ask them to gather there, please. Oh, and offer them refreshments. Madam Desire is paying. I'll be along soon to talk to them."

The steward hurried off, clearly not happy with the order but knowing that he couldn't disobey.

At the sight of the neatly arranged, sumptuous looking food An Kohli's stomach gave an impressive roar. She picked up a morsel and popped it into her mouth. Her face took on a beatific expression as the medley of flavours hit her palette. She swallowed and quickly sampled one of the other items on the tray. From the far side of the Bridge the sound of Den could be heard, demolishing his food.

"Now, Captain." An Kohli said, licking her finger tips. "Please open a channel to The Headquarters of the Guild of Bounty Hunters for me. Ask to speak to the Grand Master in person. Use my name if necessary."

It took only moments for the Grand Master's face to appear on the screen. "An Kohli, so good to hear from you. The galacticnet has been full of your name for the past couple of weeks."

"Undeserved, Grand Master. It was Gala who rescued the Ecosians. I have to keep explaining that."

"It's the price of being famous, An Kohli. You sometimes get acclaim even when you don't deserve it. So what brings you to call me at this late hour?"

"Sorry, Grand Master. I had no idea what time it is with you. I thought you would want to know; I have recovered another of the Magus eggs."

"Oh, well done. Where was this one?"

An Kohli answered the question, but didn't provide any explanation as to how she had recovered it. That could wait for her report. "However, that isn't all. There are two pirate ships on their way to Rigel. If you put together a task force I'm sure that there will be good bounties to be earned."

"What are the names of the ship's owners?"

An Kohli gave the Captain an inquiring look.

"Demetrius of Pharos and Gan Ning." He supplied.

The Grand Master looked away from the screen, obviously running some sort of query. "Ah yes. There are significant bounties for both of them. They appear to have been causing the Gargantua Enterprises Corporation some problems." As the owners of more freighters, mining ships and cruise liners than any other corporation this came as no surprise. "I'll have no trouble finding takers for the commission. I'm surprised you aren't going after them yourself."

"Not this time, Grand Master. I have other things to do. Top of the list is to deliver the Magus egg to the GCIE."

"Of course. And then?"

"I think I'll go back to Ecos. I've earned a little holiday and it would be a nice place to spend it."

"Did you encounter any members of the Fell this time? Usually they aren't far away when you recover an egg."

An Kohli arranged her face into a blank mask of innocence. "I believe that their numbers are falling." She avoided the question. "Being a member seems to be a hazardous profession these days."

"Yes, so I've heard. There were rumoured to be fourteen of them. How many do you think there might be now?"

An Kohli did a quick mental calculation, at the same time maintaining her blank look. "I think there are probably eight still at liberty and perhaps that number might soon be reduced to seven."

"You wouldn't be instrumental in reducing those numbers, would you? If you were then it's your duty to hand them over for trial; the ones that survive their encounters with you, anyway." The Grand Master reminded her, as he was duty bound to do.

"I'm aware of that." She answered non-committedly. Both of them knew that Fell members were unlikely to ever stand trial. Even if they were to face a court they would merely bribe their way to an acquittal and if convicted they would buy their way out of prison. Which was why An Kohli had devised her own way of dealing with the problem.

The Grand Master gave a wry, knowing smile but decided not pursue the subject. What he didn't know he couldn't be a party to. "Well, enjoy your holiday. You deserve it. I look forward to reading your report. They're always so… entertaining." He struggled to suppress a smile. An Kohli's reports were usually more interesting for what they didn't say than what they did, such as the whereabouts of captured members of the Fell.

The Grand Master closed the connection at his end.

"Have those pirate ships left the system yet? She asked the Captain.

"They're accelerating now. They'll be gone in a few minutes."

While An Kohli waited for the pirates to enter their wormholes for the journey to Rigel she continued to work her way through the mound of food. It really was the most delicious she had eaten in a long time. The chef could have secured a place in the kitchens of any restaurant in the galaxy. Indeed he could have opened a restaurant and have the galaxy come to him in their droves. The queue of ships bearing passengers wanting to eat at the restaurant would probably extend for several parsecs.

"They're gone." The Captain reported.

"Good. In that case please open me a ship-to-ship channel with my ship, please; the Adastra.

After a few moments Gala's face appeared on the screen. She looked tired and it reminded An Kohli that it had been more than a day since she herself had last slept.

"How are you doing?" An Kohli asked.

"Oh, great. You know, topping up my sun tan, participating in some light retail therapy. It's been a real vacation."

An Kohli suppressed a smile at her co-pilot's heavy sarcasm. "Good, nice to know you've been having fun. In case you hadn't noticed, those two pirate ships have gone."

"So Lazarus told me. Where are you now?"

"On board the Shogun. I have two Fell members under arrest and I've got the egg. We'll be coming back across to the Adastra soon. Would you like to shorten the journey by bringing the Adastra a little closer."

"No problem."

"There's another Fell member on Ecos. After I've delivered the egg to the GCIE that's where we'll go."

"And of course the fact that there's a certain Max Wallfly there has nothing to do with that decision."

An Kohli could feel herself blushing a deep maroon. "Well, seeing as we're going to be there anyway…."

"I thought so." Gala laughed at her friend's discomfort.

"I'll probably have some research for you to do on a Fell member by the name of Tiger. I'll have to interrogate these two first and I want to do that on the Adastra rather than here." She gave the two prisoners a meaningful look that suggested that the interrogation might not be a pleasant experience. They both gulped and Desire went so pale that her pink blotches disappeared leaving her with only a yellow hue. An Kohli thought that she might actually faint. Neither of them seemed to be aware of her dislike of violent interrogation methods. She had never tortured a prisoner, though of course she had threatened torture often enough. She had a feeling that Desire wouldn't be a tough nut to crack.

"OK, I'm actually on the opposite side of the system to you right now. I'll see you in a little while." Gala said as she cut the comms link.

"Thank you Captain. Now perhaps you will accompany me while I speak to your crew." She headed towards the door of the Bridge with the Captain striding to catch up with her. "Look after the prisoners Den. And don't touch my food." She shot at Den as she left the Bridge.

The crew were sat in the comfortable arm chairs and deep sofas and had to struggle to get to their feet when the Captain entered the lounge. He gave An Kohli an inquiring look. She nodded her head and the Captain ordered his crew to take their seats once more.

Some eyes were still focused on the pulsar which she still held in her hand so she hastily replaced it in the holster on her belt. She felt the tension drain from the room.

"I'm sure that news has reached you..." She looked meaningfully at the young steward, "that the person you know as Desire is no longer controlling matters on this ship. As far as I'm concerned the Captain is still in command, but I am taking the decisions with regard to the future of this ship." She paused to see what affect her words were having and was pleased to see that there were no expressions that indicated any active opposition to her.

"The twelve bodyguards that accompanied Attila down to the surface of Aragan will not be returning to the ship." This brought an excited buzz of comment to the room and there were smiles, especially from the stewards. It appeared that the bodyguards hadn't been popular. An Kohli waited patiently for the noise to abate.

"Now, you're no doubt wondering what this means for you." There were murmurings of agreement, accompanied by nodding heads. "Well, first of all I have to establish who now owns the ship. Captain, what do you know of the ship's ownership?"

The Captain cleared his throat and then launched into his explanation. "The ship is owned by a company called Benefit Enterprises Incorporated, which is registered on Falcona. Who owns Benefit Enterprises I have no idea. We received orders to pick up passengers, usually the being we knew as Shogun, and to do whatever he asked of us. I always assumed that Shogun owned Benefit Enterprises, though I don't know that for certain. When Shogun died I reported the fact in accordance with the sealed instructions with which the company had provided me. I was then told to wait the arrival of Desire and the other passengers. When she arrived she held a meeting with the bodyguards. I have no idea what was said, but there was a lot of cheering and stamping. She then came onto the bridge with two of them, fully armed and started giving orders. As with yourself, I decided against arguing with the beings who held the weapons."

"So you have no idea who now owns the Shogun?"

"None at all."

"In that case I suggest that you take her off somewhere and set up your own business. If you need help to do that I know a very influential business being who may be willing to assist." An Kohli was sure she could persuade Gib Dander to offer the resources of his organisation.

"What about our passengers?"

"They are no longer your concern. If you receive any inquiries regarding them direct them to the Guild Of Bounty Hunters. Oh, and make sure you don't tell them where you are. I suspect that anyone in a position to ask has no more claim to the Shogun than I have, or you for that matter, but there's no point in making life easy for them."

"And what if they come after us and demand the ship back?" An officer sporting three gold stripes on his uniform asked her.

"Ask the Guild for protection. Tell them what happened and they'll give you whatever help you need until the legal position is sorted out."

Under normal circumstances she would have seized the Shogun as the proceeds of crime and the courts would have decided its disposal. Whoever bought it would then almost certainly have retained the services of the crew. But to do that An Kohli would have needed to prove that the owner was Shogun and she wasn't in a position to do that right then and she didn't need the complications.

"Are you saying that we should just take the ship?" The three striper clearly doubted the advice.

"I can see no reason why you shouldn't. If Shogun was the owner he is now dead and we don't know his real identity." In fact An

Kohli had a strong suspicion as to who he might be, but wasn't about to complicate matters by revealing the information. "If anyone wants to claim ownership then let them. Let the courts decide. In the meantime I can't think of any reason why you shouldn't remain on board and do whatever you need to do to keep the ship going, which includes taking on fare paying passengers so your wages and the ship's running costs can be met. After a decent period, say five years, you can apply to the courts to be granted legal ownership."

"Actually, galactic law allows for that." The Captain said, brightly. "Ships have been found drifting in space, no one knew what happened to the crew, so ownership had to be decided by the courts."

"But that's the law of salvage, Sir." The three striper objected. "It's not the same thing as the crew taking ownership."

"I don't see why not." The Captain continued.

Deciding that she was no longer needed An Kohli slipped out of the lounge and went back onto the Bridge. She ate the last of the food on her tray before turning to Den.

"We'll have to use one of the Shogun's shuttles to get us back to the Adastra. Ours isn't big enough and I don't want either of us to be alone with two prisoners. Once we've got them safely under lock and key, would you bring the shuttle back and recover ours?"

"Sure, no problem. So you're just going to abandon this ship?"

"Not abandon. We'll call it a gift to the crew for not making life difficult for us."

"Very generous."

"Not really. I can't prove it was owned by Shogun and I can't afford to take the time to establish if it was or wasn't. Call it an investment in the future. I'm sure if we ever fancy a space cruise there won't be a problem getting a berth on this ship."

"It's still very generous. It must be worth several million nuks. Why not give it to me?"

"I did consider it, but you have no more claim than I have, so you'd have the same problem proving ownership."

"Some problems I could live with."

"Including paying the crew's wages? Or maybe you would just kick them off the ship and leave them without jobs."

"Ah, now you come to mention it, maybe I'll settle for just borrowing it from time to time."

"Good thinking. Now, let's get this pair of low-lifes back to the Adastra."

Glossary

GCIE - Galalctic Counsel In Exile. When the Magi were forced to flee, power was transferred to the GCIE pending the restoration of law and order. This is a group of senior civil servants who are the permanent heads of the departments of galactic government. They immediately took action and set up a series of committees through which to administer the galaxy. Each committee had the same members though each one had a different Chair and a different title. By coincidence each member of the GCIE chaired one committee. Because all decisions are reached by consensus it takes a long time to get anything done and then it's usually the wrong thing. For example, because of disputes over which budget would pay it took six months to agree to have biscuits served at committee meetings and then garibaldi's were chosen when the members all wanted either chocolate digestives or Hobnobs.

Parsec - An astronomical unit of length used to measure the distance of objects in space when viewed from the surface of a planet. It was developed by astrophysicists on planet Earth and is one of the few astronomical developments from that planet that have made it into the galactic system of measurement. One parsec is approximately 3.26 light years or 3.0857×10^{16} metres. Gave rise to one of the biggest bloopers in movie history when Han Solo claimed that the Millennium Falcon had done the Kessel run in 'less than 12 parsecs' which given that it is a measurement of distance is impossible. Well, that's screen writers for you – don't know the difference between measurements of distance and measurements of time. The character of Han Solo repeated the line in the 2015 sequel "The Force Awakens". This may have been an ironic reference, but it may also be that the writers still don't know what a parsec is. This entry is brought to you by the Guild Of Smug Gits, UK chapter.

14 – The Singing Faroon

Desire sat in the corner of the Adastra's holding cell. She hugged her knees and rocked back and forth in time to her sobs. This wasn't supposed to happen. The yellow patterning on her skin had gone to a greener shade; a reflection of her mood, while the pink patterning had faded almost to white. She was supposed to find An Kohli and then send lots of people to kill her and fetch the egg back to her. How had this situation possibly come about?

She wasn't a bad person. Not really. So why was she being punished as though she was? Lots of bad people went all their lives without this sort of thing happening. She was just a business person, that was all. Beings needed money, she didn't ask why, so she found the money for them and took a small commission, well perhaps not that small, for finding it for them. Then when it came to paying the money back she provided the return channel, again skimming her share off the top as it went by.

That didn't make her bad, did it? OK, some of the beings who wanted the money weren't good and some of the beings that invested also wouldn't stand up to close scrutiny, but that wasn't her fault, was it?

She should have stayed in her bunker. What in the galaxy had persuaded her that she was up to this sort of fight? In her bunker she was in control. No one came in without her say so, in fact no one came in at all. She controlled her world through her communications links and galacticnet bank accounts. It had worked for years.

It was how she had met Barbarossa, of course. Finding the finance for business deals he was setting up. Well, she met him in a virtual world even if not in the real one. When he and Odin had come up with the idea of setting up the Fell she had been a natural choice to provide some of the funding that they needed to achieve their goal. From there it had been a short step to becoming a full member. Fell members needed finance just like everyone else and their deals were measured in millions, even billions, of nuks. She had jumped at the chance.

But she hadn't thought about the price she might one day pay for that membership. It had been a one way bet as far as she was concerned, until she stupidly put herself forward to go after An Kohli. She should never have trusted the other two, of course. Attila had proved to be a blunt instrument; heavy handed in the extreme and incapable of subtlety. While Tiger… well, what about Tiger? He'd gone down to Ecos and never come back. OK, he had proved useful, but where was he now when she needed him? Maybe he had really fallen for the An Kohli bitch. Maybe that was why he hadn't come back on board. He didn't want to be involved in her killing.

Well, she hadn't wanted to be involved in An Kohli's killing, either. It was supposed to have been done at arm's length, coldly, clinically. She gave the order and the order would be obeyed. That was as close as she needed to get. Instead, here she was locked up on board An Kohli's ship. Other Fell members who had found themselves in this position had disappeared and never been seen or heard of again. Was that to be her fate?"

The cell door opened and Attila stumbled in. Behind him stood Den.

"Come on then, Desire or whatever your name is. Let's not keep the boss waiting."

Desire cuffed the tears away from her eyes before pulling her stocky frame erect. "What will she do to me?"

"If you're as co-operative as Lessar Fro here, then nothing." Den grinned.

"I didn't say anything, honest." Attila protested.

"Sang like a canary." Den grinned again. He stood to one side to let Desire step past him into the corridor then hit the big red 'close' button to secure the cell once again. He prodded Desire along the corridor as far as the Adastra's small lounge and told her to enter. An Kohli was waiting for her, standing beside a metal framed chair.

"Sit." She barked.

Desire hurried to obey. Once she was seated An Kohli secured her wrists to the chair's arms with pairs of handcuffs, before settling herself into one of the lounge's more comfortable armchairs. Den ostentatiously picked up a stout looking pair of plyers, borrowed from Gala's tool box, from an occasional table and made a show of making a close examination of them, snapping them shut several times with sharp metallic clicks.

"Now, just to put you in the picture," An Kohli leaned forward to make sure she had Desire's undivided attention, though the prisoner's eyes were riveted to the pliers in Den's hand. "I don't like hurting people. I never have. Den, on the other hand, loves it. He was the sort who pulled the wings off flies and the legs off spiders when he was a youngling. He's wanted on a dozen planets for hurting people." She lied. Den might be wanted on a dozen planets, but it was more likely to be for unpaid bar bills.

"Don't hurt me. Please don't hurt me." Desire whimpered, shrinking down in her chair, trying to look small and unthreatening.

"If you answer my questions, you have nothing to fear. Lesser Fro learnt that lesson very quickly." In fact Lesser Fro had told them little that they didn't already know, but that wasn't the point. The point was for Desire to think that he had already told everything. "Let's start with your real name."

"You won't ever have heard of me. My name is Mella Turmi. I'm from a planet called Faro in the Chorion system. I haven't even got a warrant out for my arrest. You're holding me illegally." She tried hopefully.

"Consider conspiracy to commit genocide as a holding offence." An Kohli dismissed the appeal. "I must admit your name isn't one I'm familiar with, nor your planet."

"We keep ourselves to ourselves. We like it that way."

"OK, so far so good, but now for a more tricky one. Tell me the names of the other Fell members. Don't bother with the ones who are missing or dead."

"I only know one by his real name. He uses the alias Barbarossa, but his real identity is Mentor Cross. He's a Falconan."

An Kohli narrowly avoided letting a surprised whistle escape. Mentor Cross was a popular celebrity figure, well known across the galaxy. He was often seen in images entering and leaving nightclubs with attractive females on his arm. Though, come to think of it, she couldn't remember why he was so well known. Was he one of those beings who was famous mainly for being famous? He was certainly rich, though very little information was available on how he had made his money. The vague catchall of 'business' was used to cover his activities.

"How do you know him?"

"We did a lot of business together. He knew people who wanted investors, I knew people who had money to invest. You can join the dots. We made each other a lot of money over the years. Now he acts as Secretary to the Fell. It makes him very powerful." Was An Kohli imagining it, or was there a veiled threat behind Desire's words.

"That's interesting. What about the others. You must at least know their aliases."

"Of course. There's Tiger, Chameleon, Mastermind, Drac and She Wolf." She paused while she thought some more. "Oh yes, Gunslinger. He's an odd one. He attended a couple of the early meetings but since then he's been represented by an underling who goes by the name of Florida. Finally there's Warrior."

"I'm familiar with Warrior." But what was more interesting was Gunslinger and his absence from the Fell forum. That could be significant, but she wasn't sure how or why.

"Warrior is the other key figure in the Fell right now. He's organising the election campaign."

An Kohli jerked upright in surprise. It had come so easily and without prompting. Finally, confirmation that the election was being organised by the Fell. She quickly forced herself to relax, hoping not to have given herself away.

"What are the aims of the election? What do the Fell hope to gain from them?"

"Twofold. The first is that the galaxy gets the appearance of a legitimate government that will remove the day to day burden of administration from the Fell. You have no idea how tedious it is having to organise trade talks and the like. But the more important aim is for the new government to pass laws which will benefit the Fell and its activities."

"Such as?"

"Granting mining rights on newly discovered planets, granting exemptions to existing laws; that sort of thing. Legitimising some of our more borderline operations, but above all granting us immunity from prosecution; for anything. We could just take what we want, bribe officials and so on, as we do now, but it's better if what we do is at least dressed up as being legal."

"Better for who? Never mind. I know the answer to that. OK, now tell me about Tiger."

"I doubt I can tell you any more than you already know. I don't know where he comes from or what his real name is. He's good looking, tall, quite suave. That's about it, really. We didn't talk much when he was on board the Shogun." Desire's tone suggested that their lack of socialising was a matter of considerable regret.

"Do you have an image of him?"

Desire gave her a look that suggested it was a stupid question. "No. We in the Fell try to avoid having our images taken. We find it helps when it comes to anonymity." She said wryly. "Except Barbarossa of course, but he was hogging the limelight long before the Fell were set up."

"How did you know that we were coming here, to Aragan? No, start earlier. How did you know we were going to Ecos?"

"Lessar Fro found out about Ecos. He knows someone who knows someone, that sort of thing. Apparently one of the clones let slip that your co-pilot was going to Rigel and we worked it out from there. As for how we knew you were coming here, Tiger managed to get a bug into your hotel room. We listened in on your calls to your crew. It wasn't hard."

The Faroon female was clearly terrified and An Kohli had no reason to think she had held anything back. Indeed she had revealed more than she had intended, so anxious was she to be seen to be co-operating.

"I think that's all I need from you. Den will take you back to your cell."

"What happens to me now? Do you take me off to prison?"

"No. I know that you wouldn't be in prison five minutes before someone was bribed to let you out again. I have other plans for you. Don't worry, you won't come to any harm, at least not at the hands of myself or my crew."

"What are you going to do with me?" Desire squealed as Den undid her shackles and pulled her to her feet. But An Kohli was already leaving the room.

"Join me on the command deck when you've locked her up, Den." She called over her shoulder.

When the three of them were finally assembled, squeezed tightly into the cramped space of the command deck, An Kohli summarised what she had learned.

"I'm happy we can edit the first bit of the recording. No one needs to know about that little subterfuge. The important thing is that we have the admission that she's a Fell member and that the Fell are responsible for organising the election. It should be enough to undermine any remaining credibility in the process. But I'm still worried about this Tiger character. Whoever he is he managed to get in and out of my hotel room unnoticed to plant a bug."

"Maybe it wasn't actually him. Maybe he bribed a member of staff." Den offered.

"Or maybe security on Ecos isn't as good as elsewhere. They seemed to me to be a little bit on the innocent side."

"Both are possible, of course. Desire herself wasn't there so she wouldn't know how he did it."

"Maybe it was someone who you let into your room. Did you have any visitors?"

"No, only Max."

A silence thudded into the air between them. Den was the first to break it. "How does Desire's description of Tiger match up with

Max? How did she describe him? Good looking, tall, suave. What about Max?"

An Kohli had to admit that they were words she would probably have used if she was asked to describe him. But the notion was ridiculous. She was a good judge of character. She had to be in her line of business. She could tell a good one from a bad one through an inch thick lead shield. She was well known for it.

"That's absurd." She protested. "That description matches half the males on Ecos. You might as well say that he had two legs."

"Do you have an image of him, just so we can run him through facial ident and eliminate him?" Gala gently asked.

An Kohli pulled out her communicator and went back through the recent images and realised that she didn't have one.

"How about a communicator ID?" Den asked, trying to be helpful. "With that we might be able to trace him through his comms supplier."

"Well, he gave me that, at least." An Kohli read out the number and Gala input it into a galacticnet search, but it didn't provide them with any clues. Perhaps the lack of clues was a clue itself.

The ensuing silence lay so heavily that it felt like a weight on all their shoulders, but it lay particularly heavily on An Kohli.

"OK. You don't have to say it. Max is a suspect until its proven otherwise." If nothing else An Kohli had learnt to be pragmatic. It would be wrong to place her friends' lives in danger because she refused to accept the need for caution. "Gala, do you think that you could hack into the hotel's security system? Maybe they have images of him from the security cameras."

"I'll see what I can do. But if they don't have any?"

"Then Den gets one by whatever means necessary when we get back to Ecos."

"You're serious about going back there?"

"Of course. Tiger, whoever he is, is probably still there. We have to take the opportunity to catch him if we can. We may not get another chance if we allow him to leave. Plus, if Max is innocent then I would like to see him again."

"And if he is Tiger?"

"Then I'll have to deal with it."

An Kohli set her jaw firmly and left the Command Deck before diving into her cabin and burying her face in her bedding. She wasn't going to let her fears show in front of her friends, but she felt as though the bottom had just fallen from her world.

The intercom crackled into life. It was Gala's voice she heard. "Sorry to interrupt, but what do you want us to do now? We can't just float around this planet forever."

"OK. Look, I haven't slept for more than two days so I'm going to need to catch up. Den needs to sleep as well. Then I'll go visit the GCIE and deliver the Magus egg. While I'm doing that in the Pradua I need you to take Desire and Attila to Sadr Gamma *(see The Magi and Genghis Khant)*. I'm sure they'll be quite happy there."

"That's quite a colony you're building there."

"I know, we have to hope they don't start breeding. After that you and Den can go ahead of me to Ecos and we'll meet up there."

15 – Suspicious Minds

The shuttle descended through the bright, sunlit afternoon towards the surface of Sadr Gamma. Attila glowered at Den but Desire seemed to have accepted her fate.

"Look, you have nothing to fear here except each other. The planet is uninhabited, the most dangerous creature here is you, well maybe Gypsy."

Attila's eyes lit up. "Gypsy is here?" he asked eagerly.

"You know her?"

"No, but she is known to me, shall we say."

"Well, she's here and so is Genghis, plus another that you may not know."

"Why here?"

"It has all the essentials you require to survive but no one to bribe. You are in prison but there are no bars."

"This is a PANIC warning broadcast." A calming voice oozed out of the communications speakers in the shuttle craft. "There is a severe risk of infection by neonoral virus if you continue to approach this planet."

Desire started to whimper with fear while Attila spat his defiance at Den. "So, you plan to kill us with disease."

"Don't pay any attention to that. It's just an automated system. Think of it as your prison guard. It keeps people away from the planet. No one with any sense ignores those sorts of warnings."

"Except you."

"OK, have it your way. Yes, except for me." Den mocked them, knowing that the broadcasts were just as he had described them. "Now, when we land you have a choice. You can wait where I leave you for someone to come, or you can walk towards them and meet half way. They'll see the shuttle landing and my guess is they'll be running towards it in the hope of reaching it before it takes off again. They won't make it, I've made sure of that."

Den had spent several minutes studying the infra-red scan that showed up warm blooded life forms against the cooler background of the plant life. By far the largest purple blotches had been the three clustered together around a fourth bright red blotch that was probably a cooking fire. Den had then chosen a landing site several hundred li away so that they couldn't get there before he had dropped off his passengers.

"We've made sure that you get a warm welcome by providing you with a few luxury items. It's all in a box by the door. Some soap, shampoo and such like and some tinned goods."

"Are they armed?"

"Not with anything more deadly than small knives."

"What if they try to kill us?" Desire was clearly very afraid.

"Why should they? You're from their own organisation. They'll welcome you with open arms."

"We're more mouths to feed."

"In that case I suggest you volunteer to do some of the hunting so that you aren't a burden on them."

"Look, you're a sensible sort." Desire wheedled.

Here it comes, thought Den. I'm surprised neither of them had tried it earlier.

"Why don't we cut a deal, just you and me." Desire continued, her tone descending to the almost seductive.

"And me." The effect was spoilt by Lessar Fro's shrill interjection.

"Shall we cut to the chase here?" Den interrupted, before they said anything that might actually tempt him. "If I wanted your money I would have offered you a deal before we even left the Adastra. You're far too late. If Gala even suspected that I didn't set you down on the planet she would blow us off the airlock as soon as we tried to dock."

"We don't have to do it that way. Just call a certain number and tell someone where we are. No one need ever know you were involved."

"I would know and that's all that matters. You judge me by your own standards and you've got me wrong. OK, I've pulled a few strokes in my time, but I'm not like you. I don't go down to the surface of planets and allow my hired guns to start killing and raping."

"That was him, not me." Desire shrieked, pointing an accusing finger at Attila.

"You're in it together as far as I'm concerned. You lie down with dogs and you get up with fleas. As far as I'm concerned, An Kohli has been far too lenient. It's a failing in her. I'd have put you both down on the planet and let the natives deal with you." There was a sense of finality about Den's words that prevented either Desire or Attila from trying to persuade him any further.

Silence fell as the shuttle drifted downwards in its controlled fall, fired it's landing rockets and settled onto its support legs. Den opened both the inner and outer doors then lifted the box of supplies out and walked them to the end of the ramp. Returning inside he dialled the code into the restraints that held Desire in place. With a gentle click they fell open.

"Outside, now, no funny business." Den barked, his temper frayed and his nerves jangling.

Desire stood up and meekly did as she was told. "Don't stop walking until you're at least a hundred met away." He called after her.

Turning back to Lessar Fro he could see the malevolent look in his eye. This one would be more tricky. Undoing the restraints required the use of only one hand, so he could hold a pulsar in the other, but if Lessar Fro put up a fight and the pulsar went off it could damage the shuttle and leave him stranded here with his prisoners. The Adastra only had the one shuttle and the ship wasn't suited to low level flight. At a pinch a skilled pilot like Gala could land it and take off again, but by that time the combined efforts of the prisoners might well have resulted in his capture, with or without his pulsar,

There really was only one thing he could do. Raising his pulsar he brought it around to crack against Lessar Fro's temple, stunning him and making his eyes cross. Den would have found the effect comical had the stakes not been so high. He quickly undid the restraints and bundled the small being out before dropping him a safe distance from the shuttle's ramp. He then sprinted back inside and hit the emergency take off button.

Thirty seconds later he was picking himself up off the floor before sitting down in the command seat to direct the vehicle back to the orbiting Adastra.

Why did he get all the difficult jobs? He asked himself for the millionth time.

* * *

Den dropped into the co-pilot's seat with a heavy whump of escaping air from the cushion.

"Don't tell me, it didn't go well."

"How did you guess." His heavy sigh underlined his words. "I had better tell you, because you probably already suspect it. They tried to bribe me into letting them go. Wanted me to call someone."

"Well, thanks for being honest. You didn't have to tell me that and, unless you're playing a double bluff, I guess you didn't take the bribe." Gala started to take the ship out of orbit.

"I could do that for you." The computer's voice suggested it was offended by not being asked to pilot the ship.

"Lazarus, there is something about the completion of mundane tasks that allows us sentient beings to feel that we are still in control of our lives." Gala was heartily sick of the computer's interruptions.

"Oh very well." The computer let out a theatrical sigh, not unlike the one Den had used earlier. "But don't say I didn't offer."

As the ship accelerated, Gala thought about what might be waiting for them on Ecos. "Actually, Lazarus, I do have a job that you can do for me."

"I await your command." Its tone was heavy with sarcasm.

"What is the probability that the Fell member known as Tiger and An Kohli's... friend... yes that will do, friend Max Wallfly are one and the same?"

"Tricky. That's all about sentient being's motivations, and I'm not well versed in those."

Gala was pleased to have found something that challenged the capabilities of the annoying machine.

"If you aren't up to it…."

"I didn't say that." The computer snapped back. "I just need more data."

"Such as?"

"Let's deal with factual data first: when Tiger arrived at Ecos, when An Kohli met up with Max Wallfly, that sort of thing."

Gala provided best estimates based on what she knew.

"Now I need some background on An Kohli. What is her record like with selecting suitable males with which to engage in relationships?"

"Not good." Gala had to concede. "The best ones she overlooks until it is too late." She thought about Veritan and Merkaloy as well as others. "She also engages in relationships with more unsuitable partners, without realising that they are unsuitable until it is also too late."

"Please provide data on numbers for each."

Gala thought back over the years she had known An Kohli and realised how long it had been. They had met at school as younglings, becoming inseparable friends from the first day they had sat nervously together in the classroom. Now they had been together for over thirty five years. Wow, was it really that long? Her memory flashed back to that morning and her fingers pushing at the tiny gathering of crows' feet that she had started to notice at the corners of her eyes. Yes, it had been that long.

"Four suitable males that she has let go. Twelve unsuitable males to whom she has formed attachments. That doesn't count more casual, short term dalliances."

"Dalliances? That's not what I would call them." Den sniggered. Gala scowled at him.

"Please wait." Lazarus instructed.

"How long till we get to Ecos?" Den asked.

"Just over three days according to the navi-com."

"Usual six-on-six-off watches?"

"I can't see any reason why not."

Den checked the time. "OK. That gives me time for a nap." He pushed himself slowly out of the co-pilot's chair and stepped carefully across the short distance to the door.

"Are you OK?" There was genuine concern in Gala's voice.

"Just feeling my age. I'm getting too old for the sort of shit An Kohli puts me through."

"You can always go back to being a droid bartender." Gala smirked *(see The Magi)*.

"You know, that's actually not as bad an option as it sounds." The door swished shut behind him and Gala was left with her own thoughts.

Thirty five years. Where had it gone? Some of it she could account for just by checking her bank balance. Her association with An Kohli had been a rewarding one. Her share of the bounty on the criminals they captured and the reward money paid for things they recovered for beings, including on occasion other beings, had made her quite a wealthy female. Her needs were simple so she had spent very little of her share. True, when she reached old age she would have no one with which to share her good fortune, but then again she might not get old. Being the co-pilot of a bounty hunter wasn't a secure profession. The Wall Of Remembrance at the headquarters of the Guild bore witness to that. There were very few names of deceased bounty hunters that weren't accompanied by that of their co-pilots, if they had co-pilots in the first place. The thought sent a shiver down her spine.

Trying to distract herself she selected the newsfeeds from the galacticnet and started watching. They weren't live, of course; once they entered a wormhole all forms of communication were cut off, but the ship's systems were pre-set to record selected channels so that she had something new to watch as they ploughed their lonely furrow across the immense distances of space.

The main news story was their recording of Desire admitting that the Fell were behind the forthcoming elections to a new galactic government. It was creating a sensation. It's presence on the newsfeeds meant that An Kohli had reached the GCIE and they had released the recording.

Of course, the spokesbeings for the organisers of the elections denied all connections with the Fell and claimed that the recording was fake news created by subversive elements trying to undermine a democratic election process, but their denials weren't being taken seriously. What the majority of the beings in the galaxy had long suspected now had some credibility. The only problem was that Desire couldn't be questioned about her claim. That allowed the spokesbeings to say that she was deranged and a stooge for dark forces. There were some that believed them. There are always apologists for tyrants.

Tiny Blur was shown in an interview with one of the main news channels. "You know, I'm just a regular sort of guy." he smiled an oily smile at the camera. "So when I tell you that there is no such thing as a conspiracy by the Fell you can take my word for it. I mean, do I look like the sort of person who would have anything to do with something like that?" he turned to camera and gave it a one hundred watt smile.

When you've learnt to fake sincerity you really do have it made, thought Gala.

"Where is this alleged member of the Fell? Bring her forward so that she can answer your questions and provide evidence to back up her claims. Her absence speaks volumes." He finished.

"I have a result." Lazarus's voice made Gala jump.

"Thank you Lazarus. What is it?"

"I have to be honest with you and say that there are far too many unknown variables for me to give you an answer that is completely accurate, so there is a margin of error associated with this."

"I accept that. Now, what's the result."

"There is a sixty six percent probability that Tiger and Max Wallfly are one and the same."

Gala let out a disappointed sigh, then grasped at the straw that Lazarus had given her. "What is the margin of error?" Please say plus or minus twenty percent, she thought. Please, please.

"Plus or minus one percent."

Gala's hopes deflated. "Thank you Lazarus. If I get any more data I'll let you have it so that you can refine your calculations."

"It will be my pleasure." It sounded to Gala's ears that it would be too much of a pleasure, but computers aren't capable of feeling, are they?

So, there was a two to one probability. If she was offered those odds by a bookmaker she would take the bet.

Now, did she tell An Kohli the result or not?

* * *

"Welcome back." Gala gave up the Captain's chair in favour of An Kohli, who had just re-joined the Adastra as it orbited above Ecos.

"Thanks. It's good to see you. Where's Den?"

"He's down on the surface seeing if he can catch a glimpse of Max Wallfly. According to the Ecosian immigration service he hasn't left the planet."

"They gave you that information?"

"Let's say I used up some of our credit with the authorities."

An Kohli smiled at the euphemism. "Did it go all right at Sadr Gamma?"

"Den looked a bit fed up when he came back. I don't think he's happy in his work."

"No. I was starting to get that impression when we were on Aragan. He's not really cut out for our sort of life. He finds it stressful. But it's so useful having a Gau on the team."

"Are you going to recommend him for Guild membership?"

"I already have. I sent it in with my report on the Aragan affair. I'll tell him when we're safely out of here with Tiger under lock and key."

"Will they accept him?"

"I've no idea. He has a couple of black marks against his name for helping the wrong sort of beings evade arrest. Nothing recent, of course, but the Guild has a long memory. I gave him a glowing report, naturally. 'Couldn't have done it without him', 'diamond in the rough', 'saved my life'. It's all true so far as it goes, but the Guild can be a bit funny about these things. It has to be squeaky clean and Den is…. shall we say he's little bit shop-soiled."

"He'll be gutted if he gets turned down."

"I know. We'll probably lose him when he gets the news. The only reason he came along is for that. Of course, when I promised him that I'd recommend him if he did a good job *(see The Magi)* we still thought all the eggs would be together. The job was supposed to be finished months ago. That's so negative, isn't it. If he gets turned down, not when."

"The fates laugh when mortals make plans."

"Very profound."

"I read it somewhere."

"I have this for you." She handed over a small memory device.

"What is it?"

"It's the cross reference list between the serial numbers of the eggs and the names of the Magus whose intelligence is stored inside. You did say you could decode it if you had the information, didn't you?" *(See New Earth)*.

"Of course. Nothing could be easier. Did Srumphrey give you this?"

"No. You remember that boy who was always mooning around after you at school. Du Lally? Geeky type, always writing complicated essays on socio-economic strategy?"

"Yeah. I remember him. We used to tease him a lot."

"We did. Fortunately, he doesn't bear a grudge. He works for Srumphrey now and doesn't get on with him at all. When I told him what I wanted he was only too happy to get me this."

"OK, well, I took down the serial numbers of the last two eggs so I'll check them out later."

"Erm, there's one other thing I had to do to get him to hack the information."

Gala was immediately suspicious. "Oh, and what was that?"

"I had to promise him you two would go on a date when this is all over."

"You did what?" Gala's shout would have woken the dead and An Kohli started to worry that her friend would strike her.

"Look, don't worry. Maybe he'll forget. Maybe this will never be over, who knows?"

Gala shook her head as though she wondered how her friend and employer could have landed herself in such a fix. "You better hope he does forget. And if I end up having to go out with him, you're paying"

An Kohli gave a loud laugh, then turned serious once again. "He's been very helpful about what happened when the Fell turned up and the Magi were under threat. Most of them just wanted to take a ship and go somewhere safe, a well-protected planet. It was one of their number that suggested the transfer of their intelligences to the memory eggs. Du Lally didn't know which one made the suggestion, though."

"You think that's significant?"

"I do, but I'm not sure why at the moment. I'll have to think about that. Anyway, anything else I should know?"

Gala hesitated slightly too long before answering. "No. Nothing at all." An Kohli gave her a penetrating look, causing Gala to blush slightly.

"Lazarus. What was the result of the last probability analysis that the co-pilot requested you carry out."

"There is a sixty six percent probability that Tiger and Max Wallfly are the same entity."

"Thank you, Lazarus." An Kohli gave Gala a sorrowful smile. "You could have told me. I'm a big girl and we've been together a long time now."

"Sorry. I didn't want to upset you. There's still a thirty four percent chance…"

"That he isn't. I know."

"How did you know I asked for the analysis?"

"Because it's exactly what I would have done in your position. Friends have to look out for each other and the best thing to do in these circumstances is to try to find out if he is a low life scum sucking bastard or the sweetest, cutest guy in the galaxy."

"So what are you going to do now."

"Tell Den to follow me from the shuttle port and to watch my back. I'm going to fit a tight lock on my chastity belt and go down to the planet and see if I can find out the truth."

* * *

Max Wallfly hurried across the hotel lobby, arms open wide ready to embrace An Kohli. "You look wonderful. I was starting to worry that I'd never see you again."

An Kohli allowed herself to be hugged but barely placed her own hands on Max's body. He pulled back, a puzzled look on his face. "Hey baby, what's up? Aren't you pleased to see me?"

"I'm sorry. I'm a bit bruised from my recent experiences." An Kohli evaded a direct answer.

"Why, what have you been doing? Wrestling grunties?"

"Something like that."

"Can you tell me what you were doing now that you've done it?"

"Sure, why not. Tell you what, buy me a drink and you can have the whole story."

* * *

"That's it. That's what you do for a living?"

An Kohli gave Max an appraising look. There was no doubt about it, if he was really Tiger then he was also an accomplished actor.

"Yep, that's what I do. Two more of the Fell won't be making people's lives a misery anymore and another of the Magi is safely recovered. Plus, of course, a sizeable payment into my bank account."

Max's brain worked rapidly to assess the importance of what she had just told him. It took Attila and Desire out of the game, but that wasn't what was really important. They could be rescued at a later date, if the rest of the Fell really wanted them to be rescued. More importantly, far more importantly in fact, An Kohli could lead them to the GCIE. Smash them and smash the Magi eggs that had been recovered and the Fell could rule unchallenged. It was what they had always wanted. It wouldn't matter if the other five eggs were found or not. The GCIE were right, it was all or none. Five Magi would divide the galaxy if they tried to rule. That would create chaos and people like the Fell thrived on chaos. Either way he could see no downside.

So long, of course, as An Kohli didn't suspect his true identity. That could lead to … complications.

In that instant An Kohli knew. She didn't need to wait for Den to capture an image and run it through facial recognition software. He should have been more surprised. Questions should have been tumbling from his lips; he should have been expressing concern over the dangerous nature of her employment. None of those things had happened. Instead she had sensed his brain working feverishly to try and work out what the new information meant to him. News of the disposal of two Fell members would have serious implication for him. He would be wondering what had happened to the ship, the Shogun; his escape route from Ecos.

"You've gone very quiet." An Kohli filled the gap. Let's see what he comes up with.

"Sorry, you just took me a bit by surprise, that was all. I don't meet very many bounty hunters."

"You must have had some inkling that I wasn't in a routine line of employment. After all, how many females do you know that go around with one of these strapped to their thigh?" she patted the Menafield Pulsar in its hand tooled leather holster.

"Well, I did wonder. I thought you might be police… or something. When we met your picture was all over the galacticnet and you said you were in law enforcement. But you didn't say what type of law enforcement."

Yes, thought An Kohli and the galacticnet reports all said that I was a member of the Guild of Bounty Hunters. Nice try. "Well, I am something in law enforcement. I'm a bounty hunter."

"You must think me something of a dunce."

"I think that you seemed to lack any curiosity about what I did for a living. We had plenty of time to talk before I left." She also lacked that same curiosity, she had to admit. She hadn't asked the questions that she should have.

"Yeah. Well, there seemed always to be something else to talk about."

"By the way, on that score you never told me what it is that you do for a living."

"I buy and sell. It isn't very interesting. Certainly not as glamorous as being a bounty hunter."

"What sort of things do you buy and sell?"

"I buy whatever people are selling and I sell what people are buying. Like I said, it's not that interesting."

"Well, I'm interested. Give me an example, what was the last thing you bought."

An Kohli could see his mind working to try to come up with an answer.

"I bought some information."

"Ah, well, I can appreciate that. Information is one of the most valuable commodities in the galaxy. I couldn't do my job without it. Even I've bought information from time to time. So what information was it?"

"I'm afraid I can't tell you that. It's very sensitive and if it got into the public domain it could harm the buyer's business and my reputation."

Nicely done, thought An Kohli. You've closed down that line of conversation without revealing a damn thing. "Look, I don't want to get too personal, but where is it you come from. I can't quite place you in the galaxy."

It was true that Max, she continued to think of him as Max in the absence of any other name, could pass for a member of dozens of species. No doubt it had helped him along the way. He could have passed for human, one of the inhabitants of Ecos or Earth, but she doubted that he was either.

Max considered how he might answer that question. He could answer it truthfully of course, but that would provide the start point of a trail of breadcrumbs that could lead to his true identity. On the other hand, if he provided a false location, made up on the spur of the moment, that might be just as revealing if she decided to check up on him.

He wished he had thought to create a proper cover story for himself. But why would she check up on him? She would only do that if she was suspicious and so far as he knew he had done nothing to arouse her suspicions. On the other hand why had she started asking all these questions? Was she suspicious, or was she just passing the time of day as they renewed their acquaintanceship? His head was starting to hurt as the paranoia of the criminal mind gnawed at him.

The problem for Max Wallfly was that even though he had An Kohli sitting within a few sim of him he could do nothing. There were plenty of drugs that would have her singing like a canary, some of which she might even survive, but there was no way of getting her off the planet.

He could snatch here down here, but as soon as it was noticed that she was missing there would be a search and he had no one here who could help him keep her hidden. On the other hand he had no way of getting her off the planet. If he'd had access to the Shogun's shuttle craft that would be different, but he had no idea where the Shogun was right then and the Captain wasn't answering his messages. He suspected that An Kohli was also behind that silence.

Running through An Kohli's mind were very similar thoughts. She could draw her pulsar and place him under arrest on suspicion of having committed any number of crimes, but without an identity she would have to place him into custody on Ecos while the facts were established. Eventually he would either be released because there was no proof he had committed a crime or he would bribe his way off the planet. While the Ecosians seemed to be a pretty honest bunch everyone had a price, especially if other sorts of pressure could be brought to bear. Everyone had a family to protect.

That meant getting him off the planet and then grabbing him, which was far harder to do. She would have to think about that.

Across the room a male and female strode. Had they not been a male and female they would have appeared identical. Marty and Davina, no doubt, though goodness knew which one of the many.

"An Kohli, we heard you were back. We wondered if Gala and Den were with you. You left so suddenly last time that we didn't get a chance to say goodbye."

It was at that point that Max Wallfly hit upon the solution to his conundrum.

Glossary

Grunty - (pl grunties). Large bear like animals with ferocious claws. Travelling fairs used to offer members of the public the chance to wrestle a grunty in return for a cash prize. The showman rarely had to pay out and the local accident and emergency units used to keep extra stocks of suture and needles on standby when the fair was in town. The practice has since been banned across the galaxy for being cruel to members of the public. It must be said that the public can often display incredible levels of stupidity when there is a cash prize on offer.

Neonoral virus - An extremely virulent virus that is fatal to hundreds of species in the galaxy and can cause severe long term ill effects to hundreds more. While some drugs have been found to be helpful in alleviating the symptoms of the disease the efforts of researchers throughout the galaxy have failed to identify an anti-virus capable of effecting a cure. Consequently any planet where the virus is found is immediately placed in quarantine until it has been infection free for at least fifty years.

PANIC - Pandemic Advisory Navigation Information Communication. A message broadcast by drones orbiting a planet where there is known to be an outbreak of disease in pandemic proportions. Exaggerations of the degree of risk aren't unknown, which generally cause the public to overreact. But hey – omelettes and eggs.

16 – Death At Dawn

Marty was woken by a thunderous roar, unlike anything he had ever heard before. He stumbled from his bed and staggered across his hut to the door.

Above the trees, just beyond the edge of the village, hung the ugly bulk of some sort of flying vehicle. It wasn't the familiar egg shape of a shuttle of the sort used by their friends Gala and Den, or even by the media beings that had spent so much time poking cameras and microphones into their faces, asking questions about them and their lives. Thankfully that was over; or at least he thought it was over. Maybe they had come back. Or maybe this was Gala's ship. She had said that they had another ship in orbit around the planet.

It was smaller than their own mother ship, now covered with weeds and fungus, absorbed into the forest where it would eventually be consumed by nature. But at the same time it was much bigger than the shuttles he had seen. It also had strange protrusions from which emerged long, thin, tube like objects. As he watched they started to turn until the tubes were pointing in their direction.

"What is it?" Davina arrived from her neighbouring hut, still rubbing the sleep from her eyes.

"I'm not sure. It's a space ship of some sort, I guess, but I don't know whose."

"Do you think it might be Gala?"

"I don't know. I hope so. She was nice."

"Maybe its Den." Her tone of voice suggested that might not be quite such welcome news. He had a funny way of looking at the females which made them feel as though he was undressing them with his eyes, which was weird because they didn't wear much in the way of clothes in the first place.

The rest of the village's inhabitants had started to gather, filling up the spaces between the huts on that side of the village as they strained their eyes to pierce the gloom and identify the new arrivals.

The strange craft didn't touch down, but a ramp did extend downwards, suggesting that someone was about to disembark. Marty stepped forward. As he had been the first to see the ship, the honour of greeting the new arrivals would fall to him, just as it had fallen to Marty when Gala and Den had first arrived.

There was movement at the top of the ramp and two figures ran down it. Neither was Gala nor Den. They carried objects, but they weren't cameras or microphones. Marty recognised them from images he had seen. They were long pulsars, fired from the shoulder to give greater stability and improved accuracy. He didn't like the look of that. He started to back away.

He half turned to the nearest figure behind him. It was a Davina. "Take the younglings back inside. I don't think…" It was at that point that a pulsar blast hit him in the back. Davina would never find out what he didn't think.

More figures were descending the ramp. As the echo of the first shot died away a youngling screamed, the piercing cry being quickly taken up by the other younglings. Adults started grabbing at their hands, dragging them away to the illusory safety of the nearest huts. They were already too late. The pipe-like objects on the strange ship started firing, revealing them to be ship mounted pulsars. One by one the village's buildings were blasted into atoms or set alight, removing their refuge. A Marty picked up a youngling and sprinted towards the edge of the forest, but it was too far away. He was cut down before he got even half way. The youngling flew from his arms to land with a heavy thud. The youngling set up a loud wailing, clambering to his feet and stood still, too shocked to move.

The crowd shrank backwards deeper into the village, seeking safety wherever they could find it. Adults grabbed up their ineffective hunting weapons. Someone grabbed the village's only pulsar from its charging point on the outer wall of the meeting hut. He flicked off the safety catch and levelled it at the advancing figures. He fired once and the nearest one sank to its knees, and then into a heap on the ground.

The Marty who had fired the shot dropped the weapon, horrified at having killed another being. A Davina was made of sterner stuff. There were younglings to be protected and she wasn't going to let her natural dislike of violence get in the way of that. She scooped up the weapon, handed the Marty the youngling she had been carrying and turned to defend the two of them. She fired once, twice, but before she could get off a third shot she was targeted and fell dead.

The pulsar was picked up once again, but the Marty who now held it realised that fighting the attackers in the village was untenable. They were too exposed. They had to get into the forest where they would be hidden by the foliage.

"Spread out!" He commanded as he ran. "Make for the trees." Once within the safety of their concealment he could rally them into a fighting force and perhaps mount a counter attack. Not that he actually knew what a counter attack was.

He took a last look back towards the figures of their attackers. A Davina had been caught and was now being forced to the ground. Marty had no idea what the being who held her was about to do, but he knew it wouldn't be good. He took careful aim, squeezed the trigger of the pulsar and Davina cried out in the fraction of a second before she died. The figure holding her jumped up, gesticulating in anger, directing others to find the being that had robbed him of his prize.

Marty ran. As he did so the pulsar gave out a soft beep, warning him that its charge was critically low. It had enough energy remaining for perhaps one or two more shots.

He reached the illusory safety of the forest's edge. Around him he heard the crashing and swishing of vegetation as others arrived. "The Great Tree." He called, directing his brothers and sisters to the only clear landmark available to them. The top of that monstrous growth could be seen for miles around. Some of the braver brothers and sisters had climbed it and claimed to be able to see to the other side of the planet.

It took an hour to reach it and another hour for the last of the stragglers to catch up. Most carried or held the hands of the younglings. Some of the older ones were wriggling to be let free, but the adults weren't going to let them go.

Marty did a quick count. Thirty or so adults and perhaps forty younglings. That latter figure was a relief. It accounted for most of those in the village. But only thirty adults. That wasn't so good; it was less than half.

It didn't take them long to decide what to do. To fight against weapons such as those used by their attackers was suicidal. Their only choice was to continue to flee into the vast tracts of the forest.

"We'll take a few minutes to prepare ourselves." Marty said as calmly as he could. They started to prepare the colours they need to create camouflage. With spit they smoothed soil into a brown paste. They crushed leaves into it to give them shades of green. Berries were added to give a reddish hue. Soon their bodies were daubed and streaked to allow them to blend perfectly with their background.

From the direction of the village came loud cracks of pulsar fire followed by the crashing roar of trees falling. Rather than following them through the forest it sounded as though their assailants were removing the forest met by met.

* * *

The ramp had been withdrawn from beneath the ship to allow it to pass over the wreckage of the village without it snagging on any obstructions. The attackers became more methodical, searching huts before destroying them. A female was discovered, alive and terrified. A crowd gathered around but a leader of some sort broke it up. Only the one who had discovered her was allowed to remain while the others were chivvied onwards.

Once through the village the ship started its real work, opening up the width of the pulsar beams so that they acted like a giant scythe to cut down everything that grew. Timber and vegetation was blasted away to create a route through the forest.

As they stepped forward once again an arrow flew at them, taking an attacker through the centre of his chest. The source of the attack couldn't be identified. Pulsars were fired but with no obvious result. The attackers reached to their belts and found the goggles in their pouches. They pulled them over their head, turning their world into a kaleidoscope of colours ranging from deepest blue to brightest yellow. The bright red of a living being moved amongst the darker colours of the foliage and a pulsar shot quickly terminated another life.

17 – Codeword Attitude

It was hard for An Kohli to keep Max Wallfly at arm's length. While her head said it was a definite no, her loins told her yes, yes, yes. In the end she resisted temptation more by remaining on board the Adastra than through her own willpower. She claimed other engagements, working with the local police and other authorities, but Max wasn't fooled.

It didn't matter to him. He had set things in motion and it was only a matter of time before An Kohli stuck her head into the noose entirely of her own volition.

"Here he is." Gala announced, pulling Max Wallfly's image onto the screen. "Real name Castor Macati, the son of miners on the planet Karakara in the Faron system. He's been to prison once, as a young being. Since then he's either kept his nose clean or, more likely, he hasn't been caught." She pulled up a second image. "This interesting. As you can see it's Max, but look who he's with."

"Roselee." An Kohli breathed.

"That's right. Does that make him a member of the Fell, or is it just a coincidence?"

"It's good enough for me. Can we link him directly to any crimes. I need to be able to arrest him and have him stay arrested. If I can find a planet that wants him, or wants to solve a crime for which he fits the frame, I can take him off and we're out of here."

"You know how good Roselee was at covering her tracks. If he was working for her, or with her, there won't be any smoking guns."

"Roselee went to prison, don't forget." Den interjected. It was he who had snatched the image that had allowed Lazarus to run the facial recognition software that had led to Wallfly's true identity being discovered.

"She went to prison for murder in front of a dozen witnesses. If she had just walked out of the bank, as she was supposed to, she would have got away free and clear. She was stupid, acting on the spur of the moment. I think our Tiger is a lot more circumspect." An

Kohli slumped into her chair once more. "So, we still have nothing that would support an arrest."

"Looks like it. What do you want to do now?" Gala was getting bored with Ecos. It was a nice enough place, but after playing hide and seek with pirates at Aragan she wanted to party a bit. The Ecosian idea of a party was a glass of warm wine and a hedgehog made of bits of cheese and pineapple on sticks.

Den must have been reading her mind. "You're going to be off after the next Magus egg soon and the highlight of our stay here has been the visit to the prune museum. Come on An Kohli, we need some serious fun."

"I agree with you. You deserve a break and so do I. Tell you what, if I haven't found a way of getting Wallfly off Ecos in five days from now, we go. Now we know who he is and have an image of him we can get it posted across the galaxy and if he shows up anywhere with any sort of justice system still in place we'll know about it.

"That's more like it. So what do we do in the meantime?"

"Well, there always the prune museum again."

* * *

"Gala, please help us."

The call had come unexpectedly, as do most such calls. The image on the screen was of one of the Martys, his face camouflaged, his voice frantic.

"Is that pulsar fire I can here?" Gala responded.

"Yes. We've been attacked. We saw a ship landing. We thought it was you, or perhaps some more of those media people. When we went to greet them they started shooting. Now they are pursuing us through the forest killing everyone they can find. The village is on fire, so many of us dead."

"OK, Look, we'll come to help as soon as we can. Take your people and hide in the forest. You'll be safe there."

"We are doing that, but they still find us. They seem to be able to see through the trees."

Infra-red, Gala concluded. Tracking them through their own body heat, which would stand out against the cool of the vegetation in which they sought refuge. Spears and bows against pulsars. They didn't really have a chance. It would take too long to mount a proper rescue mission. It would have to be them; An Kohli, Den and herself.

"Look, just hang on in there. We'll be there as soon as we can."

She closed the communications channel and called An Kohli.

She was sitting in a coffee bar with Max Wallfly, having one of their interminable conversations in which he tried to talk her into bed and she found more and more elaborate excuses why she couldn't comply, while at the same time trying to maintain the semblance of their relationship while she tried to come up with a plan to get Max off of Ecos and into a place where she could take him prisoner.

"Hi Gala. What can I do for you?" She said with relief, hoping the call would give her a reason to terminate her 'date' with Max.

"Can you talk freely?"

"One moment." She stood up, mouthing to Max that she needed to take the call and that she also needed a little bit of privacy.

Max tried to suppress a smile. He had no doubt what the call was about. He had been expecting it for most of the day. An Kohli, summoned to the rescue once again. Well, her grand standing desire to be a hero would be her undoing this time.

"I'm sorry Max, I've got to go. Something's come up, a work thing. Look, I probably won't be coming back here again."

"That's OK. You've got my number. When you've done whatever it is you have to do just let me know and we can arrange to meet up. My business here is about done as well, so I'll be moving on soon anyway."

"OK, that sounds good." He stood and they performed their sham farewells, An Kohli even managing to squeeze out a tear, though more at the thought of the carnage being visited on the Martys and Davinas than out of any genuine affection for Max Wallfly. That had died its final death the day she had discovered his true identity. Further investigation by Gala had revealed that he was linked to drug dealing and slavery on an industrial scale. Who knew what other miseries could be laid at his door. Unfortunately he was too clever to leave evidence behind so there were no warrants on which she could use to arrest and deport him.

* * *

"The planet's orbit is empty." Gala reported.

"Anywhere else a ship might be hidden? On the planet itself or maybe on its moon."

"No. I'm getting an ion trail. There has been something in orbit recently, but no trace of it now."

"Can you raise anyone down on the surface?"

"I'll give it a try." It took a few minutes, but at last they were able to see the image of Marty on the viewing screen.

"Thank you for coming. Thank you so much." He was in tears as he spoke.

"What's happening down there? Are you still under attack?"

"No. They left as suddenly as they arrived. One minute they were killing and… and…"

"It's OK, you don't have to go into details."

"Thank you. It's so painful. Anyway, one minute they were there and the next they weren't. That was four days ago. Since then we've been trying to clean up. Burying our dead, repairing the buildings, that sort of thing. They destroyed the medi-sys hut. We can't…. we can't…." he broke down into more sobbing.

"It's OK. We're here now. We'll be down soon to help you."

"Just one question." An Kohli leaned into vision. "Did they take anyone with them?"

"You mean prisoners?"

"Yes." She actually meant slaves, but didn't wish to say the word to someone who was already in such a fragile condition.

"No. We have accounted for everyone, living or dead."

"Thank you. As Gala said, we'll be down as soon as we can."

As Lazarus guided the ship into orbit for them they pondered the motive for the raid.

"The attack was typical of the sort of raid carried out by Meklons. But it only makes sense if they either steal or take slaves." An Kohli summarised. "The clones have nothing of value to steal and Marty said that no one was taken as a slave. I don't get it."

"There is an explanation, but you're not going to like it." Den's voice came across the communications channel from the Pradua, which he had piloted from Ecos.

"Tell me anyway."

"Well, you were struggling to find a way to lure Max off of Ecos. It could be that he was also trying to do the same to you. This was his solution. And if I'm right it appears to have worked."

The silence that greeted this conclusion told them that they all agreed it was a viable theory.

"If that's true then it means the Meklons can't have gone far."

"They don't need to. They take themselves off to the nearest star system that a wormhole will take them to and wait for us to arrive. Their navi-com can do the same sums ours will do, so they'll get a good estimate of our arrival time. Then they come back and we're supposed to be sat down there waiting to be picked off."

"And Max Wallfly?"

"He rents a ship and is probably no more than a few hours behind us."

"So all those beings down there died just to lure me here?" An Kohli's voice could hardly be heard above the quiet hum of the air conditioning system.

"You know how ruthless these beings are. Look at what they did on Aragan."

"You know, sometimes I wish I wasn't a member of the Guild. Sometimes I wish I could give them what they really deserve." Gala couldn't be sure, but she thought she saw a rare tear roll down her friend's face.

"Maybe you'll get your chance." Gala patted her arm. "They still have to take us. Many have tried, few have succeeded."

"The sensible thing to do is to get to safety and organise a hunt for the pirates."

"We've no idea who they are or where they're based. If they're working for the Fell then they're well protected. You won't get justice that way."

"But I'm placing you and Den in danger once again."

"That's what I signed up for. Besides, these beings mean something to me. They're nice, gentle beings. They hurt no one. All they want is to be left alone to get on with their lives. Rather strange lives perhaps, but we've all seen stranger. They didn't deserve this and I for one want someone to pay for what happened to them."

"What about you, Den?"

There was a long pause while Den fought with his conscience. He seemed to be doing that a lot recently. He wasn't sure he'd even had a conscience before he'd started hanging around with An Kohli.

"I'm with Gala. These beings may be the weirdest thing since that brown stuff we put on our toast when we were on Earth, but they didn't deserve what happened to them. Someone has to pay. Besides, I don't think they went to all this trouble to kill you. I think you're more valuable to them alive. You have the information that will lead you to the Magus eggs and you also know where the GCIE are hiding. That makes you valuable dead or alive."

"In that case, we'll make sure someone does pay. Lazarus. Send a message to the Guild: 'Codeword Attitude.' And add our position." That codeword required all bounty hunters who were able to do so to come to the aid of their colleague that had sent it. They may arrive too late, but they would arrive and perhaps finish the job if An Kohli, Gala and Den were no longer in a position to do so.

"What do we do now?"

"We decide whether we want to meet the Meklons up here or down there. Where do we stand the best chance?"

"Up here it only takes a lucky pulsar shot to destroy the ship. Even a small hole in the hull could be enough to kill us." That was Gala's view. She knew how vulnerable her baby might be.

"But down there we're on foot in terrain we're not suited to." That was Den's opinion.

"But down there we have the clones to help us. They do know the terrain. They also survived the attack."

"But we're putting them in danger again." Gala protested.

"They're in danger anyway. If the Meklons kill or capture us they'll go back down to finish the job, but this time they will take slaves." An Kohli had thought the issue through to its logical conclusion. "They're not going to go away and leave the clones in peace; they're worth money to them."

"So we may as well die alongside them. Is that what you're saying?" Den's voice sounded resigned to his imminent demise.

"I'm rather hoping we live alongside them." An Kohli hoped her voice sounded more confident than she felt.

Glossary

Meklon - A collective noun for a group of people who live outside the law. They live a wide variety of criminal lifestyles but one of the most common is space piracy. The origin of the term is lost in the mists of time. Some say it is taken from Mik Lon, a legendary figure who robbed from the rich, there being very few sane reasons to rob from the poor. Legend has it that he then shared the proceeds of his robberies with the poor but that is just lunacy as that would make the poor richer and he'd then have to rob them as well. Another version is that a planet called Meklon, location unknown, was a safe haven for a group of these criminals. Neither version is verified by the galacticnet, but then again very little is.

18 – Send In The Clones

From their surveillance cameras in the Adastra, cruising high above the planet, they could see the swathe that the Meklons had cut through the rain forest in their pursuit of the clones.

Once the decision had been made, Gala had contacted Marty again, to gather information on the tactics that the Meklon pirates had used. They hadn't been subtle and the scars they had left on the rainforest would take years to heal. The undergrowth would grow back quickly enough, but the trees would take generations to grow once again to their original splendour.

"Den, I want you to take the Pradua down to the surface and find a suitable landing site. We'll ask the clones to help you camouflage it. They're good at that. I'd like to keep it as a bit of a surprise for the Meklon when they come back."

"Sure thing, An Kohli. Do you just want me to sit there and wait?"

"Yes, so make sure you don't wander off. When I shout for you I need you to be there at once. Keep the engine at idle and the pulsars ready to fire. Your target is almost certainly going to be that craft they had, whatever it is."

They still hadn't worked that one out. The Meklon favoured ships that weren't suitable for low level flight, especially after they had carried out the sorts of modifications that they favoured, so whatever it was it was something new. It was also a powerful weapon, as the ruins of the rain forest testified.

But the Pradua was fast and nimble even at tree top height. Den was a good pilot; not perhaps as good as Gala, but good enough. When the time came he would make it dance around the strange craft and bring it crashing down to the planet's surface. Or so An Kohli hoped.

"We, on the other hand," An Kohli turned her attention to her co-pilot, "Are going to empty the Adastra's armoury and take very pulsar we can carry and hand them out to the clones. We're going to turn a bunch of hunter gatherers into a modern army."

"What about the infra-red capability?"

"Metal foil. They wrap it around themselves and it keeps their body heat in, so instead of shining like a beacon they will be cooler than the leaves around them."

"Metal foil reflects light. Not so good when you're trying to hide."

"We'll work on that. The pirates can't use infra-red and ordinary vision at the same time. All we have to do is keep them guessing for long enough to take them down."

"And what about Max? Or maybe I should call him Tiger." Max was a very personal name and might be a painful one for An Kohli to keep using.

"Tiger is too noble a name for that scumbag. No, just call him Max. Well, we don't know if he's going to turn up at all. Even if he does turn up he may not come down to the planet. He may stay in orbit waiting for us to be brought to him. If he does he's not our problem. That's why I sent out the codeword."

"What about the Adastra? I'm not happy leaving it up here with pirates on the loose."

"Lazarus, is the moon safe to land on?"

"The moon is an inert planetoid with no atmosphere. It has a gravity of one sixth that of the planet. If you land the Adastra on it there will be a ninety four percent probability of a safe relaunch."

"I'll take those odds. Once landed what are the chances of the Adastra being discovered?"

"In the event of a thorough scan it is a one hundred percent probability."

"Thank you Lazarus. Well, I don't think anyone is going to be looking for the Adastra until the business on the planet is concluded. By that time we will either have won or we'll be dead. If we win then we can probably get to the Adastra before anyone up here discovers its whereabouts."

Gala didn't look happy but she had to concede that they were needed on the planet first and the Adastra would have to take its chances. If they didn't survive it didn't matter anyway; the Adastra was part of the reward for the victors. "Well, I'm setting the failsafe, anyway."

An Kohli smiled. The failsafe, the small explosive charge in the fuel tank that would turn the ship into a space borne bomb if anyone entered the access code incorrectly three times. There wouldn't be a fourth time. Not for them nor for the Adastra.

"That's fine. The Adastra's insured."

"Yes. For theft and accidental damage such as being hit by a meteor or getting sucked into a black hole. Not for being blown up by a booby trap installed by the co-pilot."

"I promise not to grass on you."

As they left the command deck they just failed to hear the computer say "And I suppose it doesn't matter if I get blown up."

* * *

The wreck of the Namsat Elba provided some useful additional resources, including a stock of reflective survival blankets. The clones had never found a use for them but, conscious of the need to avoid waste, had never destroyed them. It took only a short demonstration by An Kohli, using a pair of infra-red glasses she had brought from the Adastra, for the clones to appreciate the problem.

They experimented with their homemade camouflage cream but it didn't adhere well to the surface of the shiny material. Even if they hid in thick undergrowth the foil rustled and crackled every time they moved. However, the clones were used to adapting and came up with their own solution.

Making light lattice frames they covered them with vegetation and secured the reflective blankets to one side. When they hid behind this flimsy screen they were effectively invisible on the infra-red spectrum, while at the same time the vegetation provided camouflage in the visible spectrum. It would allow them to fire their pulsars undetected.

An Kohli and Gala surveyed the ruined rain forest and planned their defences. As well as the array of pulsars they also had grenades and a single rocket launcher, complete with four missiles. The rockets weren't powerful, probably not large enough to take down the mystery craft, but they would destroy anything less substantial than a concrete blockhouse.

An Kohli decided on a funnel like defensive pattern contained within the undamaged sides of the gash the pirates had created in the forest. They would lure the pirates towards the thin end of the funnel while the clones at the side held their fire, hidden behind the reflective screens. When the pirates had moved well inside the funnel the trap would be sprung.

The dangerous part was luring the pirates into the trap.

There was a committee meeting going on to discuss this. A clone committee meeting was no short affair. All the members of the community had to have their say, even if what they had to say was a repetition of what had already been said, or even if it wasn't relevant to the topic. While An Kohli found the process frustrating she recognised that there was no way to hurry things along.

He communicator bleeped and she pulled it from its pouch in her belt. She read the message sent by the computer, then strode quickly into the centre of the circle of clones. "OK, guys and gals, sorry to interrupt, but we need a decision now. I've just had word from my ship that the pirates have returned and are entering orbit. They'll be here before long and if we're not ready, well I think we know what will happen if we're not ready."

Surprisingly it hadn't been difficult to persuade the clones of the need to fight. While they didn't really understand the concept of slavery, their presumed fate if the pirates returned, they did understand that their way of life would be destroyed forever if the pirates prevailed. They had agreed readily to fight alongside An Kohli, Gala and Den in defence of what was left of their village and their brothers and sisters.

However, the committee process was not to be subverted and after An Kohli had stopped talking the Marty who had held the floor at the time of the interruption merely continued to express his view.

Someone had to take charge.

An Kohli ground her teeth in frustration and returned to Gala's side. "They know and respect you." An Kohli whispered into her co-pilot's ear. "If you start telling them what to do I'm sure they'll do it."

"You think? Well, It's worth a try. What do you want them to do?"

"Get those that are detailed for the sides of the funnel to take up their positions, then lead the rest down to the end where the cover starts again."

"But what bait are you going to use to attract the pirates?"

"The best there is. Me."

It took three attempts for Gala to get their attention, but once she had it she discovered that An Kohli was right. A little bit of leadership went a long way. The clones allowed her to take charge and hurried to obey her instructions. One Marty and Davina herded the younglings together, picked up a bag of food, bows and quivers full of arrows. They would try to find a safe place, far from anywhere they might be discovered after the fight. If the adults fell the younglings had to have a chance to survive unmolested.

The rest of the adults took up their designated positions. Of the thirty or so clones that remained about half were armed with pulsars, the rest with their hunting bows and spears. Six were positioned at the narrow end of the funnel while the remaining twenty four spread themselves along the sides, pulling their lightweight screens in front of them and crouching down out of sight. An Kohli had made sure that the majority of the pulsars were along the sides, where they would have maximum impact.

From what had been discovered in questioning the clones about the previous attack, An Kohli knew they would face a force of between twenty and forty pirates. That matched them quite evenly. Her force would also have the element of surprise on their side.

What they didn't have, however, was the craft that transported the pirates down to the planet.

As it descended towards the wreckage of the village An Kohli peered at it through binoculars. She thought it was some sort of passenger shuttle of the type they had used to get from New Earth to the surface of planet Earth. It used conventional impulse jets to control its descent, but then appeared to use anti-gravity systems to keep it in a hover above the ground. That made it more efficient as it preserved its fuel to allow it to take off again and there was no thrust to throw dust or debris around and hamper the activities of the pirates on the ground. The main problem, for her and the clones at least, was its hedgehog like array of pulsars mounted in rotating turrets.

The craft settled into a hover over the village and the ramp descended. She counted carefully as the pirates ran down and spread out into a circular defensive ring below their ship. Whoever had trained them knew what he was doing, she admitted grudgingly. Pirates were rarely so well organised. For a start they were usually high on drink or drugs, or both, and to the forefront of their mind was women or money, depending on gender preferences, and it was the first to reach either that got the biggest share of the spoils.

As the ramp emptied she had counted thirty four. There was also the on-board crew, of course, but they were Den's problem.

She stepped out from the fringe of the forest. Hanging from a sling across her chest was the rocket launcher. She hefted it in her hands then raised it, pressing the butt into her shoulder then angling her head so that her cheek rested on the smooth plastic and she was able to take aim through the sights. She wasn't too fussy about what she hit, but that wasn't her purpose. Her purpose was to scream 'Hey, look, I'm over here'. The ramp beneath the craft was nice and big. That would serve as her aiming point.

She squeezed the trigger and the launcher leapt in her hands as the first rocket was released. At once the launcher started to whine as it recharged ready for the next shot. An Kohli was pleased to see that her aim had been true as one of the pirates flew into the air, hit the underside of the craft and dropped hard onto the ground. The ramp was a tangled mass of metal where the rocket had struck it. She immediately shifted her aim to the vast craft that hovered above the pirates. She fired the remaining three rockets in quick succession but they seemed to have no effect. Fireballs exploded on the craft's armour but when the smoke cleared there was no apparent damage. She had found the only vulnerable spot. Throwing the now useless launcher to the ground she drew her Menafield from its holster.

But the rockets had done the trick. Thirty three pairs of eyes were drawn towards her as though by a magnet. The only pirate paying her no attention was the one that lay writhing on the ground, the victim of her first rocket.

Someone must have given a command because, almost as one, they turned and started to march along the length of the clearing towards her. However, it was no headlong rush. They maintained their formation, scanning the trees on either side, their pulsars swinging in controlled arcs of fire. Some were wearing infra-red goggles and some used only their naked eyes. Above them the strange craft moved forward at a matching pace, the mangled ramp acting like a plough blade when it encountered any of the tangle of vegetation created during their previous visit. Bright metal shone from the places where the rockets had impacted. There was a screech of metal, followed by a heavy thud, as the damaged ramp hit an immovable tree-trunk. From inside the craft it was jettisoned and fell to the ground.

An Kohli watched as the turret at the front of the ship swung in her direction. She braced herself, knowing what was to come. The energy pulse would travel at close to light speed, so if she waited until she saw it coming it would already be too late.

The turret stopped and the angle of the pulsar barrels changed until all she could see of them was twin black dots. She threw herself to one side a fraction of a second before the pulsar fired. She felt the air crackle and fizz around her as she hit the ground and crawled into cover. Her long purple hair stood on end, raised by the static of the pulsar blast's passing. Getting to her knees she scuttled behind one of the screens, where she found a Marty grinning at her.

"That was close." He observed.

"Missed me by a met." She dismissed the incident, though her adrenalin levels told her it had been closer than was good for her.

Lying in the middle of the detritus of the destroyed forest a branch protruded, leafy fingers reaching skywards. To the casual eye it looked like any one of the other branches that had been left behind after the attack of the previous week, the leaves curling as they died, but it had more significance than that.

The pirates edged carefully along the broad swathe in the forest, passing by the branch and ignoring it. As the last of the thirty three pirates, at the back of the defensive circle, passed it by, the shadow of the strange craft drifted over it. Behind her screen Davina raised her pulsar and took careful aim at the rearmost pirate, just as Gala had taught her, gently squeezing the trigger. The pulsar bucked in her hand and the pirate fell dead, never knowing what had hit him.

The single shot unleashed a torrent of pulsar fire and a hailstorm of arrows. Within seconds half the pirates lay dead or wounded. The remainder threw themselves to the ground, seeking somewhere to hide.

The survivors scrabbled for their infra-red goggles but they were almost useless. The occasional bright image would show itself as one of the clones revealed themselves for an instant while they took a shot, then disappeared once again.

The pulsars in the hovering ship began to fire, ripping away the cover of the vegetation.

"Den! You're up!" An Kolhi barked into her communicator.

There was a silence and she wondered if Den had perhaps fallen asleep or maybe he had wandered away from his own communicator. She was about to start cursing him when she heard the increasing howl of the Pradua's engines as they powered up.

"On my way." She heard his reassuring voice.

"Prioritise the pulsars at the front of the ship. They're the ones causing the most damage."

"Got that."

If the pulsars at the front could be neutralised the hunted could start to become the hunters, breaking cover to haul down their prey, cowering now behind whatever minuscule cover they could find.

The Pradua thundered over An Kohli's head, its pulsars already firing. It screamed over the front of the pirate ship with seemingly no space between the two craft. Den soared upwards into steep banking turn that reversed his course and brought the Pradua back around, firing from above and behind the ship. The front turret, the one whose pulsar had been causing the most damage, disintegrated in a mass of flying metal that fell pattering to the ground. Small fires started amongst the undergrowth.

The pirate ship's nose rose as the pilot tried to get it away from the ground. If it could get higher it might be able to defend itself against this new threat, but whatever the ship was it was too slow to respond. The impulse rockets fired, but with the anti-gravity motors working at the same time it slewed sideways, tearing the tops off of the nearest trees.

Den needed no second invitation. He swung the Pradua into another tight turn that took it around to the exposed side of the ship. Skimming the tree tops he fired his pulsars and opened up a great gash in the side of his target.

Smoke started to emerge, a thin stream at first then quickly developing into billowing clouds. The ship sank gently onto the tree tops, but they couldn't support its weight. The open side tilted downwards and the great craft slid almost gently down to hit the ground with a thunderous crash. A tree fell across it, followed by loose branches, then it lay still.

There was a series of small explosions as emergency hatches flew off the upper surface of the craft. Figures started to climb out, only to be met by arrows or pulsar fire. The Pradua came screaming down at a steep angle and pumped more pulsar fire into the stricken ship, performing the coup-de-grace.

"OK, Den. Break off. Good work." From the time she had first ordered Den into the fight until that moment, barely three minutes had elapsed.

"What do you want me to do now"

"See if you can take a look at what opposition we have above us. Don't try to pick a fight, just a sneaky peek type reconnaissance. Got it?"

"You can rest assured that I have no intention of picking a fight. I'll stay inside the atmosphere until I'm around the other side of the planet and then I'll go into a low orbit and sneak back to take a look at what's up there."

The Pradua had disappeared behind the tree tops but now it shrieked back across the skies before standing on its tail and soaring upwards on the glowing disks of its rocket motors. There was a thunderous crack as the sound barrier was breached and the ship dwindled to a dot before disappearing into the high clouds.

Show off, thought An Kohli as she returned her attention to what was going on around her. The clones had split onto pairs and were now hunting their quarry across the open clearing. The pirates fought back, but without the cover from their fighting ship their confidence evaporated. One by one they discarded their weapons and threw themselves on the mercy of the clones before they could be killed.

While the clones fought like tigers they weren't cut out for revenge. They accepted the surrender of the pirates where it was offered and a growing group of prisoners, bound hand and foot, was assembled in the centre of the clearing. Soon the fighting had ceased and it was time to count the cost among the Martys and Davinas.

It wasn't as bad as An Kohli had expected. One Marty had been killed when the ship had started firing into the forest, crushed by a falling branch. Another had stayed out of the cover of their reflective shield for a fraction too long and been hit by a pulsar. There were a few suffering cuts and scratches from the vegetation over which they had fought but otherwise they were unscathed. Of the thirty four pirates that had walked down the ramp of the ship, five were wounded, ten dead and the others prisoners. Seven of the crew of the ship were dead, either as a result of Den's fire or from the impact when the craft had crashed to the ground. Three had surrendered.

An Kohli surveyed the prisoners. Several were Jackons, who were no good to her. They wouldn't succumb to intimidation and their mental capacity restricted them to point-and-shoot duties; muscle with little brain behind it. She recognised a couple of Cebalarians, a few lupines or their sub species and what may have been Earthlings. There were also two Durantines.

Durantines were so untrustworthy that their mothers placed them in maximum security kindergartens at birth. Put two Durantines in a room and lock the door and it wouldn't be long before each was offering to betray the other, even if neither of them had done anything worthy of betrayal.

"You." An Kohli pointed an accusing finger at one of them. "Come here."

A Marty helpfully cut the bindings around the ankle of the selected prisoner and helped her to her feet and over to An Kohli.

"Who is your Captain?" An Kohli demanded. She didn't threaten her. Durantines rarely had to be threatened.

"Aruj. He isn't down here with us. He stayed up on the mother ship."

"I guessed that. Is he the one giving the orders, or is he employed by someone else."

"Normally he runs things, but he accepted a commission for this job. It was worth a lot of money."

"I'm sure it was. Who hired him?"

"I don't know, honestly I don't. He came on board earlier today but no one knows who he is. Who would you like me to say he is?"

An Kohli ignored the remark. She had never framed a criminal in her life. She had no need to do so when there were so many genuine criminals with bounties to be collected. On the other hand, if the Durantine said she didn't know who had hired her boss then she genuinely didn't know.

"That ship." She pointed to the wreckage of the fighting vessel. "Where did you come by it?"

"Aruj had it built on Skopos. There are rumours of war coming and people like us… I mean people like him, are building new craft that will help when the time comes."

Skopos. That made sense. The Skopians were skilled spaceship builders and modifiers and they weren't fussy about what their ships were used for.

Rumours of war; An Kohli hadn't heard any such rumours, but then again, she had been rather busy. "Who will this war be between?"

"The Fell and whoever opposes them. Aruj says there will be easy pickings if we do as the Fell ask. Whole planets where we can live like kings and queens."

That made sense. If they couldn't win the election, as seemed less and less likely, then the obvious thing to do was to just take what they wanted. Forget all semblance of legitimate government and just rule by fear and intimidation. Take what they wanted and give nothing back. Few planets would be able to withstand a concerted attack. What had been done on a small scale here could be repeated many times over. There weren't enough people with the will, or the means, to withstand an assault. It was only the forces of law and order that stood between civilisation and anarchy and in many star systems law and order was already little more than a token.

"Do you have any more ships like that?"

"No. This was the first. We were lucky to have this planet on which to try it out." The Durantine realised she had said the wrong thing and looked downwards in embarrassment. "Not so lucky for these beings, eh?" She attempted to mollify An Kohli.

"Let me put it this way. You're very lucky that you're here. If you'd done this anywhere else I suspect you would now be dangling upside down over a slow fire praying for death. I for one wouldn't lift a finger to stop it from happening. Tie her up again." An Kohli turned angrily and stomped off in search of Gala. She found her administering first aid to a slightly injured Davina.

"According to one of the prisoners the Fell are preparing for war."

"It doesn't surprise me. Ever since they chased out the Magi it's been a possibility."

"Well, we're not going to be the ones to stop it happening, that's for sure. When this is over I'll submit a report to the Guild. The Grand Master has the contacts to get the message out there."

"How many planets are capable of mounting a defence?"

"Not many. A few have missile defence systems, to protect their own planets, but that's about all. I can't think of a single one that possesses any warships. They've come to rely too much on us and the Sentinels to do their dirty work."

"They could end up paying the price for that complacency."

An Kohli nodded her head slowly in agreement. "Not much we can do about it though, not if the Fell are serious. There are thousands of pirates and other guns for hire across the galaxy. Going after them has been very profitable business for us over the years. But I think we could be fighting for our lives and not the bounty money before long."

She turned her head, seeking out the source of the high pitched whine that had just registered on her consciousness. It didn't take her long to identify it. The familiar shape of a shuttle craft came into view, growing in size as it descended towards the clearing.

"If I'm not very much mistaken, this will be Max Wallfly."

Glossary

Sentinels - An Intra-galactic sect of mercenary warriors with very high entry standards. You don't apply to join the sentinels, you are invited.

19 – A Planet Called Hope

"I would suggest to you that our strategy for dealing with An Kohli is the wrong one." Tiger reported to his colleagues.

"You haven't gone soft on her, have you?" Over the ether, the smirk in Barbarossa's voice was almost visible.

"No I haven't 'gone soft on her'. What I am saying is that she is more use to us alive than dead. Let's face it, our attempts to kill her have all ended in failure. We started off as fourteen and now there are just eight of us."

"All the more to share between us." Drac murmured, his avatar flickering.

"Yes, but in the meantime she has found four of the Magi and there is no reason why she won't find the other five. I say that if we can take her alive we can extract the location of the GCIE from her. With that we can destroy the four eggs she has found. The other five then become irrelevant. If she finds more of them it won't matter so long as we eventually destroy the GCIE. With them gone there is no one that any of the planets can rally behind. We won't have to fight a war. We can simply crush all opposition. The galaxy is ours for the taking. So why don't we just take it?"

"I have to admit that when the Fell were first set up, that was our vision." Barbarossa clarified his own position. "We never intended to rule the galaxy, only to exploit it."

"So where did the idea of a government come from?" Asked She Wolf.

Far away across the galaxy Warrior held his tongue. The image of himself as supreme ruler of the galaxy was one that he had shared with only one other being and he wasn't available to discuss it. But he realised that his dream might have to wait. The election was a shambles now that Desire's admissions were out in the open. It would still be held, but no one would ever accept the legitimacy of the new government.

"I could check the minutes of previous meetings." Barbarossa offered.

"I don't think that will be necessary." Warrior interjected hastily. "The idea is a dead duck so no point in going around assigning blame. So, Tiger." He changed the subject, "do you think you can capture An Kohli alive."

"My forces are attempting that as we speak."

"Will they succeed?" Drac for one wasn't going to accept any more casual assurances of success.

"I see no reason why not. My forces will strip away her allies leaving only her. She will have no option but to surrender. However, if we fail this time there will be other opportunities. What I wish to ensure is that we don't sacrifice any more of our number on future attempts to kill her. She may not be indestructible, but she is certainly hard to kill." Harsh sounds were heard over the ether, coming from Tiger's channel.

"What's that?" Tiger said before switching off his microphone. They waited patiently, burning with curiosity, for his return.

"I'm sorry, something's come up. I'll talk to you at the next meeting." The connection was cut and Tiger's avatar blipped off the Fell's viewing screens.

"I don't know about you." drawled Mastermind, "but I suspect we won't be hearing from Tiger again."

"I agree." Barbarossa said. "Perhaps he is right. Perhaps it is time to re-think our strategy."

* * *

The shuttle settled into the greenery, dust and leaves flying around it until the engines finally shut down. The Martys and Davinas waited expectantly. Some nocked arrows onto the strings of their bows while others made sure that the safety catches were released from their pulsars. An Kohli allowed herself a small smile. When it came to trusting new arrivals they had learnt their lesson quickly, if the hard way.

An Kohli's communicator gave a bleep and she checked the message. A grim smile formed on her lips.

The boarding ramp hissed down and two armed pirates stepped forward. Their weapons were lowered, but the response form the clones was immediate. Every weapon was aimed directly at the two new arrivals.

"There's no need for that." Tiger said as he stepped between his two bodyguards. "We come in peace."

"Based on recent experiences you'll forgive us if we don't believe you. Hello Max. What a surprise." An Kohli's expression belied her welcoming words.

"An Kohli. You seem to have more lives than a moricon. Despite what you said you don't actually seem that surprised to see me."

"You may think of me as a dumb brunette but I can assure you that I'm anything but. You fooled me for a while, but you couldn't fool me forever."

"Just long enough to get some class action." He leered.

"To my great regret, yes. You will be one of the few convicted criminals in the galaxy able to say that you screwed An Kohli. I hope the thought gives you comfort as you live out the rest of your life behind bars."

"I suppose Desire and that idiot Attila gave me away."

"They told me that you existed and that you were on Ecos. The rest we worked out for ourselves."

"But you seem to think that I will be going to prison. I hate to contradict you, but I think you'll find we are at a stand-off. You may control this group of…. very attractive females... oh and their males, but I control the space above you. We know where your ship is. You'll never be allowed to reach it."

"How do you think we destroyed that?" An Kohli nodded towards the wreckage of the fighting craft, still leaning drunkenly against the trees."

"Yes, I know all about that. But if you think your Pradua is any match for Aruj's ship then you are very much mistaken." Tiger was worried though. An Kohli was far too confident. She should have been showing some signs of worry. What did she know that he didn't? His own communicator bleeped. What now? He could do without any further distractions.

"What?" he barked into it.

The blood drained from his face and the communicator almost slipped from his fingers as shock registered. He recovered his grip, disconnected the call and returned the communicator to its pocket in his belt.

"I take it that was Captain Aruj telling you what I already knew." An Kohli couldn't keep her triumph from showing on her face.

"Who are they?"

An Kohli could barely hear his question and he had to repeat it.

"Friends of mine. Unlike your sort we cover each other's backs. Of course, they'll want a share of the bounty on Aruj and his crew, but I think there will be plenty to go round."

"Make the most of it. Soon there will be no one willing to pay bounties." He snarled. Then he realised that she had made no mention of a bounty on him. There were no actual warrants out for his arrest, but for the crimes committed here the government of Ecos would still be prepared to reward An Kohli for his arrest.

A wry smile formed on his lips. "I'm not going to prison, am I?"

"Yes and no. Yes you're going to prison, but no, it's not one run by any government. We'll call it remand pending your eventual trial, which will come when the Fell no longer have any say in how the galaxy functions."

"Gypsy and Genghis? I take it they're already in this remand."

"Yes. And Attila and Desire. You won't be short of company. It's a very nice place. No bars, no doors. It's a bit like this but maybe not quite so hot and steamy. By the way, Desire has quite a crush on you. You'll have your work cut out resisting her advances."

Tiger grimaced. "What's to stop me just getting in my shuttle and flying off? I might make it to your ship, the Adastra"

"About a dozen tractor beams, I'm guessing, from what I've been told. I wouldn't risk trying for the Adastra, if I were you. My co-pilot has been very inventive with the anti-theft devices."

Tiger considered his options and they weren't good. If he cooperated with An Kohli he would live, but he would be imprisoned somewhere. If he tried for her ship she had made it clear that he wouldn't ever take off and going back to join Aruj was out of the question. Aruj had already told him he intended surrendering to the ships that had suddenly appeared out of wormholes.

"In that case," he said flatly, "I have very little alternative." He raised his pulsar and took very careful aim at An Kohli. She threw herself to one side just as he fired, landing heavily in the mud. A dozen pulsars spat death at Tiger and he fell, rolling along the shallow ramp and dropping off the end. His two bodyguards threw down their weapons and raised their hands, keen not to share Tiger's fate.

An Kohli stood up and ran the short distance to Tiger's body. She lifted him, resting his head on her knee. "Why? Why did you have to go and do that?"

Gala stepped up close to her and patted her friend's shoulder. "He knew what he was doing. If he had wanted to kill you he had plenty of time. He delayed the shot to give you time to get out of the way."

"Suicide?"

"I think so. He couldn't face prison. The clue is in the name he chose; Tiger. It's a creature of the wild. They don't like being locked up."

"But they don't die in captivity."

"Yes they do; eventually. He wasn't going to allow that."

"And you think he really intended his shot to miss?"

"There's no way of knowing, but I think so. In the end, I think he really did have feelings for you and didn't want to kill you."

An Kohli cuffed away a tear. "Well, I didn't have feelings for him." She let his body fall heavily to the ground. "Not after what he's done here. I could never love someone that could do that."

An Kohli stalked angrily away across the clearing, her back ramrod straight. Gala let her go. She would grieve in her own way and Tiger's own actions would make sure the grieving would be short.

* * *

Twisted metal creaked as Gala crawled out of the wreckage of the medi-sys hut. "I'm sorry, even with a fully equipped workshop I doubt I could get that back into working order."

The assembled group of clones looked glum.

"But without it we can't continue." One Marty spoke for them all. "We won't be able to have younglings and we'll just… well we'll just die out."

"You don't need a medi-sys facility to procreate." An Kohli gently interjected. "Ecos has acknowledged you as its citizens and because you have farmed here you are colonists and this planet is an Ecosian colony. They can send more colonists of your own species and you can have younglings in a more. shall we say, conventional manner."

"But colonists will change us. They'll change the way we live." There was a buzz of agreement around the group.

"Not necessarily. There are a lot of people on Ecos that understand your desire for a simple way of life. Many of them would love to come here and help you to continue to populate this planet. In fact I doubt you would be able to stop them. It's a big planet and people will come if they want to and you won't be able to prevent it. Maybe it's better if you control the arrival process."

"Can we do that?"

"Of course. If you ask the government to allow your brothers and sisters on Ecos to participate in the selection of the colonists, they will make sure that anyone who comes here is dedicated to maintaining your way of life. They can make sure that the right number of males and females come at the right times so that you procreate in a manner that won't create too shallow a gene pool, so your community becomes more diverse, but also doesn't grow at too fast a rate."

"We'll still need medical facilities."

"You will, but they can be provided in other ways. Living nurses and doctors can perform the same function, at the same time as making other contributions to your group, perhaps through teaching.

The medi-sys couldn't do that for you, so you became too dependent on it. Eventually it would have broken down or worn out, even if the pirates hadn't come."

"You would help us with that?"

"As best I can. I have other work I must do, but I can pull strings or help you find the right advisors; people that will work with you in your best interests and not against them."

"Are you leaving us now?"

"Yes, we have a job to finish. But we'll come back and visit you again. Happier times are ahead for you now and we want to be part of them." An Kohli fervently hoped that she was right about that. "Now, there is one matter outstanding. Your star and your planet don't have a name. I think it's time to rectify that and it's only right that you should choose the names."

The clones went into one of their interminable committee meetings, but eventually names were chosen. The star would be called Davina, after their mother, and the planet would be called Hope.

* * *

"Lazarus, calculate the locations of the remaining five Magi eggs. Show me only the most probable location for each egg, but do the calculations for the four next most likely for each egg, just in case."

"So you trust my algorithms now then?" An Kohli felt a strong urge to slap the computer's smug face but it didn't have a face and slapping its cabinet would just hurt her hand.

"I concede that your probability calculation for the egg that we found was fit for purpose. As you said yourself, you can now improve the algorithm based on that data and provide results with greater levels of probability. I would be a fool to turn down such an opportunity."

"Results on screen now."

"That was quick."

"I anticipated your request and completed the calculations after you abandoned me on that moon." The computer's tone was heavy with accusation.

The computer's words added to An Kohli's worries. Ship's computers weren't supposed to anticipate the Captain's requirements. It was only one step away from pre-empting the Captain's decisions. The Captain had sole responsibility for the safety of the ship and if the computer started to pre-empt his decision making it not only undermined the Captain's authority, it might select the wrong option. Decision making was a complicated business, with so many variables; not just the ship's safety, though that was important, but also the crew's mission and its outcomes. Captains were allowed to take risks, but computers couldn't be allowed to take risks on the Captain's behalf.

But that would have to wait, along with dealing with the computer's attitude.

"Thank you, Lazarus. I see that all the probability factors now exceed seventy percent."

"Correct. As each egg is found I will be able to improve on that for the next egg, and so on. I anticipate that the probability factor for the final egg will be in the reason of ninety percent or more."

"Why not one hundred percent?"

"There may have been factors in Su Mali's thought processes of which I am unaware and which can't be discerned from her navigational behaviour."

"Very good. Calculate the route from Ecos to the egg that we can reach the soonest if the starting point is Sabik." She would have liked to have said 'the closest' but wormholes didn't seem to work that way. You could reach a star system twenty light years away in days, yet it might take double that to reach one only ten light years away. No one yet knew why.

Den's voice came over the communications channel, speaking from the Pradua. "Nzite's in the area." *

"Are you sure?"

"It's either him or a ship load of Gau. I don't know anything that can make my brain hurt as much; not even a bottle of slack has that effect on me."

"Lazarus, have you detected any knew ships in the area." Since the arrival of so many bounty hunters in response to An Kohli's call the orbit around the planet had become crowded and it might have been possible for a ship to drift in unnoticed.

"Negative. There are no new ships."

"Locate the calling frequency for a ship called the Doobria Dawn."

"You're wasting your time. That ship isn't in orbit." Lazarus adopted a patronising tone.

"Just do it, computer, and less of the attitude."

The computer's sulk was almost visible, so it was with some humility that it spoke a few moments later.

"I have the Doobria Dawn. Why didn't you tell me it had a cloaking device?"

"You didn't ask and you weren't clever enough to work it out." An Kohli enjoyed her small victory.

"Hello Nzite. You may as well uncloak. We know you're there."

The result was almost instantaneous as the gleaming cone that was the Doobria Dawn appeared in a high orbit. "Greetings An Kohli." Nzites smooth voice came over the airwaves. "I see you have been busy once again."

"I have. To what do I owe the dubious pleasure of this visit."

"You can be so hurtful. Well, my employer, Gib Dander, would like to talk to you."

"He can use the galacticnet like everyone else."

"He feels that a face to face meeting would be preferable."

"I'm busy. Ask him to make an appointment." Gala let out a chuckle. It was what they would be told to do if they called on Gib Dander unexpectedly.

There was silence as Nzite puzzled over how to deal with An Kohli's hostility towards him and his employer. He settled on a direct approach. "If you refuse he could decide to make life difficult for you."

"Ah, threats. That's more like it. Look, I've got a lot on my plate right now. I have to return to Ecos to sort out some stuff for the beings down on this planet. Then I'm keen to get after the remaining Magus eggs. There's trouble brewing and if they aren't recovered quickly they may not be recovered at all."

"That is precisely why Gib Dander wishes to speak to you. He has important information with regard to the eggs. One of them in particular."

"What information?"

"He hasn't confided in me. It is for your ears only."

An Kohli mulled over that nugget. In truth, with Gib Dander providing her with almost unlimited credit, it was unwise for her to mess him around. At the same time, anything to do with the Magi was relevant to what she was trying to do and could, conceivably, make the difference between success and failure.

"Oh, very well. As soon as I've been to Ecos I'll go and see him. I presume he wants to meet on Tan Tara Beta."

"He does."

"You didn't have to come all this way to tell us this, you know. You could have communicated over the galacticnet."

"I know, but I have other business to do here for my employer."

"Forget it. This planet's resources are off limits."

"You think so?"

"I know so."

"Well, maybe we'll let the planet's inhabitants decide that."

"Yes. That's an idea. Be sure to tell them that you intend to give them lots of money and that you're going to pull down all the trees." An Kohli severed the connection.

"What do the clones want with money? And they'd do anything to protect their trees." Gala couldn't make much sense of the advice An Kohli had just given him.

"The clones don't need money and only you and I know how they feel about their ecology. It will come as a nice surprise for Nzite when he sees their reaction."

"If Gib Dander wants to mine here you know he has the clout to make it happen."

"That's something that we can discuss when we meet him."

* See The Magi and Genghis Kant.

Glossary

Moricon - The Earth species of cat is reputed to have nine lives, supposedly because they are famed for making lucky escapes from imminent death. The moricon, a similar feline species, is said to have twenty seven lives for similar reasons.

Slack - A very strong alcoholic drink made with poor quality ingredients. A few drops have been known to dissolve metal coins. Hangovers caused by drinking slack have been known to last for years.

Appendix

Galactic Species

The nature of An Kholi's work tends to bring her into contact with the worst examples of members of the billion or so species that exists in the galaxy. In order to avoid the reader creating stereotypes this appendix seeks to describe the nature of the species that she encounters in this book. Similar appendices appear in the other books in the Magi series and this version merely adds in the star systems that are referred to in this volume.

Aloisan
Star system: Alois
Planet: Gamma

A ridiculously good looking species who have a keen intellect and high moral standards. It is unthinkable that an Aloisan would ever commit a crime, tell a lie, cheat on their partner etc. They tend to find employment in academia or law enforcement. It was an Aloisan that set up the Guild of Bounty Hunters to regulate the activity of a profession whose members had become barely distinguishable from the criminals they pursued. To have an Aloisan as a friend is to have someone always ready to cover your back and who would give you the shirt off their own if you needed it. They are actually quite nauseating in large doses.

Arthurids
Star system: Arthuria
Planet: Beta

The Arthurid species evolved from the largest primates on the Beta planet of the system. The species is known for its great physical size and athleticism. However, they also have a keen intellect if they can be restrained for long enough to use it, as they are known for their impetuosity, especially if there is the prospect of a fight. They are brave and loyal. It isn't unknown for an Arthurid to commit crimes but they tend to do so only as a last resort, which has probably been caused by their own impetuosity.

Faroon
Star system: Chorian
Planet: Faro

The Chorion star system is one of the more remote and the planet Faro has benefited by being largely ignored by the galaxy. Its humanoid population are generally considered meek and unassuming, which would normally make them a magnet for exploitation by other species. However, by some quirk of galactic good fortune they escaped largely unnoticed by the rest of the galaxy. The population is mainly law abiding, content to get on with their lives and let others get on with theirs. Mella Turmi is unusual among the Faroon population firstly for having travelled outside her own star system and secondly for having made such unusual acquaintanceships. These are the basis of her business dealings of course. However, Mella Turmi has paid the price for these business dealings, now being afraid of her own shadow and, until she left to board the Shogun, living in fear in a bunker buried deep below the planet's surface.

Cebalrains
Star system: Cebalrai
Planet: Delta

This species is humanoid in appearance but has the advantage of having two livers. This means that Cebalrains are able to consume twice as much alcohol as other species. Never go drinking with a Cebalrain unless you are also of this species.

Danians
Star system: Peacock
Planet: Mun Dane

The species of An Kholi and her co-pilot Gala Sur. They evolved from primates similar to Earthlings, but where Earthlings are destructive by nature Danians are born to create and innovate.

They have produced some of the finest architects in the galaxy and are responsible for some of its greatest buildings, many of which are regarded as works of art in their own right. Because the planet is so peaceful many young Danians go seeking adventure, just as An Kholi did. After a year or two of drifting around the galaxy seeing the sights and forming dubious relationships with hippies, most return to Mun Dane to take up regular occupations. However, the odd one or two, such as An Kholi and Gala, enjoy the adventure so much that they can't give it up.

Diplopoda
Star system: Phad
Planet: All in system excluding the alpha planet, which is too hot.

The diplopoda are one of many species inhabiting the planets of the Phad system, others include arachnids and insects. These species are semi-sentient, in that they are capable of rational thought but not of grasping higher level concepts. Consequently they have never developed any form of technology. They occasionally migrate across the galaxy by stowing away on visiting space ships, but in general terms are happy to remain on the planets that they occupy in the Phad system. Surprisingly all the species have developed as vegetarians, which prevents all that messy 'catching things in webs and waiting till they dissolve' type of stuff. The diplopoda are highly skilled at the game of football but rarely win any matches. By the time they have laced up over a hundred pairs of boots each, their opponents have scored twenty goals. Their opponent's fans then stage a pitch invasion so that the match has to be abandoned before the diplopoda can score. There are rumours of match fixing as a consequence of this.

Durantines
Star system: Stromat
Planet: Durant

The Durantines are such an untrustworthy race that when the females undergo a gynaecological examination it isn't unusual for the gynaecologist to find his watch has gone missing. Durantine younglings are placed in maximum security kindergartens immediately after birth and often have to be searched to recover the obstetric instruments that were used to deliver them. If a Durantine tells you that it is daylight outside it is well worth going to the window to check.

Adult Durantines find employment as estate agents, bankers, lawyers and, of course, politicians, though they take naturally to lives of crime. They rarely commit crimes on their home planet as this would be counterproductive. Here they have developed a culture of knock-for-knock; if one steals from you then you are fully entitled to steal something back, so in the end no-one really bothers. If they steal at all it is usually just for practice. However, if they do enter a criminal profession they progress well until caught, when they end up grassing on each other and even on people they don't know. A typical death for a Durantine is to go swimming wearing concrete boots.

Earthlings
Star system: Sol
Planet: Earth

This species evolved from primates and is known mainly for its destructiveness. When not killing each other, they are killing their planet and any other planet they colonise. They run many of the larger mining, drilling, nuclear and chemical corporations. The planet is technologically backward, having developed very little of its own technology prior to the arrival of visiting species.

Earth women are known for being strong, independent types who turn to goo when confronted by a puppy or kitten. They also have a fetish for footwear and hand bags, possibly caused by their worship of the Gods Gucci and Laboutain.

Earth men are addicted to sport in any form and the best way to start a fight is to ask a seemingly innocent question, such as "What do you think of Arsenal's back four this season?". The two best things to come from Earth are Northampton Saints Rugby Club and beer, which is the best in the galaxy (except that brewed in the USA which is piss, but still better than blash, if only marginally).

Earthlings are big in banking, which is the main source of crime on their planet, however, no one is ever prosecuted for banking crime. This is why people on Earth tend to keep their money under the mattress.

Falconans
Star system: Mufrid
Planet: Falcona

The only planet on the galaxy to develop a business school before they invented the wheel. Falconans are born business people and are the entrepreneurs of the galaxy. While most of them operate ethical businesses, which benefit society as a whole there are a few Falconans for whom the law is merely a speed bump on the road to success and ethics is a county on an obscure island on an obscure planet in an even more obscure star system.

Like so many other species Falconans are evolved from primates, but unlike others their sense of community has been bred out of them, giving them an 'every being for themselves' sort of attitude. They also make natural politicians. However if, by some chance, you are able to befriend a Falconan you will have a loyal friend for life, or at least until someone makes him a better offer.

Gau
Star system: Flage
Planet: Camoo

This species is the only one in the galaxy known to have shape shifting capability and it is thought to have been a major factor in its survival as they are not noted for their fighting skills. To identify each other they retain a limited telepathic capability. Because of this they have become known for a high level of deviousness and they also make up a significant minority of criminals in the galaxy. However, a degree of fecklessness in their nature means that they are rarely successful. Su Mali is the exception to this rule and it is thought that she may have the blood of another species mixed with her Gau blood. See also Sutra

Jackon
Star system: Jackon
Planet: Awree

The Jackon are known for their extremely large feet and equally extremely low foreheads. The feet are required to keep them upright as they often forget how to balance. As this suggests, they aren't known for their intellect. Any technology they have has been imported and is usually operated and maintained by a species with a higher level of intellect.

They are very hard workers and therefore much in demand by employers, especially in the mining industry. They are very good at obeying orders as it saves them from having to think for themselves, so they are also well suited for employment as prison guards, parking wardens, back bench MPs etc. They lack ambition so they make ideal henchmen.

Non Jackon find it impossible to distinguish between male and female Jackon and Jackon males are also sometimes unable to do this, which is why the females find it necessary to release strongly scented pheromones in order to breed.

Lupine
Star System: Canis Major
Planet; Lupus

A species evolved from canines. Unlike most canine based species, the Lupines have evolved opposable thumbs which means that they, like primates, became tool users. Because of their aggressive nature Lupines replaced primates as the dominant species on their planet.

While capable of great affection and loyalty they are prone to biting the hand that feeds them, in both literal and metaphorical terms. They will become loyal to whoever provides them with employment, often abandoning previous loyalties. This means that they can be easily bought and, coupled to their aggressive nature, favour professions such as the law and selling used cars. Although not generally of a criminal bent, if they do choose that career path they are usually very successful if led by a dominant male, or a female in heat. They have a very unusual greeting ritual; well, unusual if you aren't evolved from a canine.

Sabik
Star system Sabik
Planet: Gamma

There is no true Sabik species as their planet was originally colonised by Aloisan. Evolutionary differences mean that they are slightly less attractive than pure Aloisans, but in most respects the species can be accepted as being similar.

Skopians
Star system Marut
Planet: Skopos

Skopos is a planet renowned for its excellence in engineering. If it can be built the Skopians will build it for you. They are a humanoid species and otherwise unremarkable. It is known that Skopians have travelled to distant parts of the galaxy, often in disguise, and may have lived amongst more primitive species, advancing their engineering skills without their knowledge. The sudden advance of industrialisation on Earth which started with the building of iron bridges and steam engines and culminated with the construction of the artificial planet called New Earth may well be evidence that Skopians have visited Earth and lived amongst humans.

Surchifs
Star system: Brit
Planet: Surchia

Evolved from the Pop people of the Brit star system, the Surchifs are best known for their ability to be totally forgettable. They have travelled far and wide across the galaxy and they have settlements on many planets, though the rest of the planet's occupants may not even realise it. They were present on Earth for many years before that planet commenced inter-stellar travel and their presence is credited with the speed up in the development of the necessary technology as a means of escape. The Surchifs on Earth are so instantly forgettable that they often win the same TV talent contests year after year without anyone noticing.

Sutra
Star system: Flage
Planet: Sutra

Evolution has provided a unique niche for Sutra in that they provide females whose sole desire is to have sex and whose males are only too happy to let them get on with it, while they themselves go to the pub and watch football. Being evolved from the Gau they have the shape shifting abilities and a slightly improved telepathic ability. Sutran females can enjoy their sexual freedom to the maximum. They often find employment as females of negotiable affection, which they see as an honourable calling that allows them to earn money while doing what they would be happy doing for free. The males of many species have died in the arms of a Sutran (or two, or three) with a smile on their lips.

Tacon
Star system: Taco
Planet: Bell

Tacon are one of a number of species descended from reptiles rather than primates. This is primarily because their planets are hotter and drier than those where primates evolved. Their development was aided by the evolution of opposable thumbs, which is a general rule for species that have evolved higher capabilities.

Tacon are honest and hard working and find employment in fields where having a very long tongue is considered to be both an advantage and aesthetically pleasing. Male Tacon are popular with the females of many other species.

Towie
Star system: Towie
Planet: Gamma

Perhaps the shallowest species in the known galaxy, they are obsessed with image to the point where they shun most other aspects of existence. Almost certainly evolved from butterflies, though the fossil record doesn't, as yet, prove this. The only species in the galaxy to invent the mirror before the wheel.

Education levels amongst adults is rudimentary at best, so this paragraph can be written in the certain knowledge that a Towian will never be offended because they never read books. While Towians are outwardly friendly their shallow nature means that if you give one the choice between saving a friend from drowning or getting a new spray tan, you better have the tanning lotion and paper underwear on standby. This also means that they very rarely indulge in criminal activity because it would distract from getting a vagazzle.

Most find employment where they can stand about looking good while ignoring people, so they make ideal shop assistants and receptionists.

Valon
Star system Val
Planet: Vala

A telepathic species that has evolved in such a way as to be able to live with its telepathic powers without continually having to apologise for the embarrassment caused by what it reads in the minds of other Valon. Originally evolving on one very large planet they have dispersed throughout the galaxy so as to be as far away as possible from each other. They come together only to mate, which, for a female, is a once in a lifetime activity.

Male Valon spend most of their time building models of sailing ships out of match sticks, a solitary task but it keeps them from thinking about sex more than once every few seconds. They can only read the minds of other creatures that have telepathic ability, such as Gau. Criminality is almost unheard of amongst Valon as they lead such a solitary existence, so Nzite is very much an oddity amongst an odd species.

Author's Note

Cloning is in its experimental stages here on Earth. So far scientists have managed to clone only twenty-two species of animals, starting with Dolly the sheep in 1996 and ending, at the time of writing, with a buffalo in India in 2016. Within those species, however, many more actual clones have been produced, with bovines being the most popular species for cloning.

The ethics involved in cloning humans means that it is unlikely that we will see cloning at that level for a long time. However, Davina didn't have those ethical considerations to take into account.

There have been numerous depictions of cloning in fiction, too many to mention in a short note such as this. The most memorable, for me, was in The Boys From Brazil, which has Dr Josef Mengele, the Nazi doctor, trying to rekindle the Third Reich by raising clones of Adolf Hitler in surrogate mothers.

My favourite use of cloning in a plot, however, is in Red Dwarf, series 6 episode 5, in which Rimmer arrives on an uninhabited planet and clones himself in order to try to gain some female companionship. Instead he creates a nightmare population of people identical to himself. In scientific terms, the episode is hopelessly inaccurate, because Rimmer is a hologram and therefore has no cells from which DNA can be extracted and there are no eggs available into which the DNA can be implanted and no surrogate mother available. But it was a very funny episode.

For those of you that didn't spot it, the name of the ship, Namsat Elba, is Able Tasman spelt backwards, in honour of the great Dutch explorer who was the first person to reach Australia, many years before Captain Cook set foot in Botany Bay.

I'm not an astronomer, physicist, mathematician or any sort of scientist so any errors in my understanding of the universe are purely my own. Some ideas used in this story, such as the ability to use wormholes to cross the galaxy, have been created purely to allow the story to work, though astro-physicists have proposed the idea themselves. I am indebted to Wikipedia and other websites for most of the scientific information used within the story, plus to my various science teachers at school who tried to drum some rudimentary understanding of the universe into my unwilling brain. A big shout out to Professor Brian Cox for his contribution through his excellent TV shows.

This is a work of science fiction and just as there is no such thing as an orc or an elf on Earth then there may be no such species as Aloisans, Gau, or any of the others I have created in the universe. Please don't sweat the detail, just enjoy the story if you can.

With regard to the naming of star systems I have drawn on both my imagination and existing star maps. In other words some of the names are made up and some are real. If you wish try to work out which is which then feel free, but there's no prize for being right.

Which of the real systems have planets around them and what the nature of those planets might be I also have no idea, so please don't e-mail me to tell me that Sabik only has one planet not several, or no planets at all (I do know that it's a binary star system). The same applies to many of the scientific, anthropological, zoological and botanical terms I have used (please see glossary). I can only hope that the British education system has been sufficiently effective so that readers are able to distinguish between the real facts and the made up ones.

Three more of the Fell have been neutralised and another Magus has been found but there are five more still missing. What new strategy might the Fell adopt in their pursuit of both the eggs and An Kohli? She, Gala Sur, and Den Gau have more work to do, more battles to fight and will return in Book 5 of the series, "Timeslip".

Preview

A Chance for you to take a sneak peek at Book 5 in The Magi series.

TIMESLIP

1 – A Galaxy Far, Far Away

The insistent buzzing and chatter from the intercom eventually woke An Kohli. She rubbed at her sleep filled eyes then shook her head to try to evict the befuddlement from it and make sense of the sounds she was hearing.

The buzzing sounded again followed by more unintelligible chatter. By exerting all her powers of concentration she was at last able to bring the words into focus and understand their meaning.

"….get in here and take a look at this An Kohli. Can you hear me?" The buzzing started again, insistent, clamouring for attention. She slapped her hand against the grill of the intercom, hoping to hit the right button with one of her spread fingers. The sound stopped, mid buzz.

"What the hell is going on." If Gala was unaware that An Kohli was unhappy she would now realise it.

"Sorry to wake you, but can you come in here. We have a… a situation I guess you might call it."

"Is it an emergency?"

"Not as such. Look, it's easier to show you than to tell you."

"OK, give me a couple of minutes."

An Kohli stumbled into the bathroom and splashed water onto her face. Gala wasn't easily spooked, so if she was requesting her presence then it must be important, she reasoned. On the other hand, the lack of alarms sounding and the steady hum of the engines suggested that all was normal on board the Adastra. So what in the name of the galaxy was so urgent that it warranted rousing her from her much needed rest?

She grabbed at her robe in passing and wrapped it around herself before leaving her cabin and turning onto the narrow corridor that took her, in a few short steps, to the door of the command deck. Gala had already moved into the co-pilot's seat so An Kohli threw herself into the Captain's chair, making it clear with every nuance of her body language that she was not a happy bexoth.

"So what's so dammed urgent."

Gala seemed to cower under An Kohli's stern tone, almost regretting summoning her employer, but she knew this was important. The computer had told her that.

"We've dropped out of our wormhole."

"So, that's not unusual. What caused the ship to do that?" Unlike Gala she tended to treat the craft as more of an inanimate object than a beloved member of the family.

"That's the problem. There's nothing wrong with the ship. All systems check out as functioning normally. There we were, one second zooming along towards the Tan Tara system and the next second we weren't. We're still at top speed, nought point eight five c, but no longer in a wormhole."

"OK, so where are we?"

"That's even stranger. The navi-com can't work it out."

"How long has it been working on the problem?"

"Nearly thirty minutes."

There was a sharp hiss as An Kohli sucked air through her teeth. That wasn't good. Under normal circumstances, after dropping out of a wormhole, the navi-com should be able to calculate their position within a few minutes by taking star sightings, faster if there were galacticnet node satellites in the area. If they were in an unexplored part of the galaxy it might take longer, but hardly ever more than fifteen minutes. If, however, they were to drop out of a wormhole in a different galaxy, which had been known to happen, then there were no star charts available against which to plot their position and it might take years to work out precisely where they were.

"Lazarus." An Kohli addressed the main computer. It had developed a distinct and rather disturbing personality after a main engine failure during their most recent mission *(see Cloning Around)* and the combined attempts of An Kohli and Gala had been unable to disable its voice circuits. "Lazarus, while the navi-com attempts to plot our location, can you do a cross check against the galactic star maps to establish if we are still in our own galaxy."

"Of course. Stand by."

Using the same external sensors as the navi-com, the main computer would be able to analyse the positions of the visible galaxies and establish if they were in their own or if the wormhole had collapsed leaving them in a neighbouring galaxy.

"According to the available data we are currently located in galaxy Messier 83."

That didn't sound good. An Kohli didn't recognise the designation, which meant that they weren't in any of the nearest galaxies to their own. "Where is that in relation to our own galaxy?" She was almost afraid to ask the question.

"Fourteen point seven million light years away. You will appreciate that is an approximation. Do you want me to calculate a more accurate figure?"

"No, that isn't necessary." An Kohli whispered. She exchanged looks with Gala, whose face had gone so pale that it had lost all of its lilac colouring.

"I guess we're not in Kansas anymore, Toto." Gala misquoted.*

"I think you're right Gala. Lazarus, why are we here?"

"There could be any number of reasons and it would be wrong for me to speculate without more data."

"In other words, you don't know." An Kohli felt a rush of pleasure at finally being able to expose a lack of knowledge in the computer. The embarrassed silence confirmed her assessment. The computer had got 'smug' and 'patronising' down to fine arts and if it had any inkling as to what had happened she knew it would be providing a penny lecture at that moment.

"Lazarus, based on the navi-com's known capabilities, can you give an estimate as to how long it will take to calculate our exact position."

"Two years, six months and four days, approximately."

An Kohli nodded her understanding. The navi-com worked by taking bearings on stars and comparing their properties with those held in its database: their size, brilliance, type and number of planets. In practice it looked for galacticnet nodes in the first instance and if it couldn't find any in the local area then it resorted to the star maps. It compared the properties of the stars with their neighbours to eliminate any errors introduced by similarities between star systems before using the results to calculate a position accurate to within a few li.

However, with no star maps available for galaxies other than their own the navi-com had to start from scratch and build up new maps based on observations within this galaxy and with known stars in other galaxies. It was a slow, painstaking business, even using data passed on from other ships that had found themselves in the same situation.

"OK, so we're lost in space. What do we do now?"

"Lazarus, will it help to tell the navi-com which galaxy we're in?" An Kohli asked, but already pretty sure she knew the answer.

"It always helps to provide a computer with additional data. It will shorten the processing time by three days."

"Three days. Is that all?" It was unusual for Gala to sound so despondent; a real indication of the degree of trouble they were in.

"The issue is not of which galaxy we are in, but where in that galaxy." An Kohli explained it to her before the smug computer could.

"Ship approaching." Lazarus intoned, as though it was an insignificant detail.

"Maybe this will help to provide some answers." An Kohli suggested. "I doubt it just turned up by chance and I doubt they speak Common Tongue."

"It is attempting to communicate." The computer supplied. "I have initiated the Genesis protocol."

Genesis would at least allow them to establish a line of communication, though it wouldn't necessarily provide answers.

Gala had been busy with the external cameras to locate the ship. "Would you look at this." Her awed whisper attracted An Kohli's attention as she locked a camera on to the new arrival and zoomed in.

The ship appeared to be made of nothing more substantial than light. Hard edges of light gave it an outline while the body was made up of a dim glow. Within the glow they could make out individual figures. There was a cluster of four or five in the centre which, An Kohli assumed, was where control of the vessel was exercised, while individuals were located in other parts. Some could even be seen lying down, as though resting. It was more like a projection of a ship, rather than a ship itself, but there was nowhere from which a projection could originate.

"Is it armed?"

"Who knows." An Kohli breathed. "With a ship like that the whole thing may be a weapon. It's far advanced on anything I've seen anywhere else."

"It looks like the imaginings of an artist, or maybe a writer. Something they dreamed up and turned into an image."

"Well, as well as establishing communication, the Genesis Protocol also requires that we treat the ship as friendly until it proves otherwise. If it wanted to destroy us it could do it. It's far bigger than we are. Lazarus." An Kohli addressed the computer again. "Gradually slow us down until we're stopped. Let's see how they react."

The computer cut the power, reducing the engine to idle. Then it fired retro jets in the nose, using blasts of air to apply an opposing force and reduce their forward speed so that they gradually slowed from eighty five percent of light speed and eventually stopped.

The other shipped mimicked their actions until the two hung side by side against the backdrop of the stars that made up this galaxy. The navi-com display told them that they weren't close to any, so they were now simply drifting in the vacuum of space.

"Communication established." Lazarus intoned. "Do you wish me to display the messages as text or would you prefer me to speak for them?"

"You speak please, Lazarus." She disliked the computer's voice, the reason she had disabled the speech mode originally, but it would be easier to process the messages by listening than by reading.

"Unless I now say otherwise, I will be the voice of the alien craft."

"We are the aliens here, I think." Gala observed dryly.

"We are the embassy ship Globestar. We mean you no harm. We welcome you to our galaxy."

"Thank you. We are the ship Adastra, registered on the planet we call Artemis Beta. We didn't intend to be in your galaxy at all. Now we require time to plot our position and calculate a route back to our own galaxy. Any assistance you can offer in this respect would be welcome."

"We understand. You are here because we caused you to be here. We identified your wormholes transiting our galaxy on numerous occasions and decided to intercept the next craft to use this route. You are that next craft."

"Why did you intercept us?"

"All will become clear. We invite you to cross to our ship."

"Will our shuttle craft be able to dock with your ship?"

"No, but that is irrelevant. We will create a field around your ship that will allow you to cross to us without the need for a craft."

"And if we choose not to cross."

"That will be your choice. We have the capability to disable your ship without doing you any injury." The threat was clear enough, though the computerised voice of Lazarus wasn't applying any sort of modulation to the message which would have allowed for a clearer understanding. As the messages were simply exchanges of binary information it wasn't possible to interpret tone. Given enough time Lazarus would be able to develop an auto-translate routine that would allow for direct communication.

"May we take a few moments to discuss your invitation?"

"Of course." The more carefully modulated tones of Lazarus spoke next. "The communication is now paused."

"Thank you, Lazarus. So, Gala, what do you think?"

"Well, if we want to find out why we're here we haven't any option but to accept."

"And if we want to get home I think we also have to accept. We have no idea what their capability is, but we have to assume that they can do what they say."

"Lazarus. Are you able to identify any of the properties of that ship?" Gala asked the computer.

"It is apparently made from pure light, but how it is constructed is beyond my capabilities to establish."

"In that case, I don't think we have any choice, An Kohli. We either cross over to it and find out the answers to our questions, or we sit here until we rot."

"Not much of a choice. Very well. Lazarus, re-open the communications channel."

"You have reached your decision." An Kohli was unsure whether it was a question or a statement, but decided to treat it as a question.

"Yes. We accept your invitation to cross to your ship."

"Very well. Please leave all weapons behind. There is no reason for you to be armed and they will be useless anyway."

A beam of light slowly extended its way across the gap between the two ships as though light had slowed down to walking pace. As it came closer its spread until it enveloped the whole ship.

"It is now safe for you to cross."

An Kohli and Gala made their way to the auxiliary airlock and stepped inside, closing the inner door behind them.

"Well, I don't care what they say. I'm not opening this door unless that light goes green." An Kohli indicated the red safety light that glowed above the outer airlock door. As well as providing a docking port for visiting shuttles, it was also the way they would exit the ship if it was necessary to conduct an external inspection. She waved her hand over the switch that activated the airlock pressurisation system. There was the briefest of hisses before the red light changed to green, indicating that the pressure outside the door was equal to that within.

"Well, here we go then." An Kohli unlocked the door and pulled it open. If they were opening it onto a vacuum they would have been dead within seconds as the depressurisation robbed their bodies of air and made their blood boil in their veins, while the soft tissue of their internal organs would have ruptured.

In front of them was the glow of the light and then the vastness of space. It took a huge act of faith for An Kohli to step out through the door, but she forced herself. Her foot landed firmly on nothing. According to her brain there was nothing there to support her foot, but it was quite definitely being supported by something. She took a second tentative step, placing her right foot next to her left. She still found herself being supported. The surface was firm, there was no evidence of any sort of 'give' which she had expected for some reason, The light was as solid as any metal walkway she had ever stood on. Light couldn't be solid, she told herself, but here it was as solid as the carbon and metal of her own ship.

"Go boldly, An Kohli." Gala whispered from behind her, before stepping out to follow her friend.

* The Wizard of Oz. MGM Films 1939. The correct quote is "Toto, I've a feeling we're not in Kansas anymore." This is one of the most frequently misquoted lines from films.

Glossary

Genesis Protocol - A method of establishing communications between two species where there is no common language. It starts by one party sending the other a short signal in binary format and builds a common mathematical language until their two computers can build translation interfaces so that messages can be sent in one language and read in the other. If both species are similar levels of mathematical and computer development simple levels of communication can be established within thirty minutes and more complex communication, that perhaps necessary to explain the plot of a soap opera, within an hour.

And Now

Both the author Robert Cubitt and Selfishgenie Publishing hope that you have enjoyed reading this book and that you have found it useful.

Find Robert Cubitt on Facebook at https://www.facebook.com/robertocubitt and 'like' his page; follow him on Twitter **@robert_cubitt** You can also e-mail Robert Cubitt at **robert.cubitt@selfgenie.com**

Please tell people about this eBook, write a review on Amazon or mention it on your favourite social networking sites.

For further titles that may be of interest to you please visit the Selfishgenie Publishing website at **selfishgenie.com** where you can join our mailing list so that we can keep you up to date with all our latest releases (or maybe that should be 'escapes').

Printed in Great Britain
by Amazon